MW01254259

The Haunted Room

Charlotte Maria Tucker

Copyright © 2017 Okitoks Press

ISBN: 197396886X

ISBN-13: 978-1973968863

Table of Contents

CHAPTER I.

A PLEASANT HOME.

"A pleasant nest my brother-in-law has found for his family," said Captain Arrows to himself, as, carpet-bag in hand, he walked the brief distance from a railway-station to his relative's house. "Trevor's home is near enough to London for its inmates to reach Charing-Cross by train in fifteen minutes, and yet far enough from it to be beyond reach of its smoke and noise. Not quite so," added the captain as he passed a Savoyard with hurdy-gurdy and monkey, and then was overtaken by an omnibus well filled within and without; "but I doubt if our young folk would have relished perfect rural seclusion, or would have wished to have dwelt fifty miles from the Great Exhibition and Albert Hall. As long as he holds his government office, Trevor cannot live far from London; and in choosing his residence here, he has made a pleasant compromise between town and country. This is as bright-looking a home as heart could wish," thought the captain, as from the slope of a hill he came in sight of a pretty villa, in the Elizabethan style, standing in its own grounds. "These gay flower-beds, with their geometrical shapes and blooming flowers, show the ingenuity of Bruce and the taste of Emmie. The croquet loops on the lawn, the target in the little field yonder, tell of lives passed in ease and enjoyment. It may be a question whether such lives be indeed the most desirable for our young men and maidens," thus the captain pursued his reflections as he walked down the hill. "Simply to pass youth as pleasantly as possible seems to be hardly the best preparation for the rough campaign of existence. We would not train our army recruits in Arcadia. It would be an interesting problem, had we the means of working it out, to find out how far our characters are formed by our surroundings, as physical qualities are affected by climate. Would early acquaintance with difficulties and dangers ever have braced up our lovely Emmie into a heroine, or made Vibert a reflective and self-denying man? As for Bruce, he has in him so much of the nature of the oak sapling, that the most enervating air could not rob him of all the knots and toughness of close-grained wood. Another curious problem to solve would be, how far easy, luxurious existence in youth is actually conducive to happiness; whether the prospect from a bleak hill-side be not fairer, as well as its air more bracing, than that of the garden of the Hesperides. Where the mind has no real difficulties with which to grapple, the imagination is wont to grow with the rank luxuriance of tropical vegetation. Nervousness, superstition, anxiety about trifles, take the place of serious trials; and the child of luxury, to parody the fine line of Johnson,

'Makes the misery he does not find.'"

The captain had no more leisure for his reflections, for, as he threw open the gate of Summer Villa, his approach was seen from the house, and two of its inmates hastened forth to meet a favourite uncle. A graceful maiden ran lightly down the shrubbery path, followed by her younger brother, a handsome lad of some sixteen or seventeen years of age.

"Oh, you are so welcome; we were so glad to get your telegram and know that your long cruise was over!" cried Emmie as she gave to her mother's brother an affectionate greeting.

"We've so much to tell you, captain," said Vibert Trevor, cordially shaking the hand of the newly-arrived guest. "John is away, so let me carry your carpet-bag into the house."

This, from Vibert, was rather a remarkable offer of service. The captain accepted it with a smile, for Vibert was little accustomed to act the part of a porter.

"Where is Bruce?" asked Arrows. "As for your father, I suppose that he is at his office in London."

"No; papa is not at his office," replied Emmie, slipping her arm into that of her uncle. "But come into the house and have refreshment, and while you take it—"

"We'll tell you the whole story," cried Vibert, looking like one who has a grand piece of news to impart.

While the three enter Summer Villa, let us pause and glance at them for a few moments.

Captain Arrows is a naval officer. He has scarcely reached middle age, and looks young to be addressed as "uncle" by the young lady who rests on his arm, or the tall brother at her side. The captain's face, bronzed by sun and wind, is not one to be easily forgotten, so keen and piercing are the dark eyes which glance from beneath projecting brows. An expression of satire sometimes plays around the thin lips, but of satire tempered and controlled. The impression conveyed by Arrows' appearance and manner would be, "That is a man of character, a man of decision, a keen observer, who looks as if he were making notes for a book satirizing the follies of mankind." But there is a kindly frankness about the sailor which tends to counteract the sense of restraint which might otherwise be felt in his society. If he carry the sharp rapier of wit at his side, it is sheathed in the scabbard of good-nature.

Never does Arrows look more kindly or soften his tone to more gentleness than when addressing the motherless daughter of a sister loved and mourned. Emmie is, indeed, one to draw out the affections of those around her. Not only is her face fair, but it has the sweetness of expression which is more winsome than beauty. Her soft dark-brown hair does not, in the shapeless masses prescribed by modern fashion, mar the classical contour of a gracefully formed head. Gentle, tender, and clinging, the maiden's type might be found in the fragrant white jasmine that embowers the porch of her pleasant home. Emmie's school companions have loved her; not one of them could remember a harsh or unkind word spoken by the lips of the gentle girl. Her brothers love her; Emmie has shared their interests, and joined them in their amusements, without ever brushing away that feminine softness which, as the down to the peach, is to woman one of the greatest of charms. Bruce would have disliked having "a fast girl" for his sister almost as much as Mr. Trevor would have disapproved of his daughter earning that title. The slang in which some modern ladies (?) indulge would have sounded from the lips of Emmie as startling as the blare of a child's trumpet toy breaking in on a melody of Beethoven.

Vibert Trevor in appearance resembles his sister; but what is pleasingly feminine in the woman looks somewhat effeminate in the boy. Boy! how could the word escape my pen! Vibert, in his own estimation at least, has left boyhood long ago. His auburn hair, parted carefully down the middle, falls on either side of a face which would be singularly handsome but for the somewhat too great fulness about the mouth. The lad is dressed fashionably and in good taste. If there be a little tinge of foppishness in his appearance, it is as slight as the scent which a superfine cigar has left on his clothes.

"No more refreshment for me, thanks; I have taken some in London," said the captain in reply to a question from his niece as they entered the house together.

4

"Then we will go into the drawing-room," said Emmie. "We expect papa and Bruce by the next train from Wiltshire. Papa wrote that they would reach this an hour before dinner-time."

A cheerful drawing-room was that which looked out on the lawn of Summer Villa, lighted up as it was by the rich glow of a September sun, then just at its setting. The red light sparkled on the crystal globe in which gold-fish were gliding, and lent vividness to the green of the graceful ferns which ornamented both the windows. Emmie's piano was open, with a piece of music upon it. Emmie was an enthusiast in music. She had to displace her guitar from the sofa on which she had left it, to make room for her uncle to sit by her side. Emmie's basket with its fancy work lay on the table, and traces of her late employment in the shape of dropped beads and morsels of bright German wool strewed the soft carpet. Emmie rather felt than saw that her uncle's eye detected the little untidiness; the naval officer was himself "so dreadfully neat!"

"Now for your news," said the captain, as he seated himself by his niece, while Vibert threw himself into an arm-chair. Vibert usually chose, as if by instinct, the most luxurious chair in the room.

"What would you say if papa were to throw up office, leave Summer Villa for ever and for aye, and carry us all off to be buried alive?" cried Vibert.

"In Labrador—or equatorial Africa?" inquired the captain.

"Not quite so bad as either of those distant deserts," laughed Vibert. "Myst Hall is not a hundred miles from London, and Wiltshire is not quite beyond the pale of civilized life."

"What has happened to make such a migration probable?" inquired Arrows. "You know that during our northern cruise I have had no letters, and that as regards home news, the last three months have been to me an absolute blank."

"Our story is easily told," said Emmie. "You will, I dare say, remember that papa had an aunt, Mrs. Myers, who lived in Wiltshire."

"I recollect the name, but little besides," replied Arrows.

"None of us knew much of Aunt Myers," continued his niece. "Except a hamper of home-made preserves which came to us from Myst Court every Christmas, we had little to remind us of a relative who shut herself up from her family and friends for fifty long years."

"But if we forgot the old dame, she did not forget us," interrupted Vibert. "Aunt Myers died eight or nine days ago and there came a letter from her lawyer announcing her death, and informing my father that he is the old lady's heir, executor, and the master of Myst Court, with all the fields, pleasure-grounds, cottages, copses, and I don't know what else thereto appertaining."

The captain did not look as much impressed by the announcement as his young informant expected that he would be.

"Papa, of course, went to his poor aunt's funeral," said Emmie, "and took Bruce with him to see what he thought of the place."

"There was plenty of business to be transacted," observed Vibert; "I fancy that there always is when landed property changes hands. My father asked for a week's holiday from office-work. Perhaps he will give up his appointment altogether; all depends on whether he decide to live on his own estate, or to let it and take a new lease of Summer Villa."

"You must have had letters from your father; to which decision does he appear to incline?" asked the captain, addressing himself to his niece.

"Papa has been very busy, and wrote but briefly," said Emmie. "I believe that a good deal will depend on whether papa is satisfied with what he sees of a gentleman at S——, who has been highly recommended as a private tutor for my brothers. S—— is but three miles from Myst Court, so that if we lived at that place, Vibert and Bruce could go over to Mr. Blair's for study every week-day."

"My father's plan, now that Bruce and I have left Cheltenham," interrupted Vibert, "is to keep us with him at home for a year or two, and have us prepared for Cambridge or some competitive examination by a private tutor, either in London, or at S——, if we go into Wiltshire."

"What description does Bruce give of Myst Court?" inquired Captain Arrows.

"Bruce is a lazy dog with his pen, and seldom honours me with a scratch of it," answered Vibert.

"Bruce wrote to me the day after he went into Wiltshire," said Emmie. "He knew that I should be interested to hear of the place which may soon be our home. Bruce writes that the house is of the date of the reign of Queen Anne; that it is built of red brick, and looks rather formal, but has splendid trees around it. Myst Court stands quite by itself, with no other country-house near it, and has the reputation of being *haunted*."

Arrows smiled at the gravity with which the young lady pronounced the last word.

"Myst Court must be a horridly dull place, at least for those who are not sportsmen!" cried Vibert. "Bruce and I may find a little liveliness at S——; but for you, Emmie, it will be a case of—

'And still she cried, "'Tis very dreary— 'Tis dreary and sad," she said; She said, "I am aweary, aweary; I wish I were dead!"'"

Emmie laughed, but the laugh was rather a forced one.

"Your sister will never, I hope, echo the peevish complaint of an idle girl, who had not energy enough to nail up her peaches," observed Captain Arrows. "If Emmie go to Wiltshire, it will be, I trust, to lead there an active, useful, and happy life."

"I wonder on what course papa will decide," said Emmie; "we are very anxious to know. A great deal will depend on what Bruce thinks desirable,—papa has such an opinion of the judgment of Bruce."

"Bruce has a precious good opinion of his own," said Vibert, with something like scorn.

"For shame!—how can you!" cried Emmie, in a tone of playful reproof.

"Here they are! here come my father and Bruce!" cried Vibert, rising from his easy-chair as he caught sight of two figures at the gate.

Emmie had started up, and was out of the room to receive the travellers, before Vibert had finished the sentence.

CHAPTER II.

COMING TO A DECISION.

"Yes, I am satisfied in regard to educational advantages for my sons," said Mr. Trevor, in reply to a question asked by the captain, when, a few minutes afterwards, the family were gathered together in the drawing-room. "The tutor, Mr. Blair, appears to be in every way qualified to do full justice to his pupils; I had a very satisfactory interview with him at S——."

"But Myst Court itself, what do you think of the place?" inquired Vibert.

"The house was originally handsome, but it is now utterly out of repair," replied Mr. Trevor.

"I don't suppose that painter or glazier has entered the door for these last fifty years," observed Bruce.

"The grounds are extensive," continued Mr. Trevor; "but the trees are choking each other for lack of thinning; and the brushwood, through neglect, has thickened into a jungle."

"A good cover for rabbits and hares," observed Vibert, who had an eye to sport.

"I never before saw such wretched cottages," said Bruce; "and there are sixty-one of them on the estate, besides two farms. The hovels are dotted in groups of threes and fours in every corner where one would not expect to find them. Some lean forward, as if bending under the weight of their roofs; some to one side, as if trying to get away from their neighbours; some cottages look as if they were tired of standing at all. I cannot imagine how the men and women, and swarms of bare-footed children, manage to live in such dirty dens."

"Is there no one to look after the people?" asked Captain Arrows.

"There is no church or school-house nearer than S——," replied Mr. Trevor. "The people either work for the neighbouring farmers, or in a dyeing factory which stands about a mile from Myst Court. Wages are low in that part of the country; but that is not sufficient to account for the misery which we saw there. Ignorance prevails—ignorance more dense than I could have believed to have been found in any part of our favoured land. I doubt whether of the peasants one in four is able even to read. As a matter of course, drunkenness and every other vice spread as weeds over a field so neglected."

"It is there that the labourer is called to lay his hand to the plough," observed Captain Arrows.

Vibert gave an almost imperceptible shrug of his shoulders; Bruce as slight an inclination of his head. A very faint sigh escaped from the lips of Emmie.

"I have been giving the matter serious, very serious thought," said Mr. Trevor. "My first idea, when I found that my aunt had bequeathed the property to me, was to let Myst Court, and to remain at least for some years in Summer Villa, where we have been for long so comfortably settled. But I found, on visiting Myst Court, that it would be impossible to let the house without effecting such extensive and thorough repairs as I could not at present undertake. Even if this were not so—" Mr. Trevor paused, as if to reflect.

"No mere tenant could be expected to take the same interest in the people as would be felt by you, their landlord and natural protector," observed the captain, concluding the sentence which his brother-in-law had left unfinished.

"And so you think that we are bound to act as props to the cottages that are leaning forwards or sideways, and make them hold themselves straight, as respectable cottages ought to do!" laughed Vibert.

"But what have you to say about the haunted room?" timidly inquired Emmie, who had been sitting with her hand in that of her father, a hitherto silent but much interested listener to the conversation.

"Haunted! Oh, that's all nonsense!" exclaimed Bruce. "Myst Court is no more haunted than is Summer Villa; it is simply a big, dreary-looking house that wants new mortar on its walls, new glass to replace what is cracked in its windows, and a good fairy, in the shape of a young lady, to turn it into a cheerful, comfortable home."

"What gives to Myst Court the name of being haunted," said his father, "is simply this. My aunt, who was of a nervous and highly sensitive nature, had the misfortune to lose her husband, a short time after their marriage, in a very distressing way. When on his wedding-tour, Mr. Myers was bitten by a mad dog, and a few weeks after bringing his bride to their home he died of hydrophobia."

"How dreadful!" exclaimed Emmie.

"Very dreadful indeed," said her father. "The shock of witnessing Mr. Myers' sufferings (he died in frantic delirium) almost upset the reason of his unfortunate wife. She fell into a state of morbid melancholy, making an idol of her grief. From the day of her husband's funeral to that of her own death, a period of fifty years, my poor aunt never once quitted the house, even to attend a place of worship."

"The most singular and eccentric mark of the widow's sorrow was her determination that the room in which her husband died should always remain as it was on the day of his burial," said Bruce. "Aunt Myers had the shutters closed, and the door not only locked, but actually bricked up, so that no foot might ever enter or eye look on the apartment connected in her mind with associations so painful. It is merely that closed-up chamber which gives to the house the name of being haunted."

"The sooner it is opened to heaven's light and air the better," observed Captain Arrows. "Let the first thing done in that house be to unbrick and unlock the door, fling back shutters and throw open windows, and the first time that I visit Myst Court let me sleep in the haunted chamber."

"I am afraid that I have not the power either to follow your advice or to gratify your wish," said Mr. Trevor. "My poor aunt, retaining her strange fancy to the last, actually— in a codicil to her will—made as a condition to my possession of the place that the room in which her husband died should remain as it is now, bricked up and unused."

"That condition would add not a little to the difficulty of letting or selling the house," observed the practical Bruce.

"It appears to be a law of nature that whatever is useless becomes actually noxious," remarked the captain. "That closed chamber, into which the sun never shines, will tend to make the dwelling less healthy, as well as less cheerful."

Again Emmie breathed a faint sigh.

"And now we return to my proposition," said Mr. Trevor gravely. "Shall I remain where I am, and put this large property into the hands of some agent to let or improve as he may,—with but little chance of its becoming of much more than nominal value; or shall I give up my office, take the pension to which I am now entitled, live on my own estate, look after my tenants, and gradually effect such improvements as may make the land profitable, if not to myself, to my heirs?"

"What does Bruce, who has seen the property, say on the question?" asked the captain, turning towards his elder nephew.

Bruce replied alike without haste or hesitation. "If my father leave his office in London, there are at least twenty persons ready and eager to fill his place, and to do his work; but there is not one who could be his substitute at Myst Court. It is the master's eye that is wanted there, not that of a paid agent."

Young as was Bruce, his words carried weight with his father. Mr. Trevor's elder son in most points presented a contrast to Vibert; as regarded ripeness of judgment, the fifteen months that separated their ages might have been as many years. In physical appearance the brothers were also unlike each other. Bruce, though older, was not so tall as Vibert; his frame was spare and slight. He had not, like Emmie and his brother, inherited their mother's beauty. The good sense expressed in his steady gray eyes, the decision marked in the curve of his lip, alone redeemed the countenance of Bruce from being of a commonplace type. The characteristics of the three Trevors had been thus playfully sketched by a lively girl who was a frequent guest at Summer Villa: "If I want amusement, I choose Vibert for my companion; if I need sympathy, I turn to Emmie; but if I am in difficulty or danger, commend me to Bruce, he has the cool brain and firm heart. I like Vibert; I love Emmie; but Bruce is the one whom I trust."

A brief silence succeeded the young man's reply to his father; it was broken by Vibert's inquiry, "What sort of a town is S——?"

"Like any other county town," replied Bruce shortly. The question seemed to him to be trifling, and irrelevant to the subject of conversation.

"S—— seemed to me to be a pleasant, cheerful place," said the more indulgent father.

"And I suppose that fishing and shooting are to be had at Myst Court?" inquired the youth.

"A stream runs through part of the property, and there is likely to be plenty of game in the copse," replied Mr. Trevor.

"Then I vote that we go to Myst Court!" cried Vibert.

"The only thing which makes me hesitate in coming to a decision," observed Mr. Trevor, "is the doubt as to whether my dear girl would like being taken from her present bright home. Emmie has here so many sources of innocent amusement, so many young friends and pleasant companions, that it might be trying for her to be transplanted to a place which I cannot now represent as a cheerful abode, though I hope that it in time may become such." Mr. Trevor, as he spoke, looked tenderly on his daughter, and pressed the hand which he held in his own.

"Oh, papa, do not think about me; I shall have you and my brothers," said Emmie. It did not escape the notice of Arrows that his niece spoke with a little effort, and that her lip quivered as she uttered the words.

"You shall have a pony-chaise, too," said her father; "it will be needed to carry you to church on Sundays, and on week-days you shall drive about the country, explore the neighbourhood, or indulge a lady's taste by shopping in S——."

"And carry us back from our tutor's," interrupted Vibert; "for I suppose that a hansom is not to be got for love or money; and I've no fancy for trudging six miles every day, like a horse in a mill."

By the time that the dressing-bell rang before dinner, the question of removing to Wiltshire was virtually settled. Emmie was too unselfish and high-principled to oppose a decision which approved itself both to her common sense and her conscience. She tried to hide from her father her strong repugnance to leaving Summer Villa, its pleasant associations and friendly society, in order to bury herself alive in a grand, gloomy house, quite out of repair, and with the name of being haunted besides.

CHAPTER III.

GOSSIP DOWNSTAIRS.

 The topic which excited such interest in the drawing-room was certain to be eagerly discussed in the kitchen also. At the servants' supper-table that night nothing was talked about but Myst Hall, and the probability of the Trevor family leaving Summer Villa to settle in Wiltshire.

"I'm certain that there will be a grand move soon, from what I heard while I was waiting at table," said John the footman. "I mean to give warning to-morrow," he added, shrugging his shoulders.

"You had better do nothing in a hurry," observed Susan Pearl, a sensible, pleasant-looking woman, who had been Emmie's attendant when she was a child, and who acted as her lady's-maid now. "You may find that second thoughts are best, when the matter in question is throwing up a good place."

"Then master had better have his second thoughts too," observed John, as he stretched out his hand for the walnut pickle. "A week of Myst Court was quite enough for me, I assure you. If you were to see how the mortar is starting from the brickwork, how the plaster is peeling from the ceilings, and how the furniture is faded; if you were to hear the windows shaking and rattling as if they had a fit of the ague, the boards creaking, and the long passages echoing, you would think any sensible man well out of so dreary a prison."

"Plaster and paint can be put on anew, a carpet deadens echoes, and curtains keep out draughts. As for windows rattling, a peg will stop that," observed Susan, who was not easily daunted.

"Outside the house it's as bad as within," pursued John. "The drive is green with moss and grass, and the piece of water with duckweed; the trees grow so thick together that you can't see ten yards before you; and your ears are dinned with the cawing of rooks."

"Weeding and clearing will do wonders," said Susan; "if Miss Emmie were set in a coal-yard, she would manage to make flowers grow there."

"Are there good shops near?" inquired Ann, the housemaid, who wore a cap of the newest pattern, trimmed with the gayest of ribbons.

"Shops!" echoed John, as if amazed at the question. "Why, the very baker and grocer have to come in their carts from S——, and there's nothing like a gentleman's house within several miles of Myst Court."

"I'll give warning to-morrow," said Ann. "As well be transported at once, as go to such a heathenish out-of-the-way place as that is!"

"I suppose that Myst Court is overrun with rats and mice," observed Mullins the cook.

"Not a bit of it," answered John, laughing. "Thieving rats and mice would have had a hard life of it with old Mrs. Myers' nine and thirty cats and kittens to serve as a rural police."

"La, John, you're joking! nine and thirty!" exclaimed the women-servants in a breath.

"I'm not joking," replied the footman; "I counted them,—black, white, gray, and tabby, long hair and short hair, blue eyes and green eyes! Mrs. Myers cared a deal more for her cats than she did for her tenants' children. No, no, the rats and mice would find no safe corner in that big old house, unless in the shut-up, haunted chamber."

Whenever these last two words were pronounced, curiosity was certain to be roused, and questioning to follow. Three voices now spoke at once.

"Do you think that the place is really haunted?"

"Did you see any ghosts?"

"What do the servants say about that chamber?"

The last question, which was Susan's, was that to which John gave reply.

"The cook and the housemaid at Myst Court say that for certain they've heard odd noises, a sighing, and a rattling, and a howling o' nights," said the footman, looking as mysterious as his plump, well-fed face would allow him to do.

"On windy nights, I suppose," said the sensible Susan. "I've heard a sighing, and a rattling, and a howling even here in Summer Villa."

"Let him tell us more!" cried Ann impatiently, for John's countenance showed that he had a great deal more to impart. The footman prefaced his tale by deliberately laying down his knife and fork, though cold beef lay still on his plate; this was a token that honest John was indeed in solemn earnest. He began in a lowered tone, while every head was bent forward to listen:—

"Mrs. Jael Jessel, the old lady's attendant, told me that she had twice passed a ghost in the corridor, and once on the stairs. It was a tall figure in white,—at least seven feet high,—and it had great round eyes like carriage-lamps staring upon her."

Ann and the cook uttered exclamations, and exchanged glances of horror; but Susan quietly remarked, "If Mrs. Jessel really saw such a sight once, she was a stout-hearted woman to stay to see it a second time, and a third. Did this brave lady's-maid look much the worse for meeting her ghost?"

"No," replied John, a little taken aback by the question. "Mrs. Jessel is a stout, comfortable-looking person. I suppose that she got used to seeing odd sights."

Susan burst into a merry laugh. "John, John," she cried, "this Mrs. Jessel has been taking a rise out of you. She saw that you were soft, and wanted to make an impression." Susan was helping herself to butter, which, perhaps, supplied her with the simile of which she made use.

"Mrs. Jessel did not stay at Myst Court for nothing," said John, who, possibly, wished to give a turn to the conversation; "she had not waited on Mrs. Myers for more than three years, yet the old lady left her five hundred pounds, a nice little furnished house just outside the Myst woods, and all the cats and kittens, which she could not trust to the care of strangers."

"It was made worth her while to live in a haunted house," observed Ann.

"I thought at first," continued John, who had taken up his knife and fork, and was using them to good purpose,—"I thought at first that I might as well put my best foot forward, for that it would be no bad thing to have a wife with five hundred pounds and a house to start with; and," he added slyly, "with such a live-stock to boot, one might have done a little business in the furrier's line. But—"

"But, but,—speak out!" cried Ann with impatience; "what comes after the 'but'?"

"Somehow I didn't take to Mrs. Jessel," said John, "and shouldn't have cared to have married her, had the five hundred pounds been five thousand instead."

"What's against her?" inquired the cook.

"Nothing that I know of," said John; "but when you see her, you'll understand what I mean."

"I'll not see her; I'm not going to Myst Court; I could not abide being so far from London," observed the cook.

"I shall give miss warning to-morrow!" cried Ann.

"And what will you do?" inquired John of Susan.

"Stay by the family, to be sure," was the answer. "Would I leave my young lady now, just when her heart is heavy? for heavy it is, I am certain of that. While she was dressing for dinner, Miss Emmie could hardly keep in her tears. It is no pleasure to her to leave a home like Summer Villa, where she has nothing to cross her, and everything to please. There's not a day but Miss Alice, or some other friend, comes dropping in to see her; nor a week that passes without some sight or amusement in London. At the age of nineteen, a young lady like Miss Trevor does not willingly leave such a pleasant place as this for a dreary, deserted old country-house."

"Poor miss! I pity her from my soul!" cried Ann.

"With a pity that would leave her to see none but new faces in her household!" said the indignant Susan. "No; I'll stick by my young lady through thick and thin, were she to go to the middle of Africa. I've been with her these ten years, ever since she lost her poor mother, and I will not desert her now."

"You don't believe in ghosts," observed John.

"I believe my Bible," replied Susan gravely; "I read there that I have a Maker far too wise and good to allow His servants to be troubled by visitors from another world. This ghost-fearing is all of a piece with fortune-telling, and spirit-rapping, and all such follies, after which weak-brained people run. Simple faith in God turns out faith in such nonsense, as daylight puts an end to darkness."

Susan was not laughed at for her little lecture as ten years before she might have been. Her long period of service and her tried character had given her influence, and won for her that respect which a consistent life secures even from the worldly. Her fellow-servants felt somewhat ashamed of their own credulous folly.

"I'm not a bit afraid of ghosts," said Ann; "but I don't choose to mope in the country."

"I don't care a rap for a house being haunted; but I mean to better myself," said the cook.

"Do you think, John, that the young gentlemen will like Myst Court?" inquired Susan.

"I think Master Bruce has a purpose and a plan in his head; and when he has a purpose and a plan, it's his way to go right on, steady and straight, and none can say whether he likes or don't like what he's a-doing," answered the footman. "When he looked over the house, it wasn't to say how bad things were, but to see how things could be bettered. He has a lot o' common sense, has Master Bruce; I believe that he'll make himself happy after his fashion, and that ghosts, if there be any, will take care to keep out of his way."

"He'd see through them," said Susan, laughing.

"As for Master Vibert," continued John, "if he has plenty of amusement, he'll not trouble his head about ghost or goblin. He's a light-hearted chap is Master Vibert, and a bit giddy, I take it. Perhaps his father ain't sorry to have him a bit further off from London than he is here in Summer Villa."

"The one for whom I feel sorry is my young lady," said Susan. "She'll not take a gun or a fishing-rod like her brothers, and—"

"She'll be mortally afraid of ghosts," cried Ann.

"She's timid as a hare," observed John.

"If miss screams when a puppy-dog barks at her, and hides her face under her bed-clothes if there's a peal o' thunder, how will she face ghosts ten feet high, with eyes like carriage-lamps?" cried the cook.

Susan looked annoyed and almost angry at hearing her mistress spoken of thus. "Miss Emmie is nervous and not very strong, so she is easily startled," said the maid; "but she is as good a Christian as lives, and will not, I hope, give way to any idle fancies and fears such as trouble folk who are afraid of their own shadows. I should not, however, wonder if she find Myst Court very dull."

"She'd better take to amusing herself by looking after the poor folk around her," observed the cook. "From what you've told us, John, I take it there's company enough of bare-legged brats and ragged babies."

"Miss Emmie is mighty afraid of infection," said John, doubtfully shaking his head. "She has never let me call a four-wheeler for her in London since small-pox has been going about. Miss will cross to the other side of the road if she sees a child with a spot on its face. No, no; she'll never venture to set so much as her foot in one of them dirty hovels that I saw down there in Wiltshire."

"'Tain't fit as she should," observed Ann. "Why should ladies demean themselves by going amongst dirty beggarly folk?"

"To help them out of their misery," said Susan. "In the place where I lived before I came here, I saw my mistress, and the young ladies besides, take delight in visiting the poor. They thought that it no more demeaned them to enter a cottage than to enter a church; the rich and the poor meet together in both."

"Miss Emmie is too good to be proud," observed John; "but, take my word for it, she'll never muster up courage to go within ten yards of a cottage. Kind things she'll say, ay, and do; for she has the kindest heart in the world. But she'll send you, Susan, with her baskets of groceries and bundles of cast-off clothes; she'll not hunt up cases herself. Miss would shrink from bad smells; she'd faint at the sight of a sore. She'll not dirty her fine muslin dresses, or run the risk of catching fevers, or may be the plague, by visiting the poor."

"Time will show," observed Susan. But from her knowledge of the disposition of her young lady, the faithful attendant was not without her misgivings upon the subject.

CHAPTER IV.

PREPARING TO START.

The question of a move was finally settled; Myst Court was to be the future residence of its new owner, who lost no time in making arrangements for effecting in it such repairs as were absolutely necessary to make it a tolerably comfortable dwelling. More than this Mr. Trevor did not at present attempt; his expenses, he knew, would be heavy. His newly-inherited property would yield no immediate supply; improvements must be gradually made. The life of a landed proprietor was one altogether new to Mr. Trevor, who had passed thirty years of his life in a government office, never being more than a few weeks at a time absent from London. Being a sensible man, he was aware that experience on a hitherto untried path is often dearly bought. He expected to make some mistakes, but resolved to act with such prudence that even mistakes should not involve him in serious difficulties.

The six weeks which elapsed before the departure of the family from Summer Villa were full of business and arrangements. Mr. Trevor, having to wind up his office-work, and settle the affairs of his late aunt, was, except in the evenings, very little at home. Emmie, who acted as her father's housekeeper, found a hundred small matters to arrange before making a move which must bring so complete a change. Her brothers attended a private tutor in London, and usually went and returned by the same trains as their father; so that, but for the company of her uncle, Emmie would have spent much of her time alone. But the captain was a cheerful companion and a most efficient helper to his young niece. He made up her accounts, he paid her bills, he helped her to decide which articles of furniture must be taken to the new home, which left to be sold or given away. The slow-paced John was astonished at the energy with which the naval officer would mount a ladder, and with his own hands take down family pictures and swathe them in the matting which was to secure their safe transit to Wiltshire.

"Sure the captain does the work of three. One would think he'd been 'prenticed to a carpenter by the way he handles the tools; and he runs up a ladder like a cat," observed John to another member of the household.

Captain Arrows felt strong sympathy for his niece. He saw, perhaps more clearly than did any one else, how painful to her was the change which was coming over her life. Her uncle respected Emmie's unselfish efforts to hide from her father her reluctance to leave Summer Villa and all its pleasant surroundings. Arrows noticed the shade of sadness on Emmie's fair face when she received, as she frequently did, congratulations on her father's accession to property. The acute observer could not fail to see that the acquisition of Myst Court was no source of pride or pleasure to Emmie.

Miss Trevor was perpetually reminded of her approaching departure from the home in which her life had been so much like a summer holiday. Many visits of leave-taking had to be paid, and few could be paid without more or less of pain. Emmie had numerous friends, and to some she could not bid farewell without a sharp pang of regret. Even inanimate things, dear from association, were resigned with sadness. Emmie sighed to take leave of her garden, and spent much time in procuring cuttings from her favourite plants, her geraniums, her fuchsias, her myrtles. With what pleasant memories were those flowers connected in the affectionate mind of Emmie! Summer Villa and her friends seemed dearer than ever when she was about to leave them behind.

Next to the captain, Emmie found her best helper in Susan. Active, thoughtful, the neatest of packers, the most intelligent of maids, Susan was indeed "a treasure" to her young mistress.

"You seem to like the change," said the cook to Susan, who was humming cheerfully to herself as she knelt beside a hamper which she was packing with china.

Susan did not pause to look up from her work as she answered, "I never ask myself whether I like it or not; my business is to make ready for it, and that is enough for me."

"How dismal a house looks when everything in it is being pulled down and upset!" remarked the cook, standing with her back to the wall, and watching Susan as she imbedded quaint old china tea-pot and cream-jug in white cotton wool as carefully as she might have laid a baby in a cradle. "The hall all lumbered with luggage; the whole place smelling of matting; things awanted just when they've been packed up, corded, and labelled; the walls looking without their pictures as faces would do without eyes,—there is something horrid uncomfortable about a house as has been long lived in when it's agoing to be left for good. I'm half sorry that I agreed to stay on the extra fortnight; only it was such a convenience to the family. I don't know what they'd have done had Ann and I taken ourselves off before the move was fairly over."

Susan went quietly on with her occupation, while Mrs. Mullins went on with her talking.

"P'r'aps master did wisely to keep on Mrs. Myers' servants, for he'd hardly have got London folk to stay in his dismal country house, even on double wages. We'll have you at the Soho registry before three months are over."

"Time will show," said Susan.

"Them people down at Myst Court are accustomed to the kind of life they lead there," continued the loquacious Mrs. Mullins, "and that's the reason they don't mind it. Frogs like their ditch because they've never known anything better; and I suppose that folk in a haunted house get used to ghosts, as eels are used to skinning."

"Or learn not to be frightened at shadows," said Susan.

"I'm not frightened; don't you fancy that shadows keep me from going to Myst Court," cried the cook. "But I could never stand a place where the butcher—as John says—comes but twice a week in the winter; no cook could abide that."

"It seems that Mrs. Myers' cook did," observed Susan.

"She's no cook!" exclaimed Mrs. Mullins, with an emphatic snort of disdain: "she's had nothing to keep her hand in, and don't know a *vol-au-vent* from a *soufflet!* Why, Mrs. Myers never saw company, never asked a friend to a meal! John says that for five days out of the seven the old lady dined on mutton-broth, and the other two on barley-gruel! John told me that he could hardly touch the dinners which Hannah prepared; he is used to have things so very different," added Mrs. Mullins with professional pride.

"If Hannah's cooking satisfied master and his son, John might have been satisfied too," observed Susan.

"Oh, Mr. Trevor is never partic'lar about his food; and as for Master Bruce, John says that he was so much taken up about arrangements, and alterations, and improvements, that he would not have noticed if the stew had been made of old shoes. But Master Vibert, he's not so easily pleased; he likes his dainty bits, his sauces, and his sweeties;

there is some satisfaction in dishing up a dinner for him! He'll soon find out that this Hannah knows just as much of cooking as I do of cow-milking, and there will be a worrit in the house." Mrs. Mullins folded her hands complacently at the thought of how much her own valuable services would be regretted, and then inquired, in an altered tone, "Is the captain going to Myst Court with the rest of the party?"

"No; I am sorry to say that the captain leaves this to-morrow," said Susan. "He is before long to start on another cruise, and as he has much business to do in the docks, he needs to stop for awhile in London. The carriage which takes the captain away is to drop Miss Emmie at the house of her friend, Miss Alice, to whom she wishes to say good-bye. My poor dear young lady! every day brings its good-bye to her now. It will be well when Friday comes, and the move to Myst Court is fairly over."

"I'd never go into a new house on a Friday; it's unlucky," observed Mrs. Mullins, as she turned away and went off to the kitchen.

CHAPTER V.

HAUNTED ROOMS.

 November has come with nights of drizzle and mornings of fog. The dreariness of the weather without adds to the sense of discomfort within the half-dismantled house. The carpet has been taken from the staircase, and the old family clock no longer is heard striking the hours. The drawing-room is much changed in appearance from what it was when the reader was first introduced into the Trevors' cheerful abode. It is evening, and the family are sitting together, with the exception of the master of the house, who is busy in his study with lawyers' papers and parchment deeds before him. The light of the drawing-room lamp falls on a scanty amount of furniture; for sofa, arm-chair, and piano have all been packed up for removal to the new home. No ornament of china, no graceful vase relieves the bareness of the white mantelpiece; the mirror has been taken away, no trace remains of pictures except square marks on the wall. The guitar has vanished from view; the globe of gold-fish is now the property of a friend; the ferns have been sent to the greenhouse of an aunt in Grosvenor Square.

Emmie sits at the table with her lace-work beside her, but her needle is idle. Bruce, the most actively occupied of the party, is drawing plans of cottages, and jotting down in his note-book estimates of expenses. The captain has a book in his hand, but makes slow progress with its contents. Vibert is glancing over a number of *Punch*. The party have been for the last ten minutes so silent that the pattering of the November rain on the window-panes is distinctly heard.

"I hope that we shall not have such weather as this when we go to our new home," said Vibert, as with a yawn he threw down his paper. "The place will need at least sunshine to make it look a degree more lively than a lunatic asylum. 'Tis lucky that our queer old great-aunt did not take it into her head to paint the house black, inside and outside, and put in her will that it must remain so, as a compliment to her husband, who has been dead for the last fifty years. Fancy bricking up the best bed-room!"

"Such an act proves that Mrs. Myers was in a very morbid state of mind," said the captain.

"What a misfortune!" observed Emmie.

"Misfortune! I should rather call it weakness—absurdity," said Bruce, sternly glancing up from his drawing.

"I should call it a sin, a downright sin," cried Vibert. "Such a shame it is to make what might have been a jolly country-house into a sort of rural Newgate! I'm afraid that even our best friends will not care to visit us there. Why, I asked pretty little Alice to-day whether she were coming to brighten us up at Christmas, and she actually answered that she was rather afraid of haunted houses, especially on dark winter nights."

Bruce smiled a little disdainfully; and the captain suggested that perhaps the fair lady was jesting.

"Not a bit of it," answered Vibert; "Alice was as much in earnest as were all our servants when they gave us warning, because not one of them but plucky Susan would go to Myst Court. Why, I'd bet that Emmie herself is shivery-shakery at the idea of the house being haunted, and that she'll not care to walk at night along the passages lest she should meet some tall figure in white."

Emmie coloured, and looked so uncomfortable, that her uncle, who noticed her embarrassment, effected a diversion in her favour by giving a turn to the conversation.

"I have been tracing a parallel in my mind," he observed, "between the human soul and the so-called haunted dwelling. Most persons have in the deepest recess of the spiritual man some secret chamber, where prejudice shuts out the light, where self-deception bricks up the door. Into this chamber the possessor himself in some cases never enters to search out and expel the besetting sin, which, unrecognized, perhaps lurks there in the darkness."

"You speak of our hearts?" asked Emmie.

"I do," replied her uncle. "It is my belief that not one person in ten thousand knows the ins and outs, the dark corners, the hidden chambers, of that which he bears in his own bosom."

"Every Christian must," said Bruce; "for every Christian is bound to practise the duty of self-examination."

"I hope that you don't call every one who does not practise it a heathen or a Turk," cried Vibert. "All that dreadful hunting up of petty peccadilloes, and confessing a string of them at once, is, at least to my notion, only fit work for hermits and monks!"

"We are not talking about confession, but simply about self-knowledge," observed the captain.

"Oh, where ignorance is bliss," began Vibert gaily; but his brother cut short the misapplied quotation with the remark, "Ignorance of ourselves must be folly."

Vibert took up again the comic paper which he had laid down, and pretended to re-examine the pictures. But for the captain's presence the youth would have begun to whistle, to show how little he cared for Bruce's implied rebuke; for, as Vibert had often told Emmie, he had no notion of being "put down" by his brother.

"Do you think it easy to acquire self-knowledge?" asked Arrows, fixing his penetrating glance upon Bruce, who met it with the calm steadiness which was characteristic of the young man.

17

"Like any other kind of knowledge, it requires some study," replied Bruce Trevor; "but it is not more difficult to acquire than those other kinds of knowledge would be."

"In that you come to a different conclusion from that of the writer of this book," observed Arrows; and he read aloud the following lines from Dr. Goulburn's "Thoughts on Personal Religion," the volume which he held in his hand:—

"'One of the first properties of the bosom sin with which it behoves us to be well acquainted, as our first step in the management of our spiritual warfare, is its property of concealing itself. In consequence of this property, it often happens that a man, when touched in his weak point, answers that whatever other faults he may have, this fault, at least, is no part of his character.'"

The captain read the quotation so emphatically that Vibert again threw down his paper, and listened whilst Arrows thus went on:—

"'This circumstance, then, may furnish us with a clue to the discovery: of whatever fault you feel that, if accused of it, you would be stung and nettled by the apparent injustice of the charge, suspect yourself of that fault, in that quarter very probably lies the black spot of the bosom sin. If the skin is in any part sensitive to pressure, there is probably mischief below the surface.'"

"I doubt that the author is right," observed Bruce. "Besetting sins cannot hide themselves thus from those who honestly search their own hearts."

"Perhaps some search all but the haunted chamber," suggested Vibert. Captain Arrows smiled assent to the observation.

"By way of throwing light on the question," said he, "suppose that each of you were to set down in writing what you suppose to be your besetting sin; and that I—who have watched your characters from your childhood—should also put down on paper what I believe to be the bosom temptation of each. Is it likely that your papers and mine would agree; that the same 'black spot' would be touched by your hands and mine; that we should point out the same identical fault as the one which most easily and frequently besets the soul of each of you three?"

"It would be curious to compare the two papers," cried Vibert. "I wish, captain, that you really would write down what you think of us all. It would be like consulting a phrenological professor, without the need of having a stranger's fingers reading off our characters from the bumps on our heads."

"I am not speaking of the whole character, but of the one sin that most easily besets," said the captain. "Would a close observer's view of its nature agree with that held by the person within whose heart it might lurk?"

"Perhaps not," said Bruce, after a pause for reflection. "But the person beset by the sin would know more about its existence than the most acute observer, who could judge but by outward signs."

"That is the very point on which we differ," remarked Captain Arrows. "The property of the bosom sin is to conceal itself, but only from him to whom the knowledge of its presence would be of the highest importance. I should be half afraid," the captain added with a smile, "to tell even my nephews and niece what I thought the besetting sin of each, lest they should be 'stung and nettled by the apparent injustice of the charge,' and feel, though they might not say it aloud, that 'whatever other faults they may have, this fault, at least, forms no part of the character in question.'"

The captain's hearers looked surprised at his words. Vibert burst out laughing. "You must think us a desperately bad lot!" cried he.

"Uncle, I wish that you would write down what you think is the besetting sin of each of us," said Emmie, "and give the little paper quietly to the person whom it concerns, not, of course, to be read by any one else. I am sure that I would not be offended by anything you would write, and it might do me good to know what you believe to be my greatest temptation."

"As you are going away to-morrow, you would escape the rage and fury of the indignant Emmie, however 'stung and nettled' she might be!" laughed Vibert Trevor. "Now, Bruce," added the youth sarcastically, "would you not like the captain to inform you confidentially what he considers the tiny 'black spot' in your almost perfect character?"

"I have no objection to my uncle's writing down what he chooses," replied Bruce coldly. "All that I keep to is this,—neither he nor any other man living can tell me a fact regarding my own character which I have not known perfectly well before."

"Were I to agree to write down my impressions, it would be to induce you all to give the subject serious reflection," observed the captain. "It matters little whether I am or am not correct in my conclusions; but it is of great importance that no one should be deceived regarding himself. I wish to lead you to think."

"Oh, I'll not engage to do that! I hate thinking; it's a bore!" cried Vibert gaily. "I know I'm a thoughtless dog,—ah, I've hit the 'black spot' quite unawares! Thoughtlessness is my besetting sin!"

"My difficulty would be to single out one amongst my many faults," said Emmie.

"Now that is humbug; you know that it is!" exclaimed her youngest brother. "You have no fault at all, except the fault of being a great deal too good. I should like you better if you were as lively and larky as Alice!"

"Saucy boy!" said Emmie, and she smiled.

"But, captain," continued Vibert, addressing himself to his uncle, "though we are willing enough to read what you write, we won't be driven to anything in the shape of confession. You may tell us what is your notion of what lurks in our haunted rooms, but we won't invite you in and say, 'Behold there's my besetting sin!'"

"I want no confessions," said Captain Arrows. "I repeat that my only object is to induce you to pull down your brickwork, draw back your curtains, and search for yourselves; or, to drop metaphor and speak in plain words, to lead you to make the discovery of the weakest point in your respective characters the subject of candid investigation and serious thought."

And to a certain degree this desired result was obtained. Though Vibert laughed, and Bruce looked indifferent, to their minds, as well as to that of their sister, the subject of self-knowledge recurred at different parts of the evening.

"I don't suppose that the captain can look further through a mill-stone than can any one else," thought Vibert; "yet he has uncommonly sharp eyes, and is always on the watch. No doubt he learned that habit at sea. I am glad that he can detect some fault in Master Bruce, who is a kind of pope in our house, though I, for one, don't believe in his infallibility. I wonder on what my uncle will fix as the bad spirit in my haunted room. I should say—let me think—I have never thought about the matter before. Well, I don't take to religion as earnestly as do papa and my elder brother and sister. I don't go twice to church on Sundays, nor—if the truth must be owned—do I pay much attention to the service whilst I am there. I'd rather any day read a novel than a serious book. I believe that's the worst I can say of myself. The captain would call that—let me see—would he call that irreligion? No, no; that name is too hard. I'm thoughtless, I own, but certainly not irreligious. Impiety? Why, that is worse still! I do not pretend to be in the least *pious*, but still I'd be ready to knock down any fellow who called me the reverse. I'm something between the two poles. Levity? Ah, that's the word, the precise word to describe my besetting sin, if one can call mere levity a sin. I am no man's enemy but my own; and not my own enemy either, for I spare and indulge myself in every way that I can. Levity may be a fault at sixty, but it's no fault at all at sixteen. I should decidedly object to be as sober as Bruce. He goes on his way like a steady old coach, while I am like a bicycle,"— Vibert laughed to himself as the simile occurred to his fancy. "A bicycle is quick, light, not made to carry much luggage, and a little given to coming to smash! Yes, I skim the world like a bicycle, and levity is my worst fault!" Yawning after the unusual effort of even such cursory self-examination, Vibert now set his thoughts free to ramble in any direction, satisfied that nothing of a serious nature could be laid to his charge.

"It is strange that my uncle should imagine that he can penetrate the recesses of the heart of another," such was the reflection of Bruce, as, candle in hand, he mounted the staircase that night. "Captain Arrows can but judge of my character by my outward conduct, and he can have seen but little to find fault with in that. I own—and with regret—that in many points I fail in my duty towards my Maker; but that is a secret between my conscience and God,—a secret which no man can penetrate, and with which no man has a right to meddle. Yet it is evident that my uncle has detected some visible error, whatever that error may be. I am aware that I have a defective temper, but I have lately been gaining some control over that which Calvin called an 'unruly beast.' I may, indeed, have betrayed some impatience in my manner towards Vibert in the presence of my critical uncle," thus flowed on the reflections of Bruce as he entered his room, and closed the door behind him. "I now remember my uncle's remarking to me that I might have more influence with my brother if I showed him greater indulgence. But who can have patience with Vibert's follies?" Bruce set down his candle, and threw himself on a chair. "Vibert has been a spoilt child from his cradle, and now, when nearly seventeen years of age, is no better than a spoilt child still! Our poor dear mother made her youngest-born almost an idol; my father is blind to his faults; Emmie pets and humours him to the top of his bent; and all the world does the same. Vibert is admired, courted, and welcomed wherever he goes, because, forsooth, his face is what girls call handsome, and he can rattle off any amount of nonsense to please them. Vibert does not mind playing the fool, and he plays it to the life!" Bruce paused, and conscience gave a low note of warning to the elder brother. "I am, I fear, harsh in my judgment. Want of charity, that is perhaps my besetting sin. I am too quick to perceive the faults and follies of others. That is a quality, however, which is not without its advantages in a world such as this. I am not easily taken in; mere veneer and gilding will not deceive my eye. I cannot be blind, if I wish it, either to my own faults or to those of others." Bruce thought that he knew himself thoroughly, and that there was no haunted room in his heart which he had not boldly explored.

Emmie Trevor had her heart-searchings as she sat silent before her mirror, while Susan brushed out the long glossy tresses of her young mistress's hair.

"I would fain know what my dear uncle regards as my besetting sin," mused the gentle girl. "I was so foolish as almost to fancy that one so loving and partial as he is would not notice my faults, and I am still more foolish in feeling a little mortified on finding that I was mistaken in this. What defect in my character is most likely to have struck so acute an observer? My uncle cannot possibly know how often my thoughts wander in prayer; how cold and ungrateful I sometimes am even towards Him whom I yet truly love and adore. It is something in my outward behaviour that must have displeased my uncle. Is it vanity?" Emmie raised her eyes to her mirror, and had certainly no reason to be dissatisfied with the face which she saw reflected in the glass. "Yes, I fear that I am vain; I do think myself pretty, and I cannot help knowing that I sing well,—I have been told that so often. Then I have certainly love of approbation; my uncle may have detected that, for it is so sweet to me to be admired and praised by those whom I love,—and perhaps by others also. This vanity and love of approbation may lead to jealousy, a very decided sin.

Did I not feel some slight vexation even at Vibert's playful words about Alice, his wish that I were more like that gay, giddy girl? I find Alice nice enough as a companion, but would certainly never set her up as a model. I am afraid,"—thus Emmie pursued the current of her reflections,—"I am afraid that I might be haunted by jealousy, if circumstances gave me any excuse for harbouring a passion so mean, so sinful. I have often thought that for papa to marry again would be to me such a trial. I could hardly bear that any one, even a wife, should be dearer to him than myself. I should grieve at his doing what might really add to his comfort; and oh! is not this selfish, hatefully selfish? It shows that with all my love for my only remaining parent, I care for his happiness less than my own. Certainly selfishness is in my character; it lurks in my haunted chamber, and doubtless my uncle has found it out! Then am I not conscious of giving way to indolence, and harbouring self-will? There are duties which I know to be duties, and yet from the performance of which I am always shrinking, making excuses for my neglect such as conscience tells me are weak and false. Truly mine is a very faulty character, yet am I given to self-deception; the kindness and partiality of every one round me help to blind me to my own faults, and perhaps to draw me into a little hypocrisy, to make each 'black spot' more black."

It will be observed that Emmie was no stranger to self-examination; it was to the maiden no new thing to commune with her heart and be still.

CHAPTER VI.

THREE WARNINGS.

"You are right, Bruce; it is certainly desirable for you to go down to Wiltshire to-day to make any needful arrangements, and prepare for our arrival to-morrow," said Mr. Trevor to his son on the following morning, when the family were at the breakfast-table. "New servants will need verbal directions; and you will see to the unpacking of the furniture which I have sent down from this place, and to the most suitable disposal of it in the several rooms of Myst Court." The gentleman rolled up his breakfast-napkin, and slipped it into its ring. "Your train starts at 10.30," he added, as he rose from his seat.

"Is Vibert to go with me?" inquired Bruce, glancing at his brother, who had, as usual, come down late, and was still engaged with his anchovies and muffin.

"I do not think that Vibert would give you much help," observed Mr. Trevor.

"No help at all," exclaimed Vibert quickly. "It may be just in Bruce's line to order and direct, see that there are enough of pots and pans in the kitchen, meat in the larder, and fires all over the house; but as for me—"

"You think it enough to eat the food and enjoy the fire," observed the captain drily.

"And I positively must go to Albert Hall to-night; the Nairns have asked me to make one of their party, and I really could not disappoint them," continued Vibert. "It is quite necessary that I should have a little amusement before going to bury myself in the wilds of Wiltshire. As Moore the poet sings,—

'To-night at least, to-night be gay, Whate'er to-morrow brings!'"

"That's fair enough," observed the indulgent father.

Bruce exchanged a glance with his uncle which conveyed the unuttered thought of both: "It is scarcely fair that one brother should have all the trouble and the other all the amusement." Vibert noticed the look, and laughed.

"Duty first—pleasure afterwards—that's the motto taught to all good little children!" he cried. "Bruce, you are the elder, and like to be first, so you naturally pair off with duty, whilst I am modest enough to be quite contented with pleasure."

Mr. Trevor smiled at the jest, though he shook his bald head in gentle reproof. Then turning to his brother-in-law, he observed, "Edward, I have an early engagement in London, and must be off to the station. I am afraid that I shall not find you here on my return."

"I also start early," said the captain. "Emmie has ordered the conveyance to be at the door at ten. I must therefore wish you good-bye now, thanking you for my pleasant visit to Summer Villa, and hoping next spring to find you all well and happy in your new home."

The brothers-in-law cordially shook hands and parted, Mr. Trevor going off to the station, as usual, on foot.

"I say, Bruce," observed Vibert, "if you have the settling about the rooms at Myst Court, mind that you give me a good one. I like plenty of air and light, and a cheerful view. No poky little cabin for me, nor an attic at the top of the house; long stairs are a terrible bore."

"I shall certainly give my first attention to the accommodation of my father and sister," said Bruce; "they never think of themselves."

"A hit at me, I suppose," cried Vibert with unruffled good-humour. "Ah! that reminds me of our conversation last evening. Captain, have you been hunting up the ghosts in our haunted rooms?" asked the youth as he rose from his place at the breakfast-table.

Arrows replied by drawing forth a memorandum-book from the pocket of his surtout. He unclasped it, and took out from it three minute pieces of paper, neatly folded up and addressed.

"I am going upstairs to look after my luggage," said the captain; "I leave with you—"

"These three private and confidential communications!" cried Vibert, playfully snatching the papers out of his uncle's hand. "Each one, I see, is directed: here's yours, Emmie; yours, Bruce; and here's mine!"

Captain Arrows did not wait to watch the effect produced by his little missives, but quitted the room to complete preparations for his departure.

"I'm of a frank nature," said Vibert; "I don't care if all the world hear my good uncle's opinion of me!" and, unfolding the scrap of paper which he held, the youth read aloud as follows: "*Be on your guard against the* Pride *that repels advice, resents reproof, and refuses to own a fault.* I don't recognize my likeness in this photo!" cried the youth; "if the portrait had been intended for Bruce,"—Vibert turned the paper and looked at the back—"sure enough, it *is* directed to Bruce; and the captain has hit him off to the life!"

"You made the apparent blunder on purpose," said Bruce with ill-suppressed anger, as he took the paper from Vibert, and then threw it into the fire. Then, after tossing down on the table the unopened note which had been handed to him first, Bruce Trevor turned on his heel, and quitted the apartment.

"Stung and nettled! stung and nettled! does he not wince!" cried Vibert, looking after his brother. "The captain has, sure enough, laid his finger on the sensitive spot!"

"I am so much vexed at your having read that private paper aloud," said Emmie; "it was never intended that we should know its contents."

"It told us nothing new," observed Vibert. "Bruce's pride is as plain as the nose on his face; only, like the nose, it is too close to him—too much a part of himself, for him to see it."

"Bruce is a noble, unselfish, generous fellow!" cried Emmie.

Vibert cared little to hear his brother's praises. "What is in your tiny paper?" he asked, after he had glanced at his own. "Why, Emmie, you look surprised at what our uncle has written. Tell me, just tell me what lurking mischief the sharp-eyed Mentor has ferreted out in you. Some concealed inclination to commit burglary or manslaughter?"

"I do not quite understand what my uncle means," said Emmie, gazing thoughtfully upon the little missive which she had opened and read.

"I could explain it—I could make it clear—just let me see what the oracle has written!" cried Vibert, with mirth and curiosity sparkling in his handsome dark eyes. "I'll tell you in return, Emmie, what he has put in my scrap of paper: *Beware of Selfishness.* Short but not sweet, and rather unjust. I am thoughtless and gay, I care not who says that much; but as for being selfish, it's a slander, an ungenerous slander!"

"Perhaps our uncle has again laid his finger on a sensitive spot," observed Emmie with a smile, but one so gentle that it could not offend.

"I want to know what the fault-finder lays to your charge, what solemn admonition has called up the roses on those fair cheeks!" cried the younger brother; and throwing one arm round Emmie, with his other hand Vibert possessed himself of the paper of the scarcely resisting girl, sharing her surprise as he glanced at the two words written upon it. Those words were—*Conquer Mistrust.*

"Mistrust of what or of whom?" said Vibert. "The oracle has propounded a kind of enigma: as you are going to take a *tête-à-tête* drive with the captain, you will have an opportunity of getting an explanation of your paper. As for mine, it goes after Bruce's— into the fire." Vibert suited the action to the word.

About half-an-hour afterwards the conveyance which was to take Captain Arrows from Summer Villa was driven up to the door. Emmie was ready, as arranged, to accompany her uncle part of the way. John handed up his luggage to be disposed of on the coach-box. Vibert came to the door to see the guest depart and bid him farewell. "I'll show him," said the youth to himself, "that I bear him no grudge for a warning that was not very necessary, and certainly not very polite."

"Good-bye, captain," cried Vibert, as he shook hands with his uncle; "come to Myst Court next spring, and you and I will make a raid on the haunted chamber."

"Where is Bruce? I have not wished him good-bye," said the captain, pausing when he was about to hand his niece into the carriage.

"Bruce!" called the clear voice of Emmie, as she ran back to the bottom of the staircase to let her brother know that the guest was on the point of departing.

"Bruce!" shouted Vibert with the full strength of his lungs.

There was no reply to either summons, and Emmie suggested that her brother might have gone out, not remembering that the carriage had been ordered so early. After a few minutes' delay, Arrows handed her into the carriage, with the words, "You will bid Bruce good-bye for me."

"None so deaf as those who won't hear," muttered Vibert, when the vehicle had rolled from the door. "Bruce heard us call, but he is in a huff, and did not choose to appear. He *repels advice, resents reproof,* and yet won't believe that he's proud! No more, perhaps, than I believe that I'm selfish!"

CHAPTER VII.

MISTRUST.

"I am so glad to have a little time for quiet conversation with you, dear uncle," said Emmie, as the carriage in which she was seated beside Arrows proceeded along the drive. "I want to ask you,"—she hesitated, and her voice betrayed a little nervousness as she went on,—"what it was that you meant when you bade me *conquer Mistrust?*"

"Let me refer you to our old favourite, the Pilgrim's Progress," replied the captain. "In whose company did the dreamer represent Mistrust, when he ran down the Hill of Difficulty to startle Christian with tidings of lions in the way?"

"In the company of Timorous," said Emmie.

"And have you no acquaintance with that personage?" asked the captain.

"Oh, then you only mean that I am a little timid and nervous," said Emmie, a good deal relieved. "That is no serious charge; you let me off too easily."

"Not so fast, my dear child. Let us examine the allegorical personages more closely. Timorous and Mistrust are not only found together, but they are very closely related."

"You would not have me a Boadicea or a Joan of Arc?" asked Emmie, smiling.

"I would have you—what you are—a gentle English maiden; but I would have you *more* than you now are,—that is to say, a trustful Christian maiden," replied Captain Arrows.

"Surely courage is a natural quality, which belongs to some and not to others," observed Emmie Trevor. "Besides, if it be a virtue at all, it is surely a man's rather than a woman's."

"Mere physical courage, such as 'seeks the bubble reputation e'en in the cannon's mouth,' is not a Christian virtue," said the captain; "it may be displayed by infidel or atheist. The courage which *is* a grace, a grace to be cultivated and prayed for, is that childlike trust in a Father's wisdom and love, by which the feeblest woman may glorify her Maker."

"Faith in God's wisdom and love! Oh, you do not surely think that I am so wicked as ever to doubt them! I have many faults, I know, but this one—" Emmie stopped short, startled to find on her tongue almost the very words which had been given as a sign that the bosom sin had been tracked to its lurking-place.

"You remember," said Captain Arrows, "that a few days ago I listened to your singing that fine hymn which begins with the lines,—

'Lord, it belongs not to my care
Whether I die or live.'"

"Yes," replied Emmie Trevor; "and you told me that, much as you admired that hymn, you did not think it suited for my singing. I supposed that you thought it too low for my voice."

"No, I thought it too high for your practice. Could it be consistently sung by one who that morning had been in nervous terror at the scratch of a kitten; one who owned that she would scarcely dare to nurse her best friend through the small-pox; one who, even with my escort, could not be persuaded to cross a field in which a few cows were grazing?"

"Oh, uncle, how can you take such trifles seriously!" cried Emmie, a good deal hurt.

"Because I wish you to take them a little more seriously," replied Captain Arrows. "You have hitherto regarded *unreasonable fear* as an innocent weakness, perhaps as something allied with feminine grace, and not as a foe to be resisted and conquered. I see that fear is at this time throwing a shadow over your path; that you would be happier if you had the power wholly to cast it aside."

"I have not the power," said Emmie. The words had scarcely escaped her lips when she wished them unspoken, for she was ashamed thus to plead guilty to a feeling of superstitious alarm.

"Let us then trace the parentage of unreasonable fear," said Captain Arrows. "I use the adjective advisedly. There are cases where the nerves are so shattered by illness, or enfeebled by age, that fears come on the mind, as fits on the body, not as a fault but as a heavy affliction. There are also times of extreme and awful danger, such as that of the Indian Mutiny, when faith must indeed have had a dread struggle with fear; though even then, in the hearts of tender women, faith won the victory still. But I am speaking of that fear which common sense would condemn. Such fear is, must be, the offspring of mistrust, and its effects show it to be a tempter and an enemy of the soul."

"What effects do you mean?" said Emmie.

"These three at least," answered the captain. "Unreasonable fear hinders usefulness, destroys peace, and prevents our glorifying God."

"I do not quite see how it should do so," murmured Emmie.

"It hinders usefulness," said her uncle; "like indolence, fear is ever seeing 'a lion in the street.' Does not fear hang like a clog on the spirit, *making 'I dare not' wait upon 'I would,'* even when duty to God and mercy to man is in question?"

Arrows paused as if for a reply. Emmie gave none; her eyes were gazing out of the carriage window on the smoky veil which hung over the great city which they were approaching; she knew that she dared not do, what thousands of her sex are doing, go as a child of light to carry light into the abodes of darkness. Emmie had owned in her uncle's presence that she was far too timid to visit the poor.

"Then fear destroys peace," continued the captain, "and I believe that it does so to a greater extent than does any other passion which troubles the soul, remorse only excepted. If we literally and fully obeyed the command so often repeated in Scripture, to hope and to be not afraid, a mountain of misery would be removed at once and cast into the sea. If you do not mind a personal application of the subject, would you, my dear child, feel uneasy at going to a house which is called haunted, if you realized that God fills all space, and that you are everywhere under His loving protection?"

Emmie still continued silent, looking out of the carriage window. Her feelings were those of deep mortification. That she, earnestly pious as she was, should virtually be accused of want of faith, that her deficiency in this first requisite of religion should have been so glaring as to have attracted the notice of a partial relative, was a trial the more painful from being totally unexpected.

"Bunyan represents Mistrust, the parent of unreasonable fear, as a robber," pursued the captain, referring again to that allegory which gives so wondrously true a picture of man's spiritual state. "We first meet Mistrust in company with Timorous, and their object is to discourage, to frighten, to make Christian start back from the perils which would meet him if he pursued the path of duty; when we next hear of Mistrust, he is in company with Guilt, and together they rob Little-faith of his treasure."

"Yes, mistrust does rob us of our peace," said Emmie with a sigh.

"And now, let me touch on my third point, even at the risk of giving some pain," said the captain. "Mistrust not only hinders usefulness, and mars peace, but prevents our glorifying our Maker as we might otherwise do. Is not the inconsistency of His children dishonouring to God? And is it not inconsistent to avow our belief that our Heavenly Father loves us—cares for us—is about our path and our bed, and yet to be as full of unreasonable terrors as if, like the fool, we said 'there is no God'? The Christian knows that Christ hath 'abolished death;' he knows that to depart from earth is to enter into rest; that light, and life, and glory await the redeemed of the Lord. Is it not inconsistent, I repeat, in one who believes all this, to shrink with unconcealed terror from the barest possibility that the time for his going home may be hastened, even a little? The natural effect of strong faith would be to make the righteous 'bold as a lion.'"

"Uncle, you judge me very hardly," murmured Emmie, ready to burst into tears.

"I do not judge you, dear child; I only warn you not to cherish, as an inmate, that enemy whom you have hitherto regarded but as a harmless infirmity. Bring him before the bar of reason, bind him with the strong cords of prayer. I have spoken thus frankly to you on this subject, because I foresee that on your conquest of mistrust, your victory over unreasonable fears, must depend much of your peace, happiness, and usefulness also, in the new home to which you are going. A realizing faith in God's presence, a simple trust in His love, these are the most powerful antidotes against superstitious and all other ill-grounded fears. The light that dispels shadows is the words, *I will fear no evil, for Thou art with me.*"

Captain Arrows had thus given to his sister's children his warning against what, from close observation of their characters, he deemed to be the besetting sin of each,—pride, selfishness, and mistrust. What had been the effect of his words? The monitor had given offence, he had given pain, and in one case, at least, his warning had been as the dropping into a brook of a pebble, that scarcely causes even a ripple. There are few who value gratuitous counsel; the many prefer to buy experience, though it should prove to be at the price of future pain and regret. We are seldom thankful to him who would explore for us the heart's haunted chamber, even should we not possess the candour and moral courage to search its depths for ourselves.

26

CHAPTER VIII.

THE JOURNEY.

On the following day Emmie, escorted by Vibert and attended by Susan, started for her new home. Almost at the last moment Mr. Trevor found that important business would, for another day, delay his own departure; but all arrangements for the general move having been made, he would not defer it, preferring for the single night to sleep at a hotel in London.

The bustle of departure took from its pain; Emmie left her dear old home without a tear, though not without a sigh of regret. Vibert was in high spirits, for novelty has its charm, especially to a temperament such as his. Mr. Trevor had given to each of his sons a fishing-rod and a gun; and Vibert was already, in imagination, a first-rate angler and sportsman. It would have been difficult to have been dull in Vibert's company during the journey. Sporting anecdotes, stories of adventures encountered by others, and anticipations of future ones of his own, interspersed with many a jest, amused not only Vibert's sister, but their fellow-travellers in the same railway-carriage. The youth had none of his elder brother's reserve, and took pleasure in attracting the notice of strangers, having a pleasant consciousness that in his case notice was likely to imply admiration also.

"That handsome lad seems to look on life as one long holiday, to be passed under unclouded sunshine," thought a withered old gentleman, who looked as if all his days had been spent in a fog. "Poor boy! poor boy! he will soon be roused, by stern experience, from the pleasant dream in which he indulges now!"

About half-an-hour before sunset, the train in which the Trevors were making their journey approached the station of S——, the one at which they were to alight.

"Your new pony-chaise is to meet us, Emmie, so papa arranged," observed Vibert; "but it must be a commodious chaise if it is to accommodate four persons, and all our lots of luggage. There are three boxes and a carpet-bag of mine in the van, besides I know not how many of yours. Then look here,"—Vibert glanced at the numerous et ceteras which showed that the young travellers had understood how to make themselves comfortable; "here's a shawl, and a rug, and foot-warmer, a basket, a bag, three umbrellas, and a parasol, my hat-box, and a fishing-rod besides! Are all to be stowed away in the chaise? If so, it will need nice packing."

"Bruce was to order a fly," said Emmie.

"If he was to do it, he has done it," observed Vibert; "one may count upon him as upon a church-clock. Now if I had had the arranging, I should have been so much taken up with trying the new pony-chaise, that I should have forgotten all about the old rattle-trap needed to carry the boxes. I wish that we had riding-horses. I shall never give papa peace till he buys me a hunter."

The shrill railway whistle gave notice of approach to a station; the train slackened its speed, and then stopped; doors were flung open, and a number of passengers soon thronged the platform of S——.

"There is Bruce; he is looking out for us!" cried Emmie, as she stepped on the platform.

"Where is the pony-chaise?" asked Vibert, addressing his brother, who immediately joined the party. Susan was left to collect, as best she might, the numerous articles left in the railway-carriage.

"A lad is holding the pony just outside the station, and the fly is waiting also," was the answer of Bruce. "Where is the luggage, Vibert? the train only stops for five minutes at S——."

"Susan will tell you all about it," cried Vibert; "I've a bag and three boxes, one of them a gun-case, stowed away in the van. Mind that nothing is missing. Come, Emmie, I must get you out of the crowd," and, drawing his sister's arm within his own, Vibert rapidly made his way to the outside of the station, where a pretty basket-chaise, drawn by a white pony, was waiting.

"In with you, quick, Emmie!" cried Vibert, with the eager impatience of one about to effect an escape. No sooner had the young lady taken her seat than Vibert sprang in after her, seized the reins, caught up the whip, and calling to the lad who had acted as hostler, "My brother will pay you," gave a sharp cut to the pony, which made the spirited little animal bound forward at a speed which raised a feeling of alarm in the timorous Emmie.

"Stop, Vibert, stop! you must not drive off; you must wait for Bruce!" she exclaimed.

"I'll wait for no one!" cried Vibert, still briskly plying the whip. "Bruce would be wanting to drive; but this time he has lost the chance,—ha! ha! ha! There's my brave little pony, does he not go at a spanking pace?"

"I wish that you would not drive so fast, it frightens me!" cried Emmie.

"Frightens you! nonsense, you little coward! Don't you see that thick bank of clouds in which the sun is setting? We'll have a thunderstorm soon, and that will frighten you more."

"Oh, I hope and trust that the storm will not burst till we reach shelter!" cried Emmie, whose dread of thunder and lightning is already known to the reader.

"We are running a race with it, and we'll be at the winning-post first!" exclaimed Vibert, who was enjoying the excitement, and who was rather amused than vexed to see his sister's alarm.

"But, Vibert, you don't even know the way to Myst Court! Oh, I wish that you had waited for Bruce!"

It had never occurred to the thoughtless lad that he might be driving in a wrong direction; so long as the pony went as fast as Vibert wished, he had taken it for granted that Myst Court would soon be reached. The station had been left far behind; the road was lonesome and wild; only one solitary boy was in sight; he was engaged in picking up boughs and twigs which a recent gale had blown down from the trees which bordered the way.

"We'll ask yonder bare-footed bundle of rags to direct us," said Vibert, and he drew up the panting pony when he reached the spot where the boy was standing.

"I say, young one, which is the way to Myst Court?" asked Vibert in a tone of command.

The boy stared at him, as if unaccustomed to the sight of strangers.

"Are we on the right road to the large house where Mrs. Myers used to live?" inquired Emmie.

28

"Ay, ay, but you'll have to turn down yon lane just by the stile there," said the urchin, pointing with his brown finger, and grinning as if a chaise with a lady in it were a rare and curious sight.

"I don't believe that the rustic could have told us whether to turn to left or right," said Vibert, as he whipped on the pony. "If he's a fair specimen of my father's tenants, we shall feel as if we had dropped down on the Fiji Islands."

The direction given by the finger was, however, perfectly clear, and the Trevors were soon driving along a picturesque lane, where trees, still gay with autumnal tints, overarched the narrow way, and with their brown and golden leaves carpeted the sod beneath them.

"What a pretty rural lane!" exclaimed Emmie, as the chaise first turned off from the high-road; but admiration was soon forgotten in discomfort and fear. The lane was apparently not intended as a thoroughfare for carriages, at least in the season of winter. The ground was miry and boggy, and the pony with difficulty dragged the chaise. There were violent jerks when one side or other dropped into one of the deep ruts left by the wheels of the last cart that had passed that way. Vibert plied the whip more vigorously than before, and silenced his sister's remonstrances by remarking how darkly the clouds were gathering in the evening sky. Young Trevor was but an inexperienced driver, and ever and anon the chaise was jolted violently over some loose stones, or driven so near to the hedge that Emmie had to bend sideways to avoid being struck by straggling bramble or branch. She mentally resolved never again to trust herself to Vibert's driving.

"Will this lane never come to an end?" exclaimed Emmie, as the first heavy drop from an overshadowing mass of dark cloud fell on her knee. She was but imperfectly protected from rain; for Vibert, in his haste to dash off from the station before his brother could join him, had never thought of taking with him either umbrella or shawl for his sister.

"Here comes the rain with a vengeance, and this stupid beast flounders in the mud as if it were dragging a cannon instead of a chaise," cried Vibert. "These country lanes drive one out of all patience! Ha! there's the rumbling of distant thunder!"

"Oh! I trust that we shall reach home soon," exclaimed Emmie, who, exposed to the heavy downpour, shivered alike from cold and from fear.

"I suspect that we shall never reach home at all by this lane," said Vibert. "Take my word for it, that little wretch has directed us wrong; I have a great mind to turn the pony round, and get back to the high-road."

"You can't turn, the lane is too narrow; you would land us in the hedge!" exclaimed Emmie, who thought that the attempt would inevitably lead to an upset of the chaise. On struggled the steaming pony, down poured the pattering rain; Vibert, almost blinded by the shower and the gathering darkness, could scarcely see the road before him.

"The longest lane has a turning,—there is an opening before us at last!" exclaimed the young driver, as a turn in the winding road brought a highway to view. "We shall reach Myst Court like two drowned rats. Why on earth did you not bring an umbrella, Emmie? I could not think of everything at once." Vibert had, indeed, thought but of himself.

The want of an umbrella was to Emmie by no means the worst part of her troubles; she was afraid that her brother had indeed been misdirected, and that they might be lost and benighted in a part of the country where they as yet were strangers, exposed to the perils of a thunderstorm, from which the nervous girl shrank with instinctive terror. Emmie had never hitherto even attempted to overcome her fear; and though her uncle's words now recurred to her mind, the idea of encountering a thunderstorm after nightfall, without even a roof to protect her, put to flight any good resolutions that those words might have roused in her mind.

29

"There was a flash!" exclaimed Emmie, starting and putting her hands before her eyes. She pressed closer to her brother as if for protection.

"We shall have more soon; the storm comes nearer," was the little comforting reply of Vibert. As he ended the sentence, the thunder-clap followed the flash. The pony pricked up his ears, and quickened his pace.

"I am glad that we are out of this miserable mouse-hole at last," cried Vibert, pulling the left rein sharply as the light vehicle emerged from the narrow, miry lane into the broad and comparatively smooth highway.

At this moment the darkening landscape was suddenly lighted up by a flash intensely bright, followed almost immediately by a peal over the travellers' heads. The terrified Emmie shrieked, and, losing all presence of mind, caught hold of her brother's arm. The sharp turning out of the lane, the pony's start at the flash, and the sudden grasp on the driver's arm, acting together, had the effect which might have been expected. Down went pony and chaise, down went driver and lady, precipitated into the ditch which bordered the high-road.

CHAPTER IX.

NEW ACQUAINTANCE.

 Vibert shouting for help, Emmie shrieking, the pony kicking and struggling in vain attempts to scramble out of the ditch, rain rattling, thunder rolling, all made a confused medley of sounds, while the deepening darkness was ever and anon lit up by lightning-flashes.

"Oh, Vibert! dear Vibert! are you hurt?" cried the terrified Emmie, with whom personal fear did not counterbalance anxiety for her young brother's safety.

"I'm not hurt; I lighted on a bramble-bush; I've got off with a few scratches," answered Vibert, who had regained the road. "But where on earth are you, Emmie? Can't you manage to get up?"

"No," gasped Emmie; "the chaise keeps me down. Oh, there is the lightning again!" and she shrieked.

"Never mind the lightning," cried Vibert impatiently. "How am I to get the pony on his legs? he's kicking like mad; and, oh! do stop screaming, Emmie, you're enough to drive any one wild. It was your pull and your shrieking that did all the mischief."

Vibert had had little experience with horses, and to release, almost in darkness, a kicking pony from its traces, or set free a lady imprisoned by an overturned chaise, were tasks for which he had neither sufficient presence of mind nor personal strength. Glad would the poor lad then have been to have had Bruce beside him, Bruce with his firm arm and his strong sense, and that quiet self-possession which it seemed as if nothing could shake. Vibert felt in the emergency as helpless as a girl might have done. Now he pulled at the upturned wheel of the chaise, but without lifting it even an inch; then he caught up the whip which had dropped from his hand in the shock of the fall, but he knew not whether to use it would not but make matters worse. Vibert ran a few paces to seek for assistance, stopped irresolute, then hurried back, thinking it unmanly to leave his sister alone in her helpless condition.

Happily for poor Emmie, assistance was not long delayed. Not a hundred yards from the spot where the accident had taken place, two men were sheltering themselves from the violence of the rain in a half-ruined barn. The cries of the lady, the loud calls for aid from her brother, reached the ears of these men. Two forms were seen by Vibert quickly approaching towards him, and he shouted to them to make haste to come to the help of his sister.

"There's a lady there, under the wheel," said the shorter and elder man to the other, when the two had reached the fallen chaise. "You'd better look to her while I cut the beast's traces; it's lucky I have my knife with me," and the speaker pulled a large clasp-knife out of his pocket.

The united efforts of the men, assisted by Vibert, soon were crowned with success. The pony, frightened and mud-bespattered, but not very seriously hurt, as soon as it was released from the harness, scrambled out of the ditch. The light basket-chaise was, without much difficulty, raised to its right position; and Vibert helped to lift up Emmie, who was half covered with mud, and almost in hysterics with fear.

"Come, come, there's nothing to be terrified at now; the danger is over. You're not hurt, are you?" asked Vibert, with some anxiety, for he loved his sister next to himself, though, it must be confessed, with a considerable space between.

Emmie scarcely knew whether she were injured or not. She was too much agitated at first to be able to answer her brother's question.

"I don't think that there are any bones broken; mud is soft," said the shorter man. "I guess she's more frightened than hurt."

"Be composed, dear lady; the storm is clearing off," observed the younger stranger, who had assisted Vibert in releasing Emmie from her distressing position, and who now helped to place her again in the chaise. This person's gallantry of manner contrasted with the almost coarse bluntness of his elder and shorter companion. Vibert at once concluded that the two individuals who had accidentally appeared together belonged respectively to very different grades of society.

The man who had cut the traces had had string in his capacious pocket as well as a knife, and now occupied himself in making such a rough arrangement with the harness as might enable the pony to draw the chaise. He effected his purpose with no small skill; considering the imperfect light by which he worked.

"Are we in the right road for Myst Court?" inquired Vibert of this individual, as he was tying the last firm knot in the string.

"Myst Court!" repeated the man in a harsh, croaking tone, at the same time raising his head from its stooping position. "Are you some of the new folk as are coming to the old haunted house?"

The question was asked in a manner so peculiar that it arrested the attention even of Emmie. A flash of lightning occurred at the moment, not so vivid as that which had terrified her so much, but sufficiently so to light up the features of the elderly man. Miss Trevor was again and again to see that strange face, but at no time did she behold it without recalling the impression which it made on her mind when first shown by that gleam of blue lightning. The man might be sixty years of age; his nose was hooked, so that it resembled a beak; his eyes were so sunken in his head that in that transient glimpse they looked like dark eye-holes; his hair, rough, unkempt, and grizzled, hung in wet strands as low as his shoulders, surmounted by an old battered felt hat. Emmie felt afraid of him, though she could not have given any reason for her fear.

"Yes, we are to live at Myst Court," replied Vibert. "Our father has just come into possession of the place."

"Woe to him, then, for an evil spell is upon it!" muttered the man; and a distant rumble succeeded the words like an echo. "The thunder and lightning, the darkness and storm, the mistaken way, the stumbling horse,—omens of evil—omens of evil! These things do not happen by chance."

"I wish that, instead of muttering unpleasant things, you would give a plain answer to a plain question, and not keep us shivering here!" said Vibert impatiently. "Are we, or are we not, on the direct road to Myst Court?"

"No, sir," replied the taller stranger; "but by yon lane you can reach the high-road which leads straight from S—— to the place of your destination."

"Then that urchin did misdirect us!" exclaimed Vibert. "If I meet him again, I will break every stick in his faggot over his back! Must we really return through that slough of a lane, through which we have scarcely been able to struggle?"

"You must retrace your way," said the stranger. "As far as the high-road my path is the same as your own, as I am returning to my quarters at S——. Perhaps you will permit me to occupy the vacant place in your chaise (I perceive that there is a back seat), as it would be a satisfaction to me to see the lady so far safe on the road. I shall do myself the honour of calling at Myst Court to-morrow, to inquire after her health. My name is Colonel Standish, at your service, and I serve beneath the star-spangled banner."

"We shall be glad of your company, sir," said Vibert; "and are much obliged for your ready help."

"It is lucky that old Harper and I were at hand," observed Standish, as he stepped into the low basket-chaise.

Vibert sprang into the front seat beside his sister, but before taking the reins from the hand of Harper, young Trevor pulled a shilling out of his waistcoat-pocket, and tendered it to the old man. There was light now afforded by the moon, for the rain had ceased, and through a rift in the clouds the radiant orb shone clearly.

"A silver shilling to him who has helped you to reach the haunted house," said Harper, as he took the coin and thrust it into a deep pocket. "I trow there will be gold for him who shall show you the way to leave it!"

Vibert laughed; Emmie shivered, but that may have been from cold, for the night-air was clamp and chilly, and her clothes were saturated with rain. Vibert now turned the pony into the lane, but the creature limped, and had evidently some difficulty in dragging the chaise.

"The beast is lame," observed Standish; "he has probably strained a leg in the fall. We gentlemen must walk through the lane, where the ground is so boggy." The colonel sprang from the chaise, and his example was followed by Vibert.

At a slow pace the party proceeded along the tree-overshadowed way. The recent rain had increased the heaviness of the road, and the trees dripped moisture from their wet branches over the travellers' heads. To Emmie, cold and damp as she was, and longing for shelter and rest, it seemed as if that wearisome lane would never come to an end.

Harper, uninvited, had joined himself to the party, and his peculiar croaking tones were frequently heard blending in converse with the clear voice of young Vibert, or the more manly accents of Standish. Emmie alone kept silence.

"Our friend Harper is a near neighbour of yours," observed the colonel to Vibert. "He has fixed himself just outside the gate of your father's grounds."

"But I never pass through that gate," croaked Harper. Neither Vibert nor Emmie felt any regret that their forbidding-looking neighbour should keep outside.

"You call the place haunted?" said Vibert.

"Haunted!" repeated Harper, muttering the word between his clenched teeth; and the old man shook his grizzled locks with so mysterious an air, that Vibert's curiosity was roused. He began to question Harper on the traditions connected with the place.

The old man was not loath to speak on the subject, though he imparted his information, if such it could be called, only in broken fragments; giving as it were, glimpses of grisly horrors, and leaving his hearers to imagine the rest.

Then Standish followed up the theme, and recounted strange stories from the New World,—all "well-authenticated" as he declared; stories of haunted houses and apparitions, each tale more horrible than the last. Such relations would have tried Emmie's nerves, even had the stories been told on some calm summer eve; but heard, as they were, in a dark, dreary lane, on a chilly November night, when she was wet, bruised, and trembling from the shock of a recent accident, tales of horror seemed to make the blood freeze to ice in her veins. Had Bruce been present, he would have discouraged such conversation; but sensational stories had charms for Vibert, and he never considered that they might work an evil effect on the sensitive mind of his sister.

At last the open road was regained, and Standish took leave of the Trevors. Rather to Emmie's surprise, the colonel familiarly shook hands with herself as well as her brother, as if the night's adventure had converted them into old friends. Vibert again sprang into the chaise; he was very impatient to get at last to the end of his wearisome journey, and urged the pony to as quick a pace as its lameness permitted over the smoother road.

The rest of the time of the drive was passed in silence. The way to Myst Court was clear enough from the brief directions given by Harper, of whom the travellers soon lost sight in the darkness, though he was following in the same track. Emmie had thought of inviting the old man to take the back seat in the chaise, but an intuitive feeling of repugnance prevented her from making the offer.

Glad were the weary travellers to reach the large iron gate which had been described as marking the entrance to the grounds of Myst Court. The gate had been left wide open to let them pass through. The drive up to the house was rather a long one. Emmie noticed only that it appeared to be through a thick wood, and that the chaise occasionally jolted over impediments in the way. To her great relief, the weary girl at length distinguished lights in some of the windows of a building which dimly loomed before her. There streamed forth also light from the open door, at which her brother Bruce was standing, watching for the arrival of the long-expected chaise.

CHAPTER X.

A FAINT HEART.

"What has delayed you?—where have you been?—how comes the pony to be lame, and Emmie all splashed with mud?—what insane prank have you been playing?"

Such were the questions, each successive one asked in a louder and more angry tone, which were addressed by Bruce to Vibert when the brothers met in front of the house. The lad attempted to answer the questions lightly.

"We've only had a bit of an adventure," cried he. "I've been in a dilemma, Emmie in a fright, the chaise in a ditch, and—"

"None of your foolery for me, sir! You have acted like a selfish idiot!" exclaimed Bruce, who was in a passion more towering than any to which he had given way before since the days of his boyhood. While Vibert had been speaking, Bruce had been engaged in half lifting Emmie out of the chaise; but he turned round as he was supporting her into the hall, and uttered his angry exclamation, while his eyes flashed indignation and scorn. Vibert bit his lip and cowered for an instant under his brother's rebuke, conscious that it was not altogether unmerited.

"Susan, take care of my sister; let her change her dripping garments directly," said Bruce to the maid, who was waiting in the hall, candle in hand, to receive her young mistress. "You will see that your lady has all that she wants," continued Bruce, who was ever considerate and thoughtful. "I will send up something hot for her to drink."

"I'll mix a tumblerful at once. The wine's on the table—hot water and nutmeg in the kitchen," cried a female voice that was strange to the ear of Emmie. But the poor girl was too much exhausted by the events of the evening to look much around her; she was stiff and trembling with cold, and bruised by her fall, and faintly asked Susan to show her without delay to her room.

Emmie was conducted by her maid up a broad staircase of oak, which ended in a corridor, of which the length nearly corresponded with that of the house. To the left were the apartments which had been assigned to the use of Mr. Trevor and his sons. Susan, on reaching the corridor, turned to the right, drawing back a large curtain of old-fashioned tapestry, on which the life-size figures, wrought by hands long since cold in the grave, were so faded that their outlines could scarcely be traced by the light of the candle carried by the maid. This piece of stiff tapestry had been hung across the corridor in order to keep off draughts from the aged lady who had last inhabited Myst Court. Susan held back the curtain till Miss Trevor had passed through the opening thus made, and then the tapestry again shut out one portion of the corridor from the staircase and the other side of the house.

A cheerful red light guided Emmie to a room on the right side of the passage. The light came from a blazing wood-fire in the young lady's own apartment, which she now entered, followed by Susan. Glad was the weary girl to enjoy her home comforts again. Wet clothes were quickly exchanged for dry ones; Emmie's cold hands were chafed into warmth; soft slippers were placed on her feet; and while the fire shed its kindly glow over her frame, the maiden revived, and began to survey with some interest the features of her new abode.

The room in which Emmie found herself was of good size; the ceiling had been freshly whitewashed; the walls were panelled with oak; the furniture, with one exception, had all been taken from Summer Villa, and had a familiar appearance which was pleasant to the eye of the maiden, and made her feel grateful to Bruce for his thoughtful kindness. It was Emmie's own chintz-covered sofa, which Susan had wheeled close to the fire, on which the tired traveller reclined; the screen was one specially valued as being the work of her mother; the guitar-case was seen in a corner; the rows of prettily-bound books which filled the shelves of the book-case looked as if they had made the journey to S—— without even having been moved from their accustomed places. Emmie was fond of pictures, and had collected quite a little gallery of them at Summer Villa. Bruce had taken care that his sister should not miss one of them at Myst Court. Here numbers of pictures, great and small,—portraits, prints, coloured sketches,—adorned the panelled walls, relieved by the dark background of oak, from which they took all appearance of gloom.

It has been said that, with one exception, the furniture of Miss Trevor's room had all belonged to her former home; that exception was a tall press of elaborately-carved oak, which rested against one of the side-walls, between the fireplace and the window. Bruce had not ordered the removal of this press for various reasons. It was heavy, and had probably remained in its present place since the house had first been built, as the style of the carving was antique, and the wood almost black with age. Bruce had thought that a high press was a convenient article of furniture for a young lady's room; and this one was so handsome that, though it matched nothing in the apartment except the panelled walls, its beauty as a work of art might atone for the incongruity.

The gaze of Emmie rested longer on that dark press than on anything else in the room. Perhaps she was trying to make out the meaning of the figures carved in bold relief on the front; or, perhaps, she was recalling one of the sensational stories which she had heard that night, in which just such a press as this had played a mysterious part. Absurd as it may appear, the young lady would have liked her apartment better if the handsomest article of its furniture had not been left within it.

As Emmie was languidly gazing around, while Susan, on her knees by the sofa, was chafing her young lady's feet, there was heard a tap at the door. A woman then entered the apartment, bearing a steaming tumblerful of wine and hot water. As this person will reappear in the story, I will briefly describe her appearance.

She was dressed in mourning, and wore a black bonnet covered with crape flowers and pendants of bugles. Her person was short and somewhat stout. The round eyes, above which the sandy-coloured brows formed not arches but an upward-turned angle, gave her a cat-like look, which resemblance to the feline race was increased by the peculiar form of her lower jaw, and the noiseless softness of her movements.

In an obsequious manner this personage not only gave the reviving beverage to Miss Trevor, but volunteered her unasked aid to make the young lady comfortable, beating up her pillow, stirring the fire, and making inquiries about her health in a pitying tone, as if the fear of Emmie's having caught any chill were to her a matter of tender concern. Emmie guessed that the stranger must be the confidential attendant of the late Mrs. Myers, and her conjecture was soon confirmed by the woman's introducing herself as Mrs. Jael Jessel. The young lady did not like to give Mrs. Jessel a hint to depart, though the tired girl would have been glad to have been left to the quiet attentions of Susan. Jael herself was in no haste to quit the apartment; and leaning against the mantelpiece, began to converse in a voluble way.

35

"I could not help running over from my new home to see that everything was arranged comfortable-like for the niece of my dear departed lady," began Mrs. Jessel. "I know the ins and outs of this place so well,—it seems so natural to come about a house in which one has lived for years."

"My brother has arranged everything comfortably," observed Miss Trevor. "He came down before the rest of the family on purpose to do so."

"Ah, yes; I see. Master Bruce is a clever young gentleman, and he has done all that he could *under the circumstances*," said Mrs. Jessel, lowering her tone, as she uttered the last three words, to a mysterious whisper. The black bugles in her bonnet trembled with the shake of her head, as the late attendant went on,—"But if young Mr. Trevor had taken the advice of one who knows what I know, he'd have had this room shut up as closely as the one which is next to it,—I mean *the haunted chamber!*" Jael Jessel's round eyes glanced stealthily from one side to another, as if she were afraid of being overheard by some invisible listener.

Susan saw a look of uneasiness pass over the face of her young mistress, and could not help breaking silence.

"Hannah has told me this evening," she said, "that Mrs. Myers always slept in this room, and that you, Mrs. Jessel, were on a couch beside her. Since the room was chosen for her own by the mistress of the house, it must have been considered the best one."

Mrs. Jessel did not condescend to address herself to Susan, but in speaking to Emmie virtually gave a reply to the observation made by the servant.

"My poor dear lady was perfectly deaf, she could not hear what *I* heard; her eyes were dim, she could not see what *I* saw,—or she would not have rested a second night with only a wall between her and"—again Jael glanced furtively around as she murmured—"that fearful chamber!"

"What did you see,—what did you hear?" asked Emmie, shuddering as she recalled to mind the warnings given by old Harper.

Mrs. Jessel did not wait to be asked twice; she was ready enough to impart to any credulous listener her tale of horrors. Susan was hardly restrained, by her respect for her young mistress, from repeatedly interrupting the stranger, who was doing her worst to fill the mind of a nervous girl with superstitious fears at a time when bodily weariness had prepared it for their reception. At last the indignant lady's-maid could keep silence no longer.

"What you bore for years, Mrs. Jessel, and without being any the worse for it, could have been nothing very dreadful," said Susan bluntly. "My lady knows that a good Providence is as near her in this room as anywhere else, and that they who keep a clear conscience need fear neither goblin nor ghost!"

"Ah, well, we shall see, we shall see," observed Mrs. Jessel, drawing her black shawl closer around her, as a preparation for departure. "I don't believe there's a being who knows the place that would go through the wood at night but myself; but, as you say, a clear conscience gives courage. I wish you a good night, Miss Trevor," added Jael, courtesying formally to the lady; "but, to my mind, you'd have a better chance of one if you were to sleep in a different room."

Mrs. Jessel quitted the apartment; but she left behind her the painful impression which her words were calculated to make on a mind such as Emmie's,—a mind not yet sufficiently disciplined by self-control, or influenced by faith, to bring reason and religion to bear upon superstitious fears and nervous forebodings.

Emmie rose from the sofa, and took two or three turns up and down her apartment; while Susan occupied herself in trimming the fire. The young lady then stopped abruptly in her walk.

"Susan," she said, "I cannot sleep in this room!" It was humiliating to utter such a confession, even to a domestic.

"Oh, Miss Emmie, if you would let me be beside you to-night—" began Susan; but Emmie did not heed her attendant's suggestion.

"I could not close my eyes all the night, and I do so sadly need rest. I will go to my brother and ask him to make arrangements for at once changing my room."

"But Master Bruce will be so much disappointed," expostulated Susan. "He has spared no pains to have everything just as you would like it to be."

"I cannot sleep here," repeated Emmie, who was trembling with nervous excitement. "You will soon move my things—I care not whither—so that it be to the other side of the house, as far as possible from the bricked-up room."

Emmie hastily quitted the apartment, and drawing back the tapestry curtain, passed on to the head of the staircase. The house appeared to her dreary, empty, and cold, as she glided down the broad oaken steps, almost afraid to look behind her. Emmie soon reached the wide hall, and, guided by the light of the lamp in the drawing-room, of which the door was open, she entered it, and found Bruce Trevor alone.

"I hope that you feel rested, Emmie," said her brother, advancing to meet her. The clouded brow of Bruce still showed token of the angry altercation which had passed between him and Vibert.

"I cannot rest in that room, dear," faltered Emmie, avoiding meeting her brother's inquiring gaze.

"Not rest—why not?" asked Bruce in surprise.

Emmie coloured with shame as she stammered forth her reply. "I know that you will think it so silly—it—it *is* silly, I own, but—but I would rather be in any other part of the house than next door to the haunted chamber!"

"This is folly, Emmie, pure folly," expostulated Bruce. "You know that a great part of the dwelling is at present uninhabitable, and cannot be used for months. There are but two upper rooms fitted up comfortably; the one is my father's—he chose it himself; the other is given to you. Vibert and I can put up anywhere; our two little rooms, just beyond my father's, have been left as I found them, save that the housemaid has been induced to clear a few cobwebs away. I could not possibly allow you, accustomed as you are to have comforts around you, to occupy one of those bare cells at the coldest side of the house."

"I should prefer—oh, so greatly prefer one of those small rooms to my present one!" exclaimed Emmie. "Where I now am expected to sleep, that horrid tapestry curtain divides me from every other living being, and I am so close to the bricked-up room, that if so much as a mouse stirred in it, the sound would keep me awake. Dear Bruce, you who are so firm, and brave, and wise, you cannot tell what I feel. If you love me, let us exchange our rooms at once; you are not fearful and foolish like me." Emmie was trembling; her hands were clasped, and tears rose into her eyes.

"Have your own way!" exclaimed Bruce, with some impatience of manner. He was annoyed at his sister's betraying such weakness, provoked at his own arrangements being altered, and disappointed at having taken in vain a good deal of trouble to please. Without uttering another word to Emmie, the young man quitted the room to give needful orders, and did not return till the clang of the hall gong summoned the Trevors to a late dinner.

The meal was very unsociable and dull. The storm of anger between the two brothers had not passed off, and Emmie was too much disheartened by what had occurred to be

37

able to act her usual part of peacemaker between them. Bruce had not forgiven Vibert his foolish prank of driving off with Emmie, which had been the primal cause of the accident which had occurred; and Vibert, stung to the quick, had not forgiven Bruce his bitter rebukes. During the whole of dinner-time neither of the young men addressed a word to the other.

The awkward waiting of the country lad hired as a servant, which, at another time, might have afforded some amusement to the young Trevors, now only provoked their patience. Bruce disliked the clumping tread and the creaking boots of Joe; Emmie started when the noisy clatter of plates ended at last in a crash. Vibert, whose lively conversation usually added so much to the cheerfulness of the family circle, scarcely uttered a syllable, save to find fault with the cookery, which was certainly none of the best. No one, under these circumstances, cared to prolong unnecessarily the time spent at the dinner-table.

But matters were little improved when the party had retired to the drawing-room, to spend there the remainder of the first evening passed together by them in their new home. Neither reading aloud nor music, neither playful converse nor game, lightened the heavy time which intervened before the accustomed hour for family prayers. Emmie thought that the large drawing-room of Myst Court was but dimly lighted by the lamp which had shed such cheerful radiance in Summer Villa. The light scarcely sufficed to enable her to trace the outlines of the time-darkened family portraits which hung on the dingy walls. The apartment was so spacious that one fire could hardly warm it, so that it was chilly as well as dark. The small-sized furniture which had suited Summer Villa would have looked mean in the handsome old saloon of Myst Court; therefore faded carpet and more faded tapestry remained, high-backed heavy chairs of carved oak, and narrow old-fashioned mirrors whose frames the lapse of two centuries had rendered dingy and dull. Emmie's only occupation on that first evening was examining these relics of the past. She thought to herself that Myst Court was as gloomy as any cloister could be, and sighed when she remembered that she must regard it now as her permanent home.

At last Bruce, who had repeatedly glanced at his watch, saw that it was time to call up the servants for prayers. They came in answer to the summons of the bell which he rang—the three new members of the household looking awkward and shy, being evidently unaccustomed to be present at family worship. Bruce read the prayers, as was his custom whenever his father was absent from home. But there was a coldness, on that night, even in the family devotions, of which no one was more sensible than was he who had to conduct them. It was not because the room felt dreary and cold, nor because a death-bed scene had so lately occurred in the house, that a chilling damp fell over even the observance of a religious duty: Bruce, Vibert, and their sister had all on that day been overcome by their several besetting sins, and those sins were haunting them still. Pride, selfishness, and mistrust cast deeper shadows on the pathway of life than those merely external circumstances which we connect with ideas of gloom.

The spirit of Bruce was out of tune, and the noblest words of prayer were, as it were, turned into discord by the imperfection of the human instrument that gave them sound. The leaven of hypocrisy marred petitions in which the heart had no share. Bruce had to ask for the grace of meekness, whilst he was inwardly scorning a sister for weakness and a brother for folly. Had he been struggling to subdue the pride of his heart, such a prayer would have been a cry for help from above; but Bruce was attempting no such struggle. He was not seeking to imitate One who was meek and lowly; the sinner on his knees was preferring a prayer for a grace which he did not care to possess. If a remembrance of his uncle's warning against pride had passed through Bruce's mind on that evening, it had roused anger rather than contrition. "What is Captain Arrows, that he should probe the hearts of others; let him look to his own!"

Thus the high-principled young man, who was so ready to act or to suffer for what he deemed the cause of truth; he whose character was in human sight almost without a blemish, was in a state in which, according to Scripture, all his faith, knowledge, and zeal could profit him nothing. Death, if death had met him now, would not have found Bruce with his face turned heavenwards, though he had long since, with sincerity of purpose, entered on the pilgrim's narrow path. He stood condemned by the solemn words of inspiration, *If any man have not the spirit of Christ, he is none of His.*

Emmie noticed with pain, after family prayers were over, that her brothers went to their respective apartments without so much as bidding each other good-night.

CHAPTER XI.

EVENING AND MORNING.

"How foolish—how weak—how wrong has been my conduct through this day!" murmured Emmie to herself, as, after dismissing her attendant, she sat alone in the small apartment which she had chosen for her own. The room was a contrast to that which had at first been assigned to the young maiden. The cell, as Bruce had called it, did not possess even a fireplace, and might have belonged to some cloistered ascetic. The stained, dusky, peeling-off paper on the narrow walls had its blots and patches made only more visible by the whiteness of three large unframed maps, which the practical Bruce had fastened up for his own convenience. The young man had rather a contempt for the luxuries in which Vibert always indulged if he could; to the idea of Bruce they were only suitable for ladies, or those to whom age or ill-health rendered them needful. Bruce considered it unworthy of a man in the prime of his life to care about the softness of a cushion, or the temperature of an apartment. Thus, in making household arrangements, Bruce had selected his own quarters with very little regard to personal comfort, while he had spared no pains in trying to secure that of his sister.

Emmie now suffered from her brother's unselfishness, as well as from her own nervous fears. Hasty arrangements had indeed been made to improve the appearance of the cell. Some of Emmie's books had been transferred to the bookcase by Susan, nor had footstool or guitar been forgotten; but for her sofa there was no space, and the young lady's toilette-table, draped with white muslin, looked incongruous in so mean an apartment. Perhaps the discomfort of that fireless room on a damp November night was not without its effect on the spirits of Emmie, who was accustomed to the refinements and elegances of civilized life, and who was not indifferent to them; but the melancholy which oppressed the maiden chiefly rose from a deeper source, a profound discontent with herself.

It was Emmie's custom to review, every night ere she went to rest, the events of the preceding day, with self-examination as to the part which she had acted. The review had hitherto been very imperfect, for she had never traced her errors in practice to the source from whence most of them had proceeded. Instead of recognizing *mistrust* as a besetting sin, it had hardly occurred to Emmie that it was anything meriting blame. The occurrences of that Friday had been a striking comment upon the words of her uncle, which Emmie now recalled to memory.

"Unreasonable fear,—uncontrolled fear,—what has it done for me to-day?" mused Emmie. "It has destroyed my peace, most utterly destroyed it, and cast needless gloom over my arrival in my new home. Fear has made me displease both my brothers, has lowered me in the eyes even of my servants; it has caused an accident which has been painful, and which, but for Heaven's mercy, might have even been fatal. Should I have lost self-command in the storm, had I recognized the presence of Him who grasps the lightning in His hand, and whose voice is heard in the thunder? If my heart were indeed the abode of His Spirit, would that heart fail me at the bare thought of—hark! what was that sound?" Emmie started and turned pale at the cry of an owl outside her window; in her home near London she had never heard the hoot of the bird of night. The cry was repeated, and though the nervous girl now guessed its cause, in her superstitious mind it was still linked with fearful fancies.

Emmie, to compose herself, took up her Bible, and opening it, turned to the Twenty-seventh Psalm. She read the heart-stirring verse: *The Lord is my light and my salvation; whom shall I fear? the Lord is the strength of my life; of whom shall I be afraid?*

"Why cannot I make this glorious assurance of faith my own?" thought Emmie. "Why am I, a Christian girl in an English home, troubled with fears which would better beseem some poor ignorant African, worshipping his fetich, and knowing nothing of a protecting, loving God! I must struggle against this enemy, mistrust; I must try to bring my very thoughts into subjection,—those thoughts now so full of fears dishonouring to my gracious Master. Where is my reason,—where is my faith? I cannot believe that there is real danger in sleeping next to the bricked-up room, or even my selfishness would hardly have induced me to put dear Bruce in a post of peril. I must have been secretly assured that the danger existed only in fancy. But I am now too weary to be able to reason; I need a night's rest to enable me to distinguish between facts and the creations of an excited brain. I am so tired—my nerves are so weak! I shall scarcely now be able to rouse my mind even for the exercise of prayer, and by prayer alone dare I hope to conquer mistrust."

Emmie's rest was on that night troubled by a confused medley of dreams, the natural consequences of the excitement which she had undergone through the preceding day. Nothing was distinct, but the images of Harper and Jael Jessel mixed themselves up with the phantoms which their weird stories had raised in the imaginative mind of the girl. Emmie, early deprived of the guidance of a sensible mother, had often made an unprofitable use of her leisure; she had read much of the literature which is called sensational; she had pondered over tales of horror; her mind had been fed on unwholesome food. Emmie had let fancy lead her where it list, and it would be no easy task to undo the mischief wrought in idle hours under the name of amusement.

Morning came at last, and brightness and hope with the morning. How different objects appear in sunshine from what they seem to be when only faintly visible at night! Emmie gazed from her window, and greatly admired the prospect before her. Never, perhaps, in a well-wooded country, does Nature display more exquisite beauty than in the early part of November, when the foliage, thinned indeed, but brilliant in tints of crimson and gold, varied with russet and green, is lit up by the glorious sun. The orb of day, just rising, was overhung by rosy clouds; the air was fresh and fragrant after the storm; myriads of dew-drops glittered on the lawn; all was brightness above and below! Emmie thought that she could be very happy even at Myst Court, and anticipated with pleasure looking over the mansion, exploring the grounds, and examining the state of the garden.

When Emmie quitted her little room, the sunlight was streaming through the large east window which lighted the staircase, throwing gorgeous stains of crimson and azure from its coloured panes upon the wide oaken steps. What had been dreary and ghost-like by night, had become picturesque and romantic by day. Emmie tripped lightly down to the breakfast-room, where she found Bruce looking out his place in the book of family prayers.

"Did you sleep well?" was the sister's eager greeting as she approached her brother; for Emmie had reproached herself a little for exposing Bruce to the chance of any nocturnal annoyance by the exchange of the rooms.

"I slept very well,—never better," replied Bruce with a slightly sarcastic smile. "I had no expectation of seeing goblin or ghost, and was certainly troubled by none. I never knew a place more perfectly still; so far as I could judge, not a mouse stirred or a cricket chirrupped in the so-called haunted chamber. But that west room is by far too pretty and luxurious for a student like me. As ladies are allowed to change their minds once, I would strongly advise you, Emmie, to let us resume the first arrangement: do you go back to the west room, and let me study or sulk in my own little cell."

"Not now," replied Emmie Trevor; and, to do her justice, her motive in declining the second change was as much consideration for her brother's comfort as the repugnance, which she had not yet quite overcome, to sleeping next door to the haunted chamber.

"Why has Master Vibert not made his appearance either at prayers or at breakfast?" asked Bruce, when, half an hour afterwards, he was enjoying the cup of hot coffee prepared by his sister.

"Vibert was tired last night, and has probably overslept himself," replied Emmie.

"Not he," said Bruce, "for I saw him from my window this morning, more than an hour ago, loitering about the grounds. Vibert must have heard the gong sound for breakfast. No; the fact is—you must have seen it from his manner last evening—that Vibert is in a huff because I called him a selfish idiot."

"I am so very, *very* sorry that you called him that," cried Emmie, with a look of distress. "You do not consider, dear Bruce, what real harm your sternness may do to our younger brother. Vibert is so affectionate—"

"He cares for no one on earth but himself," said Bruce. "Look at his conduct yesterday, and think what might have been its result."

"Driving off from the station without waiting for you was but a foolish, boyish prank," pleaded Emmie. "As for the accident that occurred, that cannot be laid to Vibert's charge; it was caused by my catching hold of his arm just when the pony was turning a corner."

"What made you do that?" inquired Bruce.

"I was foolishly frightened at the lightning," replied Emmie meekly.

"Frightened, always frightened, at everything and at nothing!" said Bruce, but rather in sorrow than in anger. He was far more indulgent to the failings of Emmie than he was to those of Vibert.

The gentle girl, who was very anxious to bring about a reconciliation between her two brothers continued her mild expostulation with Bruce.

"I am sure that you do not think Vibert an idiot, though he may, perhaps, be a little selfish. I have heard you say yourself that Vibert has plenty of brain."

"If he were not too lazy and self-indulgent to work it," interrupted the elder brother.

"You do not think—you never have thought poor dear Vibert a selfish idiot," persisted Emmie; "and oh! Bruce, if I could only persuade you to tell him that you are sorry for having spoken that one hasty word, if—"

41

"Apologize to Vibert! never!" cried Bruce, and he pushed his chair back from the table.

"Surely it is noble, generous, right to own to a brother that in a hasty moment we have done him a wrong!" said Emmie with an earnestness which brought the moisture into her eyes.

Bruce made no reply to his sister, but rose from his seat and left the room; not hurriedly, not passionately, but with that expression on his calm face in which Emmie easily read the unuttered thought, "I need no one's advice to guide me, and I will receive rebuke from no one."

Emmie breathed a heavy sigh. Bruce was in other points so noble, so good,—oh, why did he shut and bar so firmly against the entrance of duty and affection one haunted room of his heart! Emmie was distressed on account of Vibert; she knew that her volatile younger brother needed the support of the stronger sense, the firmer principle of the elder,—that the influence of Bruce might be of inestimable importance to Vibert. And all this influence was to be worse than thrown away, because the professed follower of Him who was meek and lowly would not bend his proud spirit to own that he had committed a fault!

CHAPTER XII.

THE STRANGER.

Bruce had scarcely quitted the breakfast-room before it was entered by Vibert.

"Quick, Emmie, a cup of your delicious hot coffee! I've been out these two hours, and have come in with a hunter's appetite!" exclaimed the youth, who was looking even handsomer than usual, with his clear complexion brightened by the invigorating effects of the fresh morning air. Vibert applied himself with energy to the work of cutting slices from the cold ham which had been placed on the side-board.

Emmie poured out the warm beverage for her brother, who turned round to bid her add plenty of cream. "Cream is the one country luxury to balance against country cookery," he laughingly observed. "If that virago-looking Hannah continue to reign in the kitchen, I shall be driven to live upon cream, or be famished!"

Vibert did not appear likely to be famished as he sat at the well-spread table, doing ample justice to his slices of ham. Emmie had finished her own breakfast, but remained to keep her brother company.

"Since you were such an early riser to-day," she observed, "why were you absent from prayers?"

"Because I can't stand hearing the prayers read by Bruce!" exclaimed Vibert with some indignation. "It's a mockery for him to call his own brother a selfish idiot, to treat him as if he were a slave or a dog, and then to kneel down and pray like a saint, asking for meekness and mercy, and all kinds of graces which he never had, and never wishes to have. If that be not downright hypocrisy, I know not what is deserving of the name."

"Bruce is the very last person in the world who would play the hypocrite," cried Emmie. "As for the harsh name which he gave you, I believe that in his heart he is sorry for what he said in a moment of ill-humour."

"Then why does he not own frankly that he is sorry?" cried Vibert. "If Bruce would but confess that he regrets his hasty words, I'd hold out my hand at once and say, 'Let by-gones be by-gones, old boy; I'm not the fellow to harbour a grudge.' But Bruce would not own a fault were it to save his life or mine. Pride—that pride that repels advice, resents reproof, and refuses to acknowledge an error (how well the captain described it!)—that is Bruce's pet sin, and he'll carry it with him to his grave."

"God forbid!" faintly murmured Emmie.

"Bruce and I are to begin daily studies at S—— next Monday," continued Vibert, who was making good progress with his breakfast whilst he kept up the conversation. "I know that papa imagines that the way to keep me safe and out of mischief, is to yoke me to one whom he considers the impersonification of sense and sobriety. He'd couple a greyhound with a surly mastiff; but the greyhound, at least, will strain hard against the connecting strap. If Bruce start early, I will start late; if he walk fast, I will walk slowly; I'll keep as wide apart from him as the tether will let me get;—in plain words, I'll have as little to do with Bruce as I possibly can."

"Vibert, dear Vibert, it so grieves me that you should feel thus towards him," cried Emmie. "Bruce is not without his faults, but he is a noble-minded, unselfish—"

"Unselfish! I deny it!" exclaimed Vibert, while he kept the morsel which he was just about to convey to his lips suspended on his fork. "Unselfish indeed! when he has taken advantage of being sent on in front to make arrangements to secure the very best room in the house for himself!"

"He never did," cried Emmie eagerly. "The west room was prepared for me, but I could not endure it, and, as a matter of kindness, Bruce exchanged our respective apartments."

"Why could you not endure that capital room?" asked Vibert in surprise.

Emmie, who had been wishing, praying that she might be enabled to act the part of a faithful counsellor and friend to her younger brother, felt painfully that she had to step down from her position of vantage, as she owned, with a blush, that she had not liked to sleep next door to the bricked-up room.

Vibert burst out laughing. "So the chivalrous Bruce took the dangerous post!" he exclaimed. "Would I not just like to give him a fright!"

"Don't, oh! don't play any foolish practical joke!" exclaimed Emmie.

"I'm afraid that it would not answer," said Vibert, still laughing. "Bruce is a hard-headed chap, who sifts everything to the bottom. He'd be as likely as not to cleave a ghost's skull with a poker, and I've no fancy to try whether he hits as hard with his hand as he yesterday did with his tongue. But let's talk no more about Bruce. As soon as I've finished my breakfast, you and I shall go into the grounds and have a ramble together. You've not yet seen the outside of our mansion, for when we arrived here last night you had not enough light to distinguish Aladdin's palace from a Hottentot kraal."

The brother and sister soon sauntered out on the terrace on the east side of the house, which was bathed in glowing sunshine. The air was so mild that Emmie had merely thrown a light blue scarf over her head and shoulders as a protection from the breeze; winter wraps would have been oppressive, and she enjoyed the luxury of being able to go out without donning bonnet or gloves. The terrace overlooked the lawn and the garden: the latter had once been fine, and had still a prim grace of its own.

43

"I rather like this old family mansion," cried Vibert, glancing up at the building, which had been constructed of dark red brick, with handsome facings of stone. "There is something stately about it, as if it had seen better days, and remembered them still. Myst Court looks something like William and Mary's part of Hampton Court Palace."

"Oh, a mere miniature of that grand old building," said Emmie.

"I can just fancy the kind of people who walked on this terrace when first it was laid out," continued Vibert. "There were gentlemen in huge, full-bottomed wigs, long coats, embroidered waistcoats and ruffles of old point-lace, with rapiers hanging at their sides. There were ladies like those whom Sir Godfrey Kneller painted, stiff and stately, each smelling a rose which she held in her hand; ladies in hoops, who looked as if they could never dance anything more lively than a *minuet de la cour*. We seem too modern, Emmie, to match our mansion. Let's return to the olden times, forget that Queen Anne is dead, and fancy her yet with the sharp-tongued Duchess Sarah playing the game of romantic friendship. Let's imagine ourselves as we would have appeared some hundred and fifty years ago. I'm a young Tory gallant (of course, I'm a Jacobite at heart, and drink to 'the king over the water'); Bruce is a decided Whig,—I'm not sure that he is not a Dutchman, and has come over from Holland in the train of the Prince of Orange."

Emmie laughed at Vibert's playful fancies, and wondered how her handsome young brother would have looked in a full-bottomed wig.

"Whig and Tory must unite," she observed, "to get that garden into order. The walks are overrun with shepherd's purse and chickweed, and the beds seem to grow little but nettles."

"But these beds were clearly laid out at the time when Dutch taste prevailed," said Vibert; "it reminds one of the poet's description,—

'Grove nods at grove, each alley has its brother, One half the garden just reflects the other.'"

"Rather a mournful reflection now," observed Emmie with a smile.

"But easily changed to a bright one!" cried Vibert; "we'll set plenty of hands to work, and get everything right before spring. These old straggling bushes must come up; we'll have new plants from a nursery-garden, and fill those beds with geraniums, fuchsias, and calceolaria. An orangery, as at Hampton Court, shall be at one end of the house; and we must fix on a site for a conservatory, in which some huge vine shall spread out its branches, heavy with delicious bunches of grapes."

"My dear boy, you speak as if papa had the purse of Fortunatus," said Emmie. "You know that he will have all kinds of expense in getting the property into tolerable order,—draining, and that sort of thing. The garden must wait for new plants, and we for conservatory and orangery, till more important matters are settled. Think of the cottages out of repair—"

"Hang the cottages!" cried Vibert. "Leave them alone, and they'll tumble down of their own accord. Why should we trouble ourselves about them?"

"We must care for the tenants that live in them," observed Emmie.

"They've never done anything for us, why should we do anything for them?" said Vibert. "I don't believe that half of them ever think of paying their rents. If I were master here," continued Vibert, "I'd make a law that no dirty, ragged creature should come within a mile of the house. If these folk are miserable, I'm sorry for it; but that's no reason why I should be miserable too. Charity begins at home, and the first thing to be done at Myst Court is to put house and garden into tip-top order,—buy new carpets and a good billiard-table, set up a fountain yonder on the lawn (we'll consider about statues and vases), and then invite Alice and a merry party of young people down to the place. We'd

44

drive out ghosts to the sound of fiddle and dancing, and depend upon it, you dear little coward, we should never again hear a word about Myst Court being haunted."

"Ah, Vibert, we must remember our uncle's warnings," said Emmie, gently laying her hand on her brother's arm.

"*Beware of selfishness!*—eh? well, I'll think about that when I see you *conquer mistrust*. But to be gay is my nature, as it is yours to be timid, and Bruce's to be proud. One cannot alter nature."

"Can it not be improved?" asked Emmie. "Look at your garden,—it has been left for years to nature, so bears but a crop of weeds."

"Oh, if you are going to moralize, I'll be off!" cried Vibert. "I have not tried my new gun yet, and I expect capital sport. I warrant you that I will bring home a brace of pheasants to mend our fare!"

Mr. Trevor came down to Wiltshire by an early train, and was gladly welcomed at Myst Court. His presence greatly added to the harmony of the family circle; for his sons seldom exchanged bitter words when their father's eye was upon them. Emmie's spirits rose. When the family were gathered together at the luncheon-table, the young lady playfully rallied Vibert on his "capital sport," for she had seen him return with an empty bag from his shooting.

Vibert laughed good-humouredly at his own want of success. "I thought that pheasants and partridges would be plentiful as blackberries in the brushwood," said he; "but I lighted on no bird more aristocratic than a crow. I think that there must be poachers abroad, or perhaps four-footed poachers, in the shape of those starved, disreputable-looking cats which come prowling about the place."

"I suppose some of those left by my aunt as a legacy to her maid," observed Mr. Trevor.

"The legatee does not value the keepsakes," said Vibert, "to judge by the looks of the cats that crossed my path to-day, sneaking back to their old quarters as if in search for scraps."

"Does Mrs. Jessel live far from here?" inquired Emmie.

"About a mile from Myst Court by the road, but not half that distance by the path through the wood," answered Bruce. "The house left to her by Mrs. Myers is a two-storied, shallow building, standing very near the high-road, and looking like a Cockney villa that had somehow strayed into the country, and could not find its way back."

"So the cats have the good taste to prefer the antique beauties of Myst Court embowered in woods," said Vibert; "and their new mistress has no objection to their living here at free quarters. I fired at one of the miserable creatures, out of pure benevolence, but unhappily missed my mark."

"Your shooting is on a par with your driving," remarked Bruce satirically; "but Emmie's pony came off worse than the cat."

"That was not my fault!" exclaimed Vibert. "I managed the pony famously, in the dark too, and over a road expressly contrived to break the springs of a carriage. I was turning a sharp corner with consummate skill, when Emmie took it into her head to scream and catch hold of my arm. Of course, chaise and all went into the ditch, and how long they might have stayed there I know not, had not those two men come to our help."

"Do you know who they were?" asked Mr. Trevor, who had already heard something of the yesterday's adventure from Emmie.

"The one is called Harper, a strange, weird-looking old man, with long grizzled hair, and croaking voice," replied Vibert. "I don't care if I never set eyes on him again,—but he lives just outside our gate. The other was a very different sort of person, evidently quite a gentleman."

"Did you think so?" said Emmie, in a tone suggestive of a doubt on the subject.

"Why, he is a colonel," cried Vibert; "you heard him say so himself,—a colonel belonging to the American army."

"It is easy enough for a man to call himself an American colonel," said Bruce.

"I don't think it fair to disbelieve a gentleman's account of himself until one has cause to doubt his truthfulness," remarked Vibert. "Certainly," he added, glancing at Emmie, "Colonel Standish did tell us rather wonderful stories. You remember that one of the murdered Red Indian's ghost keeping watch over buried treasure?"

"It was a horrible story," said Emmie.

"And so graphically told!" exclaimed Vibert. "I'll let you hear the tale, papa; but I shall tell it to great disadvantage. A ghost story must lose all its thrilling effect when heard at a luncheon-table. Fancy being interrupted at the crisis by a request for 'a little more mutton!'"

After the tale had been told, and the meal concluded, Vibert went out again with his gun, to seek better success in the woods which surrounded Myst Court. The youth was wont to enter eagerly into any new kind of amusement, but three days were usually sufficient to make him tired of any pursuit.

Mr. Trevor, Emmie, and Bruce went into the drawing-room together, to talk over future plans. They had scarcely seated themselves by the table, on which Bruce had placed some papers of estimates, when the old-fashioned knocker on the front door gave a loud announcement that a visitor had come to the house.

"Who can have found us out already?" said Mr. Trevor. "We are scarcely prepared yet to receive calls from strangers."

Joe flung open the drawing-room door, and announced Colonel Standish.

Emmie's glimpses of the stranger on the preceding evening had been by such uncertain light, and she had been so unfitted by nervous fear to exercise her powers of observation, that she would scarcely have recognized her new acquaintance had not his name been announced. Colonel Standish was a tall and rather good-looking man, apparently about thirty years of age, with large bushy black whiskers, connected with each other by a well-trimmed beard, which, like a dark ruff, surrounded the chin. He was dressed in the height of modern fashion, with no small amount of jewellery displayed in brilliant studs, coins and other ornaments dangling from a handsome gold chain, and rings sparkling on more than one finger of his large gloveless hand. The colonel had a martial step, and an air of assurance which might be mistaken for that of ease. He advanced at once towards Miss Trevor, shook hands with her, and in a tone of gallantry inquired whether she had perfectly recovered from the effects of her late adventure. Emmie only replied by an inclination of her head, and at once introduced Colonel Standish to her father and brother. The stranger shook them both by the hand, with a familiar heartiness to which neither of the English gentlemen felt inclined to respond. Mr. Trevor, however, with grave courtesy, expressed his obligations to the colonel for the help which he had afforded on the preceding night.

"I am only too happy to rush to the rescue whenever so fair a lady is in peril," cried the colonel, turning and bowing to Emmie. "As for your son,—I don't think that it was this son—"

"Certainly not," interrupted Bruce.

"I must congratulate his father on the uncommon spirit and pluck shown by the young gentleman whom I met last night, under circumstances calculated to try the mettle of the boldest."

Emmie and Bruce exchanged glances; the faintest approach to a smile rose on the lips of each on hearing such exaggerated praise.

"As for this fair lady, she played the heroine," continued the colonel, again turning gallantly towards Emmie, whose smile was exchanged for a blush.

"Who is this vulgar flatterer?" thought Mr. Trevor and Bruce. Emmie took an early opportunity of gliding out of the room, to which she did not return till the colonel's visit was ended.

Standish was sufficiently a man of the world to see that he had overacted his part, and had not made a favourable impression. Mr. Trevor and his son became more and more coldly civil. The visitor took the chief share of the conversation, gave his anecdotes, and cracked his jokes. The Englishmen thought his jokes coarse, and his anecdotes of questionable authenticity. Conversation slackened, and in about half an hour the colonel rose to take his departure.

"I put up at the White Hart at S——," said he, as he threw down on the table a card for Vibert. "I find the accommodation fair, very fair, but my stay in the town is uncertain. I hope that we shall soon meet again," and the colonel shook the hand of Mr. Trevor, but a good deal less cordially than he had done on his first introduction to the father of Emmie.

"We do not echo his hope," observed Bruce, as soon as the visitor had tramped out of the house.

"Who can this low-bred talkative fellow be?" said Mr. Trevor. "It is not difficult for an impostor to pass himself off as a colonel, when those who would have proofs of his being so must seek for them at the other side of the Atlantic Ocean."

"I doubt this man's being American at all," observed Bruce. "I did not detect in his speech the peculiar Yankee accent, though it was interlarded with Yankee phrases."

"I shall not encourage this colonel's coming about the house," said Mr. Trevor, walking up to the window. "Why, there's Vibert accompanying him down the drive!"

"And they look hand and glove," added Bruce. "How they are laughing and talking together!"

"Vibert is young and unsuspicious," observed Mr. Trevor, as he turned from the window; "his generous, frank disposition lays him peculiarly open to deception. We must make some inquiries at S—— regarding this Colonel Standish. Your tutor, Mr. Blair, may know something of the man, and the character which he bears."

"I will not forget to gain what information I can," said Bruce Trevor.

CHAPTER XIII.

WORK.

On the following Sunday afternoon Emmie was sitting alone by the drawing-room window, with a devotional book in her hand, but her eyes resting on the fading glories of the woodland landscape, and her thoughts on her childhood's home, when she was joined by her brother Bruce.

"I am glad to find you alone," said Bruce, as he took a seat by his sister's side; "I want to consult you, I need your help."

Such words from the lips of the speaker were gratifying to Emmie; Bruce was ever more ready to give help than to ask it. Emmie closed her book, put it down, and was at once all attention.

"I have been making a little chart of the estate," said Bruce, unrolling a paper which he placed before his sister.

"What are those square marks on it?" inquired Emmie, looking with interest at the neatly executed chart.

"These are cottages,—some larger, some smaller," was the reply. "Those buildings marked in red are public-houses; those in green are farms. You observe that there is not a church or a school in the place; there is not one nearer than S——."

"More's the pity!" said Emmie.

"If you count, you will find that there are eighty-seven tenements of various kinds, and the dwellers in them are, of course, all tenants of our father. Give five individuals to each family, and you have four hundred and thirty-five souls on this estate, without a resident clergyman."

"And what can bring so many people around us?" asked Emmie.

"I believe the dye-works," answered her brother. "They give employment to most of the men who are not farm-labourers, and, as far as I have ascertained, to some of the women also."

"Then the people are not very poor," observed Emmie, with a look of relief; for she had been alarmed at the idea of more than four hundred beggars being quartered on her father's estate.

"The men in work ought not to be very poor," said Bruce; "but then there are sure to be widows, sick folk, and some too old for work. Besides this, improvidence, ignorance, and vice always bring misery in their train, and, from all that I have heard or seen, the people here are little better than heathens. The children run about like wild creatures; there is no one to teach them their duty to God or to man."

"I hope that papa may in time set up a school," said Emmie.—Compulsory education was a thing not yet introduced into England.

"I hope that he may; but he cannot do so at present," observed Bruce. "I was talking with him on the subject on our way from church this morning. Our father's expenses in educating Vibert and myself are heavy, and if either or both of us go to college they will be heavier still. Yet for these wretched tenants something should be done, and at once."

"Papa intends gradually to repair or rebuild some of the cottages."

"I am speaking of the people who inhabit the cottages," interrupted Bruce; "the dirty, ignorant, swearing, lying creatures who are dropping off, year by year, from misery on this side of the grave to worse misery beyond it."

Emmie looked distressed and perplexed. "What can be done for them?" she inquired.

"We must, in the first place, know them better, and so find out how to help them," said Bruce. "You are aware that I have little time to spare from my studies, which it is my duty to prosecute vigorously. I can give but my Sunday evenings, and my father is quite willing that on them I should hold a night-school for boys in our barn."

Emmie looked with smiling admiration on her young brother, about to undertake with characteristic resolution what she regarded as a Herculean task. But no trace of a smile lingered on her lips as Bruce calmly went on,—

"I can thus do something for the boys, but the care of the women and the girls naturally falls upon you."

"Upon me!" cried Emmie, looking aghast.

"Visiting the poor," continued Bruce, "is not a kind of business which our father can undertake; he has been accustomed to office-work all his life, and, as he told me to-day, he cannot begin at his age an occupation which is to him so utterly new."

"It would be utterly new to me, and I dare not attempt cottage-visiting!" cried Emmie, whose benevolent efforts had hitherto been confined to subscribing to charities or missions, and working delicate trifles to be sold at fancy bazaars.

"You are young, dear," observed Bruce Trevor.

"And that is just the reason why I should not be sent amongst all those dreadful people!" cried Emmie. "I might meet with rudeness, or drunkenness, or infectious cases. I cannot think how you could ever wish me to undertake such a work! Wait till I am forty or fifty years old before you ask me to visit these poor."

"And in the meantime," said Bruce, "children are growing up ignorant of the very first truths of religion; wretched women, who know no joy in this world, see no prospect of peace in another; the sick lack medicine, the hungry, food; the widow has no one to comfort her, and the dying—die without hope!"

Emmie clasped her hands, and looked pleadingly into the face of her brother. "Oh! what do you ask me to do?" she exclaimed; "do you want me to visit all these cottages, and the public-houses as well!"

"Not all the cottages, and most certainly not the public-houses," answered Bruce with a smile. "See," he continued, pointing to different parts of his chart, "I have marked with an E those dwellings which I thought that a lady might visit."

"There are a fearful number of E's," said poor Emmie, very gravely surveying the paper.

"Nay, if you took but two cottages each day (that would be scarce half-an-hour's work), in a month you would have visited all that I have marked for you," said the methodical Bruce; "and in each you would have left some little book or striking tract, if you had found that the inmates could read."

"I should be afraid to ask them if they could read or not," cried Emmie. Bruce went on without heeding the interruption.

"You would keep a book, and mark down each day where you had called, with a slight notice of the state of each cottage, the name of its tenant, the number of the children, and

49

such other particulars as would be of the utmost value to our father when he affords relief in money. It would be better, perhaps, for you to make it a rule not to give money yourself."

"That is just the only thing that I could do!" exclaimed Emmie; "I dare not intrude into cottage homes without the excuse of coming to give charity to those who want."

"The visits of a lady would not be deemed an intrusion," said Bruce. He had some practical knowledge on the subject, having been for years at a private school where the ladies of the master's family constantly visited the poor. "Your gentle courtesy will make you welcome wherever you go. Nor need you go alone, you can always take Susan with you."

"Why not let Susan go by herself?" said Emmie, grasping eagerly at an idea which afforded a hope of escape from work which she disliked and dreaded.

"Susan has been trained for a lady's-maid, and not for a Bible-woman," said Bruce; "she is not fitted to act as your substitute, useful as she may prove as your helper. Nor would Susan be as readily welcomed amongst our tenants as would be a real lady, their landlord's only daughter. Your position and education, Emmie, give you advantages which Susan would not possess; they are talents intrusted to you, which it would be a sin to bury."

Emmie heaved a disconsolate sigh.

"Let me put the subject in a clearer light," pursued Bruce. "What would you call the conduct of one of your servants who should, without your leave, ask another person to do the work which she herself had been engaged to perform?"

"I should call it indolence," replied Emmie. Her brother added the word "presumption."

"And if a soldier on the eve of a battle should hire a substitute to fight in his stead," continued Bruce, "what would such an act appear to his comrades and captain?"

"Cowardice," answered Emmie.

"There have been instances," said Bruce, "of pilgrimages and penances, imposed on the wealthy, *being performed by proxy!* A poor man endured, for the sake of money, what the rich man believed to be the penalty of his own sins. What were such penances or pilgrimages, Emmie?"

"A mockery," was the faltered reply.

"And if in man's sight there are duties which we cannot make over to others without presumption, cowardice, and rendering the performance of them a solemn mockery, think you that the Divine Master looks with favour on services done *by proxy?* He intends the rich to come in contact with their poorer brethren. He claims from us not merely the money which we can easily give, but the words of our lips, the strength of our limbs, the thoughts of our brains, the time which is far more precious than gold. The work which your Master gives you to do, the special work, no substitute can perform."

"Oh! I wish with all my heart and soul that we had never left Summer Villa, never come to Myst Hall!" exclaimed Emmie.

Bruce was a little disappointed that such an exclamation should be the only reply to his serious words. "You would surely not desire to pass through life putting aside every cross but the fanciful ornament which it is the fashion to wear!" he remarked with slight severity in his manner. "You have given yourself, body and soul, to a heavenly Master,— is it for Him or for you to choose your work? Is it a very hard command if He say to you now, 'Work for one half-hour each day in My vineyard'?"

"I would rather work for six hours with my fingers quietly in my own room," murmured Emmie.

"That is, you would select your own favourite kind of work, take merely what is pleasant and easy, and what suits your natural temper," said Bruce. "There is nothing to thwart your will or try your temper in making pretty trifles, cultivating your accomplishments, or managing a small household such as ours."

"There you are mistaken, Bruce," observed Emmie, raising her head, which had drooped as she had uttered her former sentence. "It does try my courage to speak to our new servant Hannah, that masculine, loud-voiced, ill-tempered woman. I did but say to her this morning, in as gentle a way as I could, that I have a book of recipes, and that perhaps she could get some hints from it, as one of the gentlemen is rather particular as to cookery, and Hannah looked ready to fly at my face. I shall never venture to find fault with her again."

"Emmie, Emmie, is this miserable timidity to meet you at every turn?" exclaimed Bruce. "Have you no spirit, no strength of will to wrestle it down, to rise above it?"

"I cannot help being timid," sighed Emmie.

"Vibert might as well say that he cannot help being selfish," said Bruce. "If you know that you have a besetting fault, it is not that you should sit down with folded hands and let it bind you, without so much as a struggle to shake yourself free."

Bruce spoke with some warmth, for he spoke from his heart. It is so easy to point out what is the plain duty of others; it is so difficult frankly to acknowledge our own. The young man justly accused Emmie of neglecting the special work appointed for her by her Great Master, and of shrinking from fighting the good fight of faith. Himself resolute and courageous, with great power of self-control and self-denial, Bruce could make little allowance for failings which were not his own. But had Bruce no special work to do from which the natural man recoiled? had he no battle to fight against a besetting sin? Bruce's appointed work lay close to him, though he did not choose to perceive it, and was virtually repeating Cain's question, *Am I my brother's keeper?* Bruce suffered pride to control his actions, and mar the work of grace in his soul. It would have been as arduous a work for him to "wrestle it down, to rise above it," as it would have been to his timid sister to go forth and minister to the poor in the hovels surrounding Myst Court.

Emmie's conscience was tender; she had a sincere desire to do what was right, blended with a natural wish to stand well in the opinion of a brother whom she admired and loved. Before the interview between them was ended, Emmie had promised to "attempt to break the ice" on the following day; but she inwardly shivered at the thought of the effort before her. How many have experienced this repugnance, this dread of obeying the Master's call and entering His vineyard!—how many of those who have afterwards found in His work their joy and delight! Duty often, when viewed from a distance, wears an aspect forbidding and stern; but on closer approach she is found to have treasures in her hand, and flowers spring up in her path.

CHAPTER XIV.

EARLY IMPRESSIONS.

Vibert had not finished his breakfast when Bruce, on the Monday morning, started on his walk to the town. Notwithstanding sundry remonstrances and hints from his father and Emmie, it was a full half-hour before the younger brother followed in the track of the elder. And very different was the careless, sauntering step of Vibert from the firm, quick tread of Bruce.

Mr. Trevor's elder son returned alone in the dusk of evening, but this time Vibert was scarcely ten minutes behind him.

"Mr. Blair has a capital method of imparting knowledge; it will be our own fault if we do not make progress under him," said Bruce to Emmie when he rejoined her in the drawing-room. "My tutor has given me plenty of work to do this evening, but I must spare an hour to refresh myself by hearing you sing. And you, dear, what have you been doing during my absence, and where have you been?"

Bruce was a little curious to know whether his fair sister had had courage to "break the ice."

"Oh! I do not know what you will think of me, Bruce," said Emmie, dropping her soft brown eyes. "I did intend to make a beginning of visiting the tenants; I had ruled lines in a book, that I might set down in order their names and all that you want to know; but—but—"

"Let's hear all about it," said Bruce good-humouredly, taking a seat by his sister's side: it was pleasant to the student to unbend after the hard work of the day.

"I could not go out in the morning,—that is to say, not conveniently," began Emmie. "I had a long, long letter to write to Alice, and another to my aunt in Grosvenor Square; and I had orders to give to Hannah, and then to arrange with Susan about hanging pictures to adorn, or rather to hide the untidy walls of my own little room."

"It would be far better to give up that room," said Bruce. "You do not consider, Emmie, in what a bad position you put me by obliging me to occupy the other apartment."

"How?—what do you mean?" cried Emmie, looking up with an expression of uneasiness on her face; "you do not find that you are disturbed by—"

"Not by spectres," replied Bruce, smiling; "but no one likes to appear to be the most selfish fellow in the world."

"No one would ever think you selfish, dear Bruce; the cap does not fit you at all."

"Therefore I have an objection to putting it on," said Bruce Trevor; "I would leave the cap to Vibert, who, to judge by his conduct, may actually think it becoming. But enough of this. You know that I dislike retaining my luxurious quarters, but if you really prefer the small room, everything possible must be done to make it a gem of a room. Now tell me how you passed the rest of the day."

"After luncheon papa called me to his study to copy out something for him," said Emmie; "however, that did not take me long. Then I glanced over the *Times*, and read about such a horrible murder, committed in a country lane, that it made me feel more than ever afraid to venture beyond our grounds. Yet, to please you, dear Bruce, I rang the bell for Susan, and bade her get ready to accompany me in a walk to the hamlet."

"I hope that you had a higher motive than that of pleasing me," said her brother.

"I am not sure that I had, at least not then," replied the truthful Emmie. "But, whatever my motive might be, it took Susan and me along the shrubbery as far as the entrance gate. At the further side of that gate, looking through the iron bars, as it seemed to me—like a bird of prey on the watch, stood Harper, with his beak-like nose, his hollow eyes, and his long shaggy hair. You know whom I mean, he is the strange old man whom we met on the night of the storm."

"And who did good service by cutting the pony's traces," said Bruce.

"I wish that I felt more grateful to him for it," observed Miss Trevor; "but I cannot without nervous dread think of Harper as I saw him on Friday night, with the gleam of blue lightning on his strange face and his flashing knife. Then he gave me such dreadful hints and warnings regarding the haunted room in Myst Court,—I shudder whenever I think of them now!"

"Cast them from your mind, they are rubbish," said Bruce.

"As Susan and I advanced to the gate," resumed Emmie, "I felt sure that Harper was sharply watching our movements. I hoped that he would soon go away, so, turning aside, I took three or four turns in the wood with Susan; but every time that we again approached the entrance, I saw that Harper was there. I so much disliked having to pass him, I so much feared that he would address me, that at last I gave up my intention of going to the hamlet to-day. I told Susan that the air felt damp and cold, and that I should put off paying my visits. So feeling, I must own, rather ashamed of myself, I returned to the house."

"This is too absurd!" exclaimed Bruce, a little provoked, and yet at the same time amused by the frank confession of Emmie. "The hovel in which lives that man Harper is just outside the gate, so that if you are afraid of passing him, even when you have the trusty Susan to act as a bodyguard, you may as well consider yourself a state prisoner at once. So nothing was done to-day?"

"I wrote to London for two packets of Partridge's illustrated fly-leaves," said Emmie. "Uncle Arrows recommended them to me as very attractive and useful, and suited for cottage homes. I shall not attempt visiting until I receive the packets by post."

"I have forestalled you," said Bruce, "and have laid in already a fair stock of such ammunition to serve us in our warfare against ignorance and intemperance here. I can supply you at once with as many of the fly-leaves as there are homes in the hamlet."

"Then I am not to have a day's reprieve," sighed the unwilling recruit.

"When a duty is before us, the sooner it is done the better," observed Bruce; "repugnance towards it only grows by delay. And I would advise you, dear Emmie, should you meet either of those men whose acquaintance you made in the storm, to be courteous—that you always are—but to avoid entering into conversation with them, especially with the so-called American colonel."

"Why, have you learned anything more about him?" inquired Emmie with interest.

"I made inquiries regarding him of Mr. Blair, as my father desired me to do," replied Bruce. "I find that this Standish has been for some weeks at S——; but where he comes from, why he came, and wherefore he remains in the place, nobody seems to know. He has had no introduction, as far as my tutor is aware, to any of the county families; but he has, it is said, been seen more than once quitting the small house which our great-aunt bequeathed to Mrs. Jessel."

"What can have taken him there?" cried Emmie.

"My tutor could throw no light on that subject, and told me that he spoke from mere hearsay, and put little faith in such gossip. One thing, however, is certain,—this colonel lives at the best hotel in the town, and in most luxurious style. He spares himself no indulgence, hires his hunter and follows the hounds, or drives about the country in a curricle and pair, and seems to be rolling in wealth. He is never seen in a place of worship, and, pushing as he is, has not made his way into any respectable circle. The less we have to say to this pseudo-colonel the better; I suspect him to be a charlatan and impostor."

"There's charity for you, and gratitude!" exclaimed Vibert, who, entering the room while Bruce was speaking, had heard his concluding sentence. "Here is a gentleman who came to our aid when we were in a dilemma, who has shown us courtesy and kindness, and he is to be condemned, unheard, as an impostor, because a pedant, who has never put foot in stirrup or fired a shot in his life, cannot understand a frank, bold, chivalrous nature. Blair thinks that all must be evil that does not just square with his old-fashioned notions. Emmie, you should stand up for your friend," added the youth more playfully, as he threw himself on an arm-chair, and stretched himself, after what he considered to be a long and tiresome walk, "for the colonel not only helped to pull you out of your ditch, but he told me that my sister is the prettiest girl that he has seen on this side of the big fish-pond."

"I hope that you do not encourage such impertinence," observed Bruce sternly.

"Oh, if the colonel dare to hint that my brother is the pleasantest fellow that he has met with, I'll resent the impertinence, I promise you," laughed Vibert.

Emmie foresaw, with uneasiness, more angry sparring between her two brothers, and, to turn the current of conversation, asked Vibert what he thought of the Blairs.

"Oh, our tutor is a learned professor, who has pored over books, and puzzled over problems, till he has grown into the shape of a note of interrogation," replied Vibert lightly. "As for his wife, she's a homely body, as clever men's wives usually are; Mrs. Blair looks like a housekeeper, but has not the merit of being a good one."

Bruce, whom the conversation did not greatly interest, had taken up a book.

"And her family?" inquired Emmie; "I suppose that you have made their acquaintance."

"We were all gathered together at early dinner, if one could call that a dinner at which there was nothing eatable," said the fastidious Vibert. "There was old Blair at one end of the table, hacking at a shoulder of mutton, and talking, as he did so, to Bruce about Sophocles and Euripides. There was Mrs. Blair at the other end, ladling out the potatoes. Bruce and I sat on one side, and three demure little chaps in pinafores on the other, like degrees of comparison, small, smaller, and smallest; dull, duller, and dullest. The children were so terribly well-behaved, that they never asked for anything (not that there was much to ask for), they never spoke a word, nor lifted their eyes from their plates, but wielded with propriety their forks and spoons; I think that only the eldest of the three was trusted with a knife. The little fellows' looks seemed to say, 'It is a matter of business, and not of play, to eat shoulder of mutton and boiled rice pudding, and drink water out of horn mugs.' The whole affair had such a nursery look about it, that I half expected to be provided with a pinafore, instead of a dinner napkin."

"You incorrigible boy!" laughed Emmie; "I think that the three degrees of comparison will become merry, merrier, and merriest in your company soon."

"They will have precious little of it, I can tell you that," said Vibert; "one such meal is enough for me. To say nothing of its intolerable dulness, the wine of Blair's table is insufferably bad, the mere washing out of casks, cheap trash!"—the lad distorted his handsome features into an expression of strong disgust. "Oh, *you* did not mind it, Bruce," continued Vibert, as his brother glanced up from his book; "you are a water-drinker and no judge on the subject, but *I* know what is what, and cheap wine of all things I detest. It ruins the constitution. I shall try if I cannot get something eatable and drinkable in the town; I hear that there is a capital *table d'hôte* at the White Hart."

"You are aware that the arrangement for our having luncheon at our tutor's being concluded, your taking the meal elsewhere must involve double expense," observed Bruce.

"Can't help that," said the youthful epicurean, shrugging his shoulders; "I can't work on coarse mutton and plain rice pudding, served up on plates of the old willow-pattern; specially as I seem likely to be starved at Myst Court, if we are to have no cook but Hannah. I am certain," continued Vibert, his bright eyes sparkling with fun as he turned to his sister—"I am certain that yesterday's boiled rabbits were my great-aunt's cats in disguise, and that the soup—faugh!—was simply the water in which they had been boiled! Why did we not bring our old cook to Myst Court?"

"We did not bring her, because she would not come," replied Emmie.

"I suppose that in an old haunted house, country cooks and country footmen are necessary evils, and must be endured," said Vibert, attempting to look philosophic. "But I hope that you, as mistress of the establishment, have spoken pretty sharply to Hannah. I hope that you have given her a fright."

"Hannah is a good deal more likely to give me one," answered the smiling Emmie. "I think of making over to you, Vibert, the office of scolding the cook."

"I should find that a more formidable task than that of facing all the ghosts of Myst Court," was the merry lad's playful reply.

CHAPTER XV.

THE FIRST VISIT.

 "Bruce is right; whenever a disagreeable duty is to be done, the sooner we get over it the better," said Emmie to herself, as, accompanied by Susan, she started on her walk before luncheon on the following day. A cloud of care was on the youthful face which looked so fair and gentle under the shade of the broad-brimmed garden-hat which the maiden wore. Emmie had "screwed up her courage to the sticking-point," and had resolved not to return home without having performed her self-allotted task of, at least, entering two of the cottages inhabited by her father's tenants. The young lady had a couple of fly-leaves in her hand, with their attractive pictures outermost,—these were

what Bruce had called her ammunition; but the timid recruit had a reserve, on which she counted more, in the form of a half-crown slipped into her left glove, ready to be produced in a moment. There are many district visitors who may remember the time when they started on their first campaign as reluctantly and as timidly as did the inexperienced Emmie.

It may have been observed that the maiden undertook her work simply as a hard duty. She was urged onwards by a brother's counsels, and pricked by the goad of conscience. There was in Miss Trevor none of the hopeful, earnest spirit which hears the Master's call, and answers it with the cry, "Here am I; send me!" Emmie had indeed prayed for help in entering on her new sphere, but her prayer was not the prayer of faith. She did not realize that God could indeed make her a channel through which His stream of blessing might flow on a parched and thirsty land. She did not believe that her dumb lips might be so opened that her mouth might show forth His praise. Emmie had a profound mistrust of her own powers. Such mistrust is safe and may be salutary; but she confounded that innocent diffidence with what was really mistrust of God. The girl knew her own weakness; so far, all was well; but there was unbelief in not resting on the almighty strength of her God. Emmie would have been startled and shocked had the truth been clothed in words, but she was really regarding the Most High as a Master who commands that bricks should be made without giving the needful straw, as a Leader who sends forth feeble recruits to the fight all unprovided with armour. The maiden's courage was not sustained by the thought, *I will go in the strength of the Lord God;* nor did she rest on His promise, *My grace is sufficient for thee, for My strength is made perfect in weakness.* It was not the love of God, but the dread of incurring His displeasure, which made the poor, hesitating, unwilling girl combat the fear of man.

And if Emmie was not impelled forwards by a loving desire to please a loving Master, still less was she influenced by tender concern for the souls of those whom she felt that she ought to visit. The child of luxury, in her pleasant home, had scarcely regarded the poor as being of the same class of beings as herself. They were creatures to be pitied, to be helped, to be taught by those trained for the work; but as beings to be objects of sympathy and love, as children of the one Great Father, Emmie could not regard them. Charity was thus to her but a cold dry duty, like the timber which may be shaped into a thousand useful purposes; but not like the living tree whose branches are bright with blossoms or rich in fruit, because through it flows the life-giving sap. Such Christian charity belongs not to fallen nature; it is a special gift of God, and comes through close union, by faith, with Him whose nature is love. Emmie's faith was so weak, that it is no marvel that her prayers for guidance were little more than forms, and that her compassion for her poor fellow-sinners was cold. The young Christian had *not* conquered mistrust.

"Susan, have you not told me that the ladies with whom you once lived used to visit the poor?" said Emmie to her attendant as the two proceeded along the drive.

"Yes, constantly, miss," was the answer.

"I wish that I knew how they made their way with the cottagers. Did they not find it very difficult at first?" asked Emmie.

"I do not know how they found it at first," replied Susan; "for when I entered the service of the vicar's lady, even her little ones were accustomed to go to the homes of the poor whom they knew, to make some good old creature happy with a jug of warm broth, or a bit of flannel, or, perhaps, a text in large letters, painted by themselves, to be hung up in a sick person's room."

"But there is just the difficult point," observed Emmie,—"how did the family come to know the poor so well? If one were once acquainted with the 'good old creature,' there might be some pleasure in taking the broth or the flannel."

"My young ladies used to go on their regular rounds, miss, and exchange the books which they lent to the poor. I have often gone with the ladies to carry the books," said Susan. "The visitors were always asked to sit down in the cottages, the people were so much pleased to see them."

"And when the ladies sat down, what happened next?" asked Emmie, who felt herself to be ignorant of the very alphabet of district visiting, and who was not too proud to learn from her maid. "What did your ladies say? Did they begin directly to teach and to preach?"

"Oh dear, no, miss!" cried Susan, a little surprised at the question; "I think that my ladies talked to the poor much as they would have talked to other people. They spoke to the cottagers about their health and the weather, and to the mothers about their children, and they gave any little bit of news, perhaps out of a missionary paper, that they thought would amuse the poor folk. The talking came all quite natural-like."

"It would never come natural-like with me," observed Emmie; "nor, to own the truth, do I see that much good is gained by that kind of talk. One does not make the effort of going into the dirty homes of the poor just to gossip with them, as one might do with a friend, but to teach them their duty and make them better."

Susan knew her proper place too well to reply to this observation of her young mistress; the maid thought, however, to herself that her former ladies had found real friends and dear friends too amongst the poor, and that to form a tie of sympathy between the higher and lower classes *did do good*, even if there were no direct religious teaching. Susan remembered also that she had heard the most pious of her young ladies observe that she had herself learned more from the poor than she had ever been able to teach them. The district visitor should recognize the possibility of mutual benefit when she goes on her charity rounds.

"Did your ladies never talk to the people about their souls?" inquired Emmie. "Was nothing said about religion in these visits which they paid to the poor?"

"Oh yes, miss," answered Susan, "but it came so natural-like. A blind woman would like to be read to; then the visitor read from the Bible, and afterwards the two talked over what had been read. Or a mother, may be, had lost a baby; and then the lady would speak of Him who carries the lambs in His arms. The poor liked to open their hearts to the ladies and tell them their troubles, because, you see, miss, they felt that the ladies cared. I'm sure when little Amy Fisher died, Miss Mary cried for her as much as her own mother did. Mrs. Fisher had been a hard sort of woman,—I think she was given to drink,—but after her little one's death Miss Mary got her quite round. But all that came quite natural-like," added Susan, again using her favourite phrase, by which Emmie understood that there had been no forced talk on religious subjects, no hard dogmatical teaching.

"I wish that I could acquire this art of comforting and helping and sympathizing," thought Emmie; "but I feel sure that I never shall do so."

Emmie and her maid had now reached the entrance gate. The young lady was relieved not to see at it the figure of Harper, whom she regarded with almost a superstitious dread. She passed his hovel, a mere tenement of mud, with a thatched roof, green with moss and stained with yellow lichen. The door was shut, and no smoke rose from the single chimney of the dilapidated dwelling.

Picking her way along the muddy road, Emmie, with a beating heart, proceeded towards the next cottage, which, though it was far from being neat and clean in its appearance, had at least glass in its windows, and was able to stand upright. Her conversation with Susan had been rather encouraging on the whole to the inexperienced lady visitor. A faint hope sprang up in the breast of Emmie that after a while district work might come "natural-like" to her as it had done to other ladies. The fair girl could not but be conscious that she possessed a more than common power of pleasing, such a power as might smooth down some of her difficulties in winning her way to the hearts of the poor.

Emmie went up to the door of the cottage, hesitated a moment, murmured to herself, "Now for an effort!" and gently tapped with the end of her parasol. No brief silent prayer was darted up from her heart,—that prayer which is as the child's upward glance at the parent who holds his hand to support and guide him. When first entering on what she regarded as work for God, Emmie's thoughts were not rising to God.

There was a slight stir audible within the cottage after the lady had knocked, followed by the click of the latch, and a woman threw open the door. A scent of bacon, greens, and porter pervaded the cottage, and Emmie saw that the family were seated at dinner. A burly-looking man in shirt-sleeves, whose back had been towards the door, turned round his unshaven, unwashed face to see who had tapped for admittance. Several dirty, untidy children stared open-mouthed at the unexpected appearance of a well-dressed lady. Emmie shrank back, for with intuitive delicacy she felt that to enter a cottage at meal-time was an intrusion.

"Won't you step in, miss?" said the woman who had opened the door, with that civility which is generally met with in the cottage homes of England.

"Oh—not now—I did not know—I never meant—" stammered forth poor Emmie, as nervously polite as if she had by mistake intruded herself at the repast of a duchess. The gruff looks of the man, who did not rise from his chair, took from the timid girl all self-possession. Emmie expected him to growl out, "What brings you here?" And as the only apology which occurred to her mind for calling at all, she nervously thrust her half-crown into the hand of the astonished woman, and with a muttered "I thought you might want it," made her retreat from the door. Emmie in her confusion dropped her papers; they were picked up and returned to her by Susan.

"You might have left them by the door," observed Emmie.

Susan thought, though too respectful to say what she thought, that her young ladies had never *dropped* tracts in the mud for the poor to stoop to pick up; the vicar's daughters had always given such papers with the pleasant smile which had insured for them a welcome. In distributing religious literature, as in most other matters, success greatly depends on the manner in which a thing is done.

Emmie was not satisfied with this her first essay in cottage-visiting. "I never thought of finding workmen at home," she observed to Susan.

"I think, miss, that twelve is a common dinner-hour," said Susan, "and that then some of the men come home from their work."

"Then assuredly twelve is a bad visiting hour," cried Emmie; "we had better return home directly." The young lady walked back to Myst Court at a much quicker pace than had been hers when she had started on her little expedition. She was glad to find herself within the gate and in the shrubbery again.

"I have not had much success, but still I can tell Bruce that I have made a beginning, that I have broken the ice," thought Emmie. "That woman was civil enough; I should not have much minded going into the cottage had I chanced to find her alone."

As Emmie's brothers were, as usual, passing the day at S——, Mr. Trevor was his daughter's only companion at luncheon. The master of Myst Court was a pleasant, kindly-looking man, who had reached the shady side of fifty, but with a form yet unbent and hair but lightly touched with gray. He had been from youth a steady hard-working man, and Bruce had probably derived his habits of business from his father's example. But with Mr. Trevor the wheel of labour had hitherto run in one groove, or rather, one may say, on a tramway made smooth by habit. It had been as natural to Mr. Trevor to go to his office, as it had been to partake of his breakfast. The complete change in his mode of life caused by the removal to Wiltshire, was like the jarring caused by turning suddenly off the tramway into a stone-paved road. Mr. Trevor had not been trained to perform the duties of a landlord and country squire, and he more than suspected that what he might have gained in dignity of position he had lost in comfort. Now as he sat at table in the lofty dining-room of his stately mansion, Mr. Trevor's brow wore an expression of worry which Emmie had never seen upon it when the family had resided in Summer Villa.

"You look tired, dear papa," she observed.

"I have had a good deal to annoy me, Emmie," said her father, who was making very slow progress indeed with his plateful of beef, tough and not much more than warmed through. "I find that Farmer Vesey has been taking, in a most unscrupulous manner, a slice off my west field which borders upon his lands. The steward says that I shall have to go to law about it. I detest going to law! Why are not boundaries clearly marked! Then I've had endless complaints from the people whose cottages border the brook below Bullen's dye-works; they say that the dye kills all the fish, and makes the water unfit for drinking. Really the complaints have good foundation. I walked down to-day to the place, and saw that the water is so discoloured that I would not let a dog slake his thirst in a stream so polluted."

"And are the cottagers your tenants, papa?"

"Yes; so it is my business to defend their rights," observed Mr. Trevor. "I went at once to Bullen, hoping that we might come to some satisfactory arrangement, without having recourse to the lawyers."

"And I hope that you found the manufacturer open to reason?" said Emmie.

"I found him to be a low, vulgar, money-making man, who would not care if he dyed all the rivers in England scarlet and blue, so that he could fish his profits out of them. I have heard that Bullen gives infidel lectures in S——, so that he tries to poison the springs of knowledge as well as the waters of the brook."

"What a dreadful man!" exclaimed Emmie.

"I shall have to go to law with him," observed Mr. Trevor, with a yet more troubled look; "I cannot let my tenants be poisoned, and yet I hate the worry and expense of a suit. I shall wait a while, and see if this fellow Bullen will not come to terms. Then I've had another annoying thing brought to my notice this morning: it is certain that there is poaching on my estate. There has been no proper care taken to preserve the game during the time of my predecessor, and if matters go on in the same way, pheasants will be as rare here as black swans. Really the cheapest and easiest way to get game is from a London market!"

The same reflection had just occurred to Emmie. Joe, in his noisy way, now entered the room, and told Miss Trevor, with awkward bluntness, that a woman was asking to see her.

"What is her name?" inquired Emmie.

"She didn't give none, miss," said Joe; "but she has brought a lot of children with her."

"Miss Trevor is engaged; desire the woman to wait a little," said the master of Myst Court.

Joe went out, banging the door behind him, but in less than three minutes returned.

"There be two other women come to see you, miss," said he. "One says as you told her to call."

"I bade no one call," said Emmie. "I am sorry, papa, that you should be thus disturbed at your meal."

"I had better myself see what is the cause of this irruption of the Goths and Vandals," observed Mr. Trevor, rising from his seat, and then quitting the room. Mr. Trevor had scarcely more experience than his daughter in dealing personally with the poor, but he felt heavy upon his conscience the responsibility belonging to the owner of landed property.

Mr. Trevor in a short time returned, looking grave and somewhat perplexed. "How one misses clergy, and district visitors, and organized societies in a place like this!" he exclaimed, as he resumed his seat at the table. "All these women declare that they are in want, that their husbands are out of work; and how am I to tell whether this be or be not the fact? I have given each of the beggars a trifle, and told them not to come here again, that we will make inquiries about them. I cannot have my door thus besieged. I wonder what brought on us this sudden invasion!"

"I'm afraid that it was my unlucky half-crown," observed Emmie.

"To whom did you give a half-crown?" asked her father.

"I gave it at the first cottage to the left of the gate, beyond Harper's wretched little den," replied Emmie. She read something very unlike approbation in the eyes of her parent, and shrank from their questioning gaze.

"What! you gave it at the cottage of Blunt, the man who earns higher wages than almost any one else in the place!" cried Mr. Trevor, slightly raising his voice.

"The cottage did not look *very* comfortable," said Emmie in an apologetic tone. She felt that the excuse was scarcely sincere, for the comfort or discomfort of the abode had had little to do with her giving the money.

"Of course the cottage is not comfortable, for the man Blunt is notoriously given to drinking," said Mr. Trevor, "and doubtless your half-crown is already turned into gin. You must really exert your common sense in visiting my tenants, my dear child," he continued in a tone of vexation, "or you will do incalculable mischief where you intend to do good."

It was so strange a thing to Emmie to receive anything like reproof from her tender indulgent parent, that her eyes glistened with tears of distress and mortification. Mr. Trevor could not bear to give her pain, and instantly softened his tone to that of kindness.

"You had the best intentions, my darling, and we shall all in time understand our new duties better. But you must be a little more careful in future where you visit, and how you give alms. I wish that instead of Blunt's cottage you had taken the one to the right of the gate. A poor respectable widow lives there; if I recollect rightly, her name is Brant. I have seen her several times at her cottage-door, looking tidy, but so poor and so ill that she has been rather upon my mind. It is not in my way to visit sick women, but I should like you to call with Susan, and ascertain whether the poor creature be really in want."

"Yes, papa, I will go," said Emmie humbly; "I will this afternoon visit the poor respectable widow, and try to keep my half-crowns in future for those who need and deserve them."

CHAPTER XVI.

TRY AGAIN.

Again Emmie, with her attendant, passed through the gateway at the entrance to the grounds of Myst Court. Miss Trevor had scarcely done so ere she became uncomfortably conscious that her movements now attracted a good deal of attention amongst the inmates of the cottages near. A rabble of children, all dirty and some of them barefoot, clustered near the gate, and when the lady had passed it, formed a kind of volunteer escort with which Emmie would have gladly dispensed. Some begged, and all stared at the lady; while two or three urchins, more impudent than the rest, pressed so closely upon her, that Susan could scarcely prevent them from impeding her mistress's progress. Emmie walked fast to rid herself of her unwelcome companions, but the children quickened their pace to keep up with the lady. Women stood at the entrances of their cottages, dropping courtesies, and evidently full of hope that the dispenser of half-crowns would visit their homes. Emmie was experimentally learning one of the most important of lessons for a district visitor, especially a rich one, that the worst way to begin is to give money without inquiry, merely to smooth our own way, and to buy that civility from the poor which is usually offered freely. The indiscriminating giver of alms, instead of improving the class whom he visits, rouses their evil passions. He makes the poor beggars, if he finds them not beggars already. Cupidity, jealousy, hypocrisy, these are the seeds which the careless, indolent almsgiver sows; and then, when he sees the harvest, he bitterly complains of the ingratitude which has requited his generous kindness. To help effectually those who require help, to sow a blessing and reap a blessing, we need to receive, we need to ask for the wisdom that cometh down from above.

"I wish that I had flung that unlucky half-crown into the brook, instead of throwing it away on those Blunts!" thought Emmie. "It was my nervous timidity that made me do so foolish a thing."

There was no difficulty in finding the cottage of Widow Brant; nor had Emmie even to knock, for the poor woman stood at her open door, only too glad to welcome the lady in. The widow was dressed neatly, but very poorly; her mourning was faded, and many a patch showed the work of industrious fingers. The inside of the cottage was so clean, that Emmie felt no reluctance to sit down on the chair which was offered to her, after a rapid dusting which it did not seem to require. Mrs. Brant was a small, thin, sickly-looking woman, with weak voice and timid manner; not even Emmie could possibly feel afraid of "breaking the ice" with one who excited no feeling but that of compassion. A good commencement was made; Emmie admired the flowers in the window, she herself was so fond of flowers; there was the point of similarity of taste on which the rich and poor could touch each other without undue familiarity on the one side, or sense of condescension on the other. The face of the widow brightened, and the young visitor felt encouraged. Miss Trevor went on to make inquiries regarding the widow's state of health, and listened with interest unfeigned to the story of long years passed in weakness and pain. The patient endurance of the poor invalid interested and touched the heart of her hearer.

"But have you had no medical advice?" inquired Emmie.

"Years agone I'd the parish doctor, miss; but he didn't do me no good," replied the meek little widow. "But now I'm in hopes as I'll soon get better. There's a wonderful clever man as has come to this place; they says as he has been in Ireland, and he has scraped the dust off the tombstones of saints, and mixed it up with holy water, and when we've crossed his palm with a shilling, miss, he hangs a bag of the dust round our necks, and mutters a charm to wile away all our pains. See, miss," and the poor creature showed a small linen bag fastened round her neck by a morsel of string, "I gave my last shilling for this."

"And has it done you good?" asked Emmie, a little amused at the simplicity of the woman, and more than a little indignant at the advantage taken of it by some heartless impostor.

"I can't say as how I feels much better yet," replied the sufferer, "but I hopes as in time the charm will work a cure."

"It will never work anything but disappointment!" cried Miss Trevor; "the food which that shilling might have bought would have done more for your health than all the charms in the world made up by a superstitious, ignorant quack!"

"Ignorant—superstitious!" croaked out a voice at the slowly opening door, which made Emmie start to her feet in alarm. She knew the tones, and she knew the hard features and long grizzled hair of him who had crossed the threshold, and who now stood surveying her with a fixed malignant gaze. "Do you talk of *ignorance*, child," continued Harper, making a stride towards Emmie, who instantly backed as far as the narrow space of the room would admit, "you who know not even the secrets of your own dwelling, nor dare to ask what things of darkness may haunt it! *Superstition!*—if it be superstition to dread the unseen, to tremble before the unknown, is it for *you* to talk of superstition in another?"

Emmie was too much terrified to attempt a reply. Her one desire was to quit the cottage directly, and she made a movement as if to do so; but Harper was between her and the door, and she did not dare to brush past him. Happily her attendant Susan was much more self-possessed than was her young mistress.

"Please to make way for my lady," said the maid with a decision of manner which caused Harper to draw a little to one side. Emmie did not even wait to wish the widow good-day; trembling like an aspen, the timid girl made her escape from the cottage, resolved never to run the risk of encountering Harper again, unless she were under the immediate protection of her father or Bruce.

Returning rapidly towards the entrance gate, like one who fears pursuit, Emmie, when almost close to it, came upon Mrs. Jessel, attired as before in black dress, with crape-flowers and bugles.

"Ah! Miss Trevor, good afternoon," said the late attendant on Mrs. Myers, with the mixture of obsequiousness and forwardness which marked the manner of one long accustomed to flatter and fawn, but who felt herself to be now greatly raised in social position by having a house of her own. "How good you are to go visiting the cottages round!"

"I cannot visit in cottages," said poor Emmie with something like a gasp, as she passed through the gateway and then stopped, as if she now felt herself safe.

"Ah! that's what my poor dear lady was always saying, Miss Trevor," observed Jael Jessel, who had followed her into the grounds. "Mrs. Myers was the kindest of creatures;

but she was too nervous to visit her tenants. 'You go for me, Jessel,' was always her words; 'you know every one here, you know who is sick, and who has had twins, who wants soup, and who would like a hundred of coals. It is you that must visit for me.'"

"I wish that some one would visit for me!" escaped from the unwary lips of Emmie.

"Oh! I'll do it with all the pleasure in life, miss!" cried Mrs. Jessel, her bugles trembling with the eagerness with which she clinched what she chose to regard as an offer of employment. "There is nothing that I like better than looking after the poor dear folk round about. You see I've now a deal of time on my hands. You have only to tell Hannah, miss, to let me have what goes from your table, or a drop of broth now and then, and there shall be no trouble to any one; I'll bring my own basket to carry the food, and you'll have the satisfaction, Miss Trevor, of knowing that every one here is well looked after."

"You are very kind," said Emmie, who thought that it would indeed be a comfort to have a substitute to do the work for which she herself was proved to be so unfit.

"I was just going up to the Court, Miss Trevor, to hunt after the tabby of which my poor dear lady was so fond," observed Mrs. Jessel; "the creature misses her so—every one misses her so! I can't keep my cats from wandering back to the old house, where she used to feed them with her own hands. I'll just tell Hannah your wishes, Miss Trevor, she'll understand what you want. You'd have the cottagers cared for, and you make over the care of them all to me."

"Pray take some food at once to poor Mrs. Brant," said Emmie.

"She shan't go to bed without a good supper, and I'll tell her who sends it," cried Mrs. Jessel; "meat is the physic she wants. It's not for ladies like you, Miss Trevor, to be soiling their nice dresses by going in and out of dirty cottages, and may be hearing bad language, or meeting, perhaps, with rudeness. It's for those who are used to the work, like me; those who know the ins and the outs, the whys and the wherefores; who are neither easily taken in, nor easily frightened. Yes, I'll do all that is wanted,—you may rest quite easy, Miss Trevor."

CHAPTER XVII.

CARES AND MISTAKES.

 If, even while the arrangement with Mrs. Jessel was thus hastily concluded, Miss Trevor had her doubts as to whether it were a wise or a good one, as days and weeks rolled on the young lady became more certain that a great mistake had been made. Emmie had given to one of whose character she knew very little a footing in the house from which it would not be easy to displace her. Mrs. Jessel had now a fair excuse for "dropping in" at Myst Court at any hour, and she almost invariably chose the hours after dark. Her basket, by no means a small one, was Jael's unfailing companion. Emmie

63

wondered, but never ventured to inquire, how much of the food which left Myst Court really found its way to the homes of the poor. What made Emmie more uneasy were the words occasionally dropped by her trustworthy Susan, who evidently disliked Mrs. Jessel's coming so much about the place, and who had no faith in her qualifications for the office of almoner into which she had installed herself by taking advantage of the timidity of Miss Trevor.

Mr. Trevor had made it his invariable rule to pay his bills weekly, and his daughter kept his household accounts. Emmie was startled at the amount of the bills now run up by the butcher and grocer who served the family at Myst Court. The young lady mustered up courage one day to express to Hannah her surprise at the heavy expense incurred at a time when the household was not large, and there was no entertaining of guests. Hannah had found out from the first her lady's weakness, and had laughingly observed to Lizzy, "The way to manage young miss is to flare up at the first word; she don't dare to bring out a second." Hannah did not fail to put her tactics into practice on the present occasion.

"I don't know what you mean by expense, miss," she growled out, like a surly dog ready to snap; "Mrs. Jessel must have what she wants for the poor, and it's a lot as her basket holds; one can't fill it with soap-suds or shavings!"

Emmie retreated discomfited from the kitchen, and with a mortified, downcast look carried the tradesmen's books to her father.

Mr. Trevor was in his study, writing out a statement to his lawyer of the wrong inflicted on some of his tenants by the dye-works of Messrs. Bullen and Co.

"I am sorry to interrupt you, papa," said Emmie, as, after gently closing the door behind her, she approached the table at which her father was seated, "but I am afraid that I shall want more money to pay these bills."

"You told me that you had enough," observed Mr. Trevor, looking up from his writing, with his ready-dipped pen in his hand.

"I thought so, till I saw the amount of the bills," and, as she spoke, Emmie placed the open books on the desk before her father.

"This is absurd!" cried Mr. Trevor, after a rapid glance at the summings-up; "Hannah must either be dishonest or wasteful. We appear to live at more expense than we did at Summer Villa, where we had far more comfort, and had friends to share our meals. You must speak to Hannah, my love."

"I have spoken to her," replied Emmie. "Hannah accounts for the expense by the quantity of food which Mrs. Jessel takes to the poor."

"I hope that you keep a sharp look-out after that woman," observed Mr. Trevor gravely. "It passes my comprehension why you should ever employ her at all to visit the tenants."

Emmie was ashamed to answer what was the truth,—"I did so because I did not dare to visit them myself."

"There seems to be no end to the drains upon my purse at present," said Mr. Trevor, leaning back on his chair; "workmen to pay in the house, fields to drain, county-hospital and schools to assist, and two law-suits looming before me! Vibert came to me for more money to-day. How that boy runs through his allowance! I thought that when he was beyond reach of London amusements, he would be able to draw in a little; and, after arranging for his meals with his tutor, I never expected to have to pay hotel-bills for my son."

Mr. Trevor had touched on a cause of uneasiness which was more and more pressing on the spirits of Emmie. The sister knew, both from light words dropped by Vibert and grave ones spoken by his brother, that the youth was by no means giving due attention to his studies at S——. Vibert was always late at his tutor's house, never remained there to luncheon, and not infrequently did not return for afternoon study at all. Emmie was aware that Vibert was sometimes driven back from S—— in a curricle by Colonel Standish, arriving at Myst Court long after Bruce had reached the place on foot. Vibert was enthusiastic in praise of his American friend, dilating on his talent, his courage, his generosity,—perhaps admiring him all the more from a spirit of opposition to Bruce, who did not admire him at all.

Emmie saw little of her brothers on week-days, except at breakfast-time, and during the evenings; the young lady, therefore, led a somewhat solitary life. She took occasional drives with her father, but, except in his company, rarely quitted the grounds. Time hung very heavily on the fair maiden's hands; Myst Court was a dreary place in November to one accustomed to cheerful society, who had now to pass many hours alone.

Bruce went on steadily with his studies on week-days, and with his class of boys on Sunday evenings, learning himself or teaching others with the same characteristic perseverance and strength of will. He never again asked Emmie to visit the poor. The two brothers rarely met each other except at meals, when the presence of their father prevented unseemly disputes between them. But both Mr. Trevor and his daughter were painfully conscious of the coldness which existed between Vibert and Bruce. The father was disappointed and displeased to find that his elder son was not, as the parent had so hoped that he would be,—a friend, protector, and guide to the younger.

"If Vibert go on as he is doing, he'll come to ruin," said Bruce one day to his sister, in the early part of December, when Emmie was accompanying him as far as the entrance-gate on his way to S——.

"Oh, Bruce, I am very, very unhappy about Vibert," sighed Emmie; "I cannot think that he has a safe companion in that American colonel."

"Standish is Vibert's evil genius," muttered Bruce Trevor.

"Do you not think that it would be only right for you to speak seriously to papa about Vibert's present way of going on?" suggested Emmie.

Bruce abruptly stopped short in his walk.

"No," he replied emphatically; "I will never say anything again to my father concerning Vibert, let the boy do what he may. I began to speak last night on the subject; I began to tell my father what I thought that he ought to know. I had scarcely spoken two sentences, when he said coldly—you know his manner when he is vexed—'Bruce, you are jealous of your younger brother.' I jealous!—and of Vibert!" exclaimed Bruce, resuming his walk at a quick pace which expressed mortification and anger. "That's all the credit that I got for speaking the truth so I mean henceforth to keep silence. Our father is utterly blind when Vibert is concerned; every one else must be blamed, rather than a fault be found in the precious young scapegrace! I may plod on, study, save, deny myself any indulgence, while Vibert quaffs his champagne, plays at billiards,—or worse, squanders his money and his time; and if I so much as venture to hint that matters are going wrong, why I, forsooth, am jealous—jealous of one whom I despise—jealous of a selfish prodigal, who would sacrifice anything or any one for the sake of an hour's amusement!"

Bruce had reached the iron gate, and he now flung it wide open with a vehement action, which was the outward expression of the indignation burning within his breast. The young man strode forth from his father's grounds full of that pride of spirit which is altogether inconsistent with Christian profession. Yet was Bruce scarcely conscious that he was proud, because his besetting sin was so closely shrouded up in his heart's haunted chamber. Bruce could not accuse himself of being self-righteous, because he truly acknowledged himself to be a sinner before his God. He was more free than most young men in his station from pride of talent, pride of birth, pride which glories in any personal gift. Bruce hated ostentation, and was not keenly eager for praise. Where, then, was young Trevor's pride to be found? It was interwoven in the very fabric of his character; but so interwoven that it did not appear glaringly on the surface. Pride, with Bruce, was as the vein which pervades the marble,—only faintly visible here and there, scarcely marring its beauty, but penetrating deep, yea, to the utmost depth of the firm and solid mass. If Emmie was self-indulgent, Vibert self-engrossed, Bruce was pre-eminently self-willed. His besetting sin was the more dangerous because it did not startle his conscience. Bruce knew that his faith in God was steadfast, his sincerity not to be questioned, that on the path of duty he walked with a step unswerving and firm. He compared his own conduct with that of Vibert, and it was impossible that such a comparison should not be to the advantage of the elder brother, who was singularly free from the selfishness which marred the character of the younger. Yet Bruce was not safe in his orthodox creed, his stainless life, his useful labours; he was not walking humbly before his God. His was not the charity which thinks no evil, which loves, and hopes, and endures; the scorn which he felt for a brother's weakness, the anger roused by a brother's sin, were tokens—had he closely examined their source—of the baneful presence of pride.

CHAPTER XVIII.

YES OR NO.

"Everything seems to have gone wrong with me here!" sighed Emmie, as she sat alone by the drawing-room window, watching the descent of large flakes of snow, which melted as they came in contact with earth. "I have been at Myst Court for a month, and what have I to look back upon since I came here but feeble attempts to do what is right, melting into failure, even like those flakes? Yes, my uncle's warning was not unneeded by me. Fear, the child of Mistrust, is indeed the haunting spirit that mars my peace, cripples my usefulness, and takes from me the power of glorifying God. I am afraid to rule my own household; I shrink from meeting an angry look; I wink at what I know to be wrong,—because I am too timid to enforce what I know to be right. I am afraid to enter the dwellings of the poor, though conscience pricks me whenever I drive past those wretched hovels which it is my duty to enter as a messenger of mercy and comfort. The good which I might have done, I do not; and oh! is it not written, *To him that knoweth to do good and doeth it not, it is sin?* I have given up my own appointed work to a substitute in whom I have no trust, all through fear—my mistrustful fear! Timidity haunts me in my house—in my family. I cannot conquer my foolish repugnance even to drawing back that curtain which divides the right wing of Myst Court from the more inhabited part of the dwelling, though my brother every night passes beyond that curtain to sleep without fear or harm in that room which I dreaded to enter. Reason tells me that my misgivings are folly, but superstitious fear is too strong for reason. And, though it appear in a different form, is it not the same mistrust that makes me so fearful to offend my brothers by speaking, in tender love, truths which they are unwilling to hear? Vibert, my own dear

Vibert, whom I remember as the bright beautiful boy who was my mother's darling, the very sunshine of our home, Vibert has entered, I fear, on a course that imperils his peace here and his happiness hereafter. I might exert an elder sister's influence over his frank and kindly nature; but I dread to rouse his anger, and risk the loss of his affection. And, alas! I am conscious that the weakness of character at which Vibert so often has laughed, has lessened my influence with him for good. Vibert loves—but he does not look up to his sister; on one point, at least, I am in his eyes but as a silly, unreasoning child!"

Emmie possessed, as has been observed, a sensitive conscience, and was no stranger to the duty of self-examination: she had made the first step in spiritual warfare, she had seen and recognized her besetting foe. But to see and to recognize an enemy is not the same thing as to fight him. A deeply spiritual writer has given directions to the Christian soldier in face of his besetting sin, directions so practical that I shall quote them instead of giving words of my own. The writer supposes the presence of the enemy to have been found out by honest searching of the heart:—

"When the discovery is made, the path of the spiritual combatant becomes clear, however arduous. Your fighting is to be no longer a flourishing of the arms in the air; it is to assume a definite form, it is to be a combat with the bosom sin. Appropriate mortifications must be adopted, such as common sense will suggest, varying with the nature of the sin, and combined always with a heartfelt acknowledgment of our utter weakness, and with a silent but fervent prayer for the grace of Almighty God.... What is the warfare of many earnest and well-intentioned Christians but the sending of shafts at a venture? They have a certain notion that they must resist the evil within and without them; but then this evil presents itself in so many forms that they are bewildered and confused, and know not where to begin.... The first work of the politic spiritual warrior will be to discover his besetting sin, and having discovered it, to *concentrate* all his disposable force before this fortress."

Let me illustrate the author's meaning by referring to the characters in my story, whose counterparts may be found amongst my various readers. Bruce, being once aware that his bosom sin was pride, should have taken every opportunity of mortifying that pride, not only by owning his sins before God, but by frankly acknowledging his own mistakes and errors in the presence of men. Vibert, if not by literal fasting, yet by the practice of self-denial in every sensual indulgence, should have sought to give the spirit the victory over the flesh. Emmie, wrestling down her mistrust by prayer, should have forced her unwilling spirit to "nobly dare the thing which nature shrinks from."

But the maiden chose a middle course. She would not attack the fortress, but go round it; she would try to do her duty, but rather by evading than by conquering the enemy who opposed her. Emmie felt like one who has made a pleasant discovery when a means of reaching her father's tenants, without trying her own courage, suggested itself to her mind.

"Yes, that will do—that will do!" exclaimed the maiden, as with a brightening countenance she rose from her seat, and then crossed the room with light step to ring the small bell by which she was accustomed to summon her maid. "Christmas-time is at hand,—that blessed time when all who have the power should seek to make those around them happy. My father and Bruce will, I am sure, approve of my little plan."

Emmie remained standing until Susan entered the room. Smilingly the young lady confided her intentions to one who would be her ready assistant in carrying them out. "Susan," she said, "I mean to give a feast at Christmas to the younger children of my father's tenants. We will prepare a German tree, to be loaded with little gifts, most of them made up by your hands and mine."

"I should be delighted to help, miss," said Susan.

"And mine should not merely be a treat for a day," continued Emmie; "I think of something beyond the mere amusement of the children whom I invite. Say that fifty little ones come; I would procure fifty New Testaments, that each child might carry back one to his home, wrapped up in one of these illustrated fly-leaves with which my brother has already provided me."

Those leaves gave Emmie a feeling of shame whenever her glance chanced to fall on the almost undiminished packet.

"I wish that more of the children knew how to read," observed Susan in a doubtful tone.

"If they cannot read, surely most of their parents can," said Emmie, her wish being father to her thought. "If such good seed be sown broadcast, certainly some benefit must result. Yes," she continued cheerfully, "I will make friends with the little children, and through them assist the parents whose homes I cannot visit."

Then came the question of ways and means. Miss Trevor was rather pleased than otherwise to find that her little project would involve some need of self-denial. She had five pounds remaining of her allowance, money which she had intended to spend in other ways, but which she would devote to the Christmas treat.

"I'll not send this," said Emmie, tearing up a note which she had written to a circulating library in London; "I will do without new books for a time. Then as for the warm dress which I meant to purchase, your clever fingers, Susan, will make my present blue cashmere serve me for another winter in a quiet place like this."

The pleasure of seeing the eyes of fifty children sparkling with delight at the feast to which she would invite them, the joy of imparting so much innocent joy, would, as Emmie truly thought, out-weigh the small gratification of buying that with which she so easily could dispense.

"And now, Susan, bring down my basket of odds and ends, and—stay—you will find pieces of muslin and ribbon in my left-hand drawer. We must see what we can make use of in dressing dolls, making pincushions and needle-books, and devise something suitable as gifts for the little boys."

Susan went, and soon returned with a basketful of such materials as woman's taste and skill can transform into a thousand attractive forms.

The snow-flakes were falling faster and thicker; grassy lawn and gravel path were now covered with a sheet of spotless white, which hid every roughness and smoothed away every blemish. Emmie was no longer troubling herself with thoughts of her follies and failings. With the eagerness natural to youth, she was preparing for the pleasant task which she had set herself to perform, a task which would at the same time employ her fingers, amuse her mind, and quiet her conscience. See her on her knees on the hearth-rug beside the blazing fire, with her basket of odds and ends beside her, and a pile of half-worn-out clothes placed on a chair. Emmie is sorting and arranging, planning and preparing, cutting out work for herself and Susan that will keep them both happily and usefully engaged for weeks. It is wonderful how care is lightened, and what mental sunshine comes with occupations such as this. Emmie's thoughts, instead of brooding over imaginary terrors, are full of ingenious devices for improving this and altering that, making old things look new, and astonishing simple rustics by elegant trifles such as they never before could have seen.

"Now take up these clothes and look to the patching," said Emmie, dismissing her maid.—"I will send at once to London for the Testaments," she added to herself after Susan had left the apartment. "My five pounds will cover that expense, as well as the cost of my simple feast,—tea and cake, oranges and buns; and then there must be a trifle for lights for my tree."

Humming cheerfully to herself, Emmie rose from her kneeling position and went to her desk, which lay on the drawing-room table. She unlocked and opened it, and then took out a pocket-book within which was her five-pound note. Joe was to take the pony that day to be shod at S——, so Emmie drew out a form for a money-order for the Bible Society to be procured at the same time. Emmie, with the order and bank-note in her hand, was about to ring the bell for the footman, when Vibert entered the drawing-room. He looked at the hearth-rug, strewn with many-coloured scraps and cuttings from the overflowing basket which Emmie had been ransacking for materials for her charity work.

"You here still, Vibert!" exclaimed his sister, pausing with her hand on the old-fashioned bell-rope which hung by the fire-place. "I thought that you had been for the last hour poring over your books at S——. Were you afraid of the snow that you stopped at home this morning?"

"Afraid!" echoed Vibert. "No; I leave that word, like bodkins and hair-pins, for the use of the ladies. The truth is, that I wanted, before I set off for the town, to ask,—but what is that which you have in your hand?" asked the youth as his glance, and an eager glance it was, fell on his sister's five-pound note.

"I am going to tell Joe to procure me a money-order," said Emmie, making a movement to ring the bell; but a quick sign from Vibert prevented her from drawing down the heavy bell-rope.

"Stop, Emmie!" cried her brother; "you would do me such a kindness if you were to lend me that five-pound note."

Emmie, for more than one reason, was annoyed at her brother's request. This was by no means the first time that Vibert had wanted to borrow money, and he had a very indifferent memory as regarded payment of debts. Vibert saw his sister's look of vexation and the slight frown which for a moment ruffled the smoothness of her fair brow.

"I assure you, darling," he said in a coaxing manner, "that the loan would be a great, a very great convenience to me. I hate asking papa for more money; he seems to feel more pinched now than he did before he came in for a fortune. When I tell him that I can't manage to keep within my allowance, he twits me with the prudence and moderation of Bruce, as if I could skin flints or count farthings like Bruce."

There was scorn in the tone of Vibert as he uttered the last sentence, which roused the spirit of Emmie in defence of her absent brother. "Bruce is no skin-flint!" she cried; "he does many a kind and generous thing. If he saves, it is on himself; there is not a particle of selfishness in his nature!"

Emmie had not intended to strike at one brother whilst defending the other; but Vibert was in an excited, irritable mood, and took his sister's words as a palpable hit at himself.

"You are the last person from whom I should have expected such a taunt," said the spendthrift bitterly. "I thought that if I had no other friend in the world I should find one, Emmie, in you."

"Always! always!" cried his sister eagerly; "I would do anything for you, dear Vibert."

"Will you lend me that five-pound note?"

Again Emmie hesitated and looked vexed. "I had laid it all out already in my mind," she replied. "It is to give pleasure to so many poor children at Christmas."

"Christmas! why, you shall have it back long before Christmas," cried Vibert; and he held out his hand for the note. But Emmie retained it still in her clasp. She was doubtful as to the use which the young prodigal might make of the money, and whether it might not be rather an injury than a kindness to Vibert to replenish his empty purse.

The youth read the doubt on the maiden's expressive face, and it made him indignant and angry.

"Emmie, can you not trust me?" exclaimed Vibert in an irritable tone; and, as no answer immediately came, he passionately repeated the question.

"Oh for courage to speak the truth faithfully!" thought Emmie; but the courage came not with the wish. Her lips formed a scarcely articulate "yes;" and having said "yes" to her brother's question, she could hardly say "no" to his demand for a loan.

Vibert rather took than received the bank-note from Emmie; he saw that his sister was reluctant to give it, but he thought that a kiss, and the assurance that she was "the dearest girl in the world," had set all right between them.

"Of course the money is as safe with me as if it were in the Bank of England!" cried Vibert; "you shall have it back in a week;" and nodding good-bye to Emmie, Vibert quitted the drawing-room, and was soon on his way to S——.

Emmie watched from the window the light and graceful form of her brother, as he tramped over the new-fallen snow, leaving brown footprints behind him. The poor girl's eyes were full of tears, and her heart of self-reproach.

"I have been no true friend to my thoughtless young brother," said Emmie to herself; "it was mere selfish cowardice which made me yield to his wishes, and put in his hands money of which I fear that he will make no good use."

The maiden left the window, but not to resume her employment; all her pleasure in it was gone: she had sacrificed her means of doing good to her fear of offending her brother. Emmie knelt down on the hearth-rug and hastily gathered up her scraps of ribbons, chintz, and silk, tossing them back into the basket, as trash to be thrust out of sight, or thrown away as useless. The cares which pressed on Emmie's mind were not now to be banished by thoughts of Christmas amusements, and the hope of imparting innocent pleasure to the children of her father's tenants.

On the afternoon of that day, Miss Trevor took possession of that apartment which, by means of thorough repairs, had been prepared for her reception. It was spacious enough to receive all the furniture which had been originally placed in the room now occupied by Bruce. Amongst other articles, the tall press of richly-carved oak occupied a conspicuous place; it had been moved with some difficulty from the position which it had held for two centuries, and now added to the stateliness, though not perhaps to the cheerfulness, of Miss Trevor's apartment.

CHAPTER XIX.

THE ECLIPSE.

The demeanour of Mr. Trevor's two sons, when they met at the dinner-table on that evening, was in strong contrast to each other. Bruce looked grave and stern, and had the appearance of one who is pale and weary from too close attention to study. Vibert, on the contrary, was in the highest spirits.

"Bruce, you look as the moon will look to-night under an eclipse!" cried Vibert; "you mean to tack to your name M.A. or D.L. or A.S.S., or some other mystical letters of the alphabet, and the shadow of coming distinction is falling on you already!"

"Is this the night of the eclipse?" asked Emmie, interposing, as was her wont, some indifferent remark to prevent any interchange of bitter words between her brothers.

"Yes; had you forgotten it?" said Vibert. "It is to be an almost total eclipse. We can hardly see it from any window in the house, the place is so smothered with trees; but there is a spot on the lawn from which we can get a very good view."

"I wish that we had a telescope here," observed Mr. Trevor.

"That's just what I said to my friend Standish," cried Vibert; "for, as you know, I'm desperately eager in pursuit of scientific knowledge. 'I'll lend you mine,' said the colonel; 'it has prodigious magnifying power. It was my travelling companion when I journeyed northward, in a sledge, with only an Eskimo guide, and reached the high latitude of'—I really don't remember the latitude that Standish mentioned, but it was something that would make our Arctic explorers stare."

"Perhaps it was degree one hundred and one," said Bruce sarcastically. "I suspect that the colonel's telescope is not with him the only instrument that has high magnifying power."

"You are always sneering at Standish," cried Vibert angrily; "you give him credit for nothing, simply, I believe, because he has chosen me for his friend. But others appreciate him better," continued the youth, addressing his conversation to Emmie. "Standish had grand news to-day from Washington; he has only been waiting at S—— till he should know how his suit in America has prospered."

"A law-suit?" inquired Mr. Trevor.

"Oh no; a suit more interesting by far than any regarding field-boundaries or dye-works!" laughed Vibert. "Standish is an illustration of the proverb, 'None but the brave deserve the fair.' He has wooed and won the greatest belle in the West, a cousin of the president of the United States, a lady with a dowry of half a million of dollars!" Vibert glanced triumphantly at Bruce, and raising a glass of claret, pledged the health of the colonel's destined bride.

"I suppose that as the lady is in Washington, the colonel will not remain long in Wiltshire," observed Mr. Trevor, who had no wish for his longer stay.

"That's the worst part of the business,—at least for me," replied Vibert, setting down the glass, which he had drained. "Standish leaves England almost directly. He has already secured his passage in an American steamer, and has only now to get what he wants to take with him, amongst other things wedding-gifts for his bride. Standish is prodigiously liberal as well as enormously rich; so the fair lady will have her caskets of diamonds and 'ropes of pearl,' such as a duchess might envy. The colonel asked me to-day what London jeweller I would recommend," continued the youth with a self-complacency which made his auditors smile, "and I told him that our family had dealt for twenty years with Messrs. Golding. I showed Standish the watch, studs, and signet-ring which I had bought at their shop, and he declared that he had never seen anything in the jewellery line more tasteful." It was evident that the boy's vanity had been tickled by his being consulted on such a matter by one who was the accepted suitor of a president's cousin. "But here am I talking about these sublunary affairs, when the eclipse will be beginning," cried Vibert. "It is quarter past seven now,"—he glanced at his watch as he spoke; "the night is splendid, not a breath of wind is stirring, while moonlight is silvering the snow. Who will come out with me and look at the queen of night under a shadow? Emmie, you will certainly make one of the party; we all know your taste for the beautiful and sublime."

71

"My girl must be well wrapped up if she venture out in the snow," observed Mr. Trevor.

"We'll case her in fur like a squirrel!" cried Vibert. "Come, Emmie, or we shall be late."

Emmie rose from her seat at table; her life at Myst Court afforded so little variety, that the sight of an eclipse on a clear wintry night was not one that she would willingly miss.

"I suppose that you, Bruce, will go too," said his father. "For my part, I have seen so many lunar eclipses already, that I shall return to my desk. I want to finish the perusal of that paper sent by my lawyer which I was showing to you when the dinner-gong sounded."

"I should like to look over the paper with you," said Bruce. "I do not care to go out to-night."

The young man was feeling ill, though he did not complain.

"We'll leave them to their musty-fusty law; as for us, we prefer meditation and moonlight!" said Vibert playfully, as a few minutes afterwards he stood in the hall with Emmie, assisting his sister to mantle her slight form in her fur-lined mantilla. "I don't see why papa should bother himself with Bullen and his horrible dyes; the stream is clear enough where it flows through our woods. If Bullen had poisoned our coffee, or killed our trout, the matter might have required a lawyer. There now, just let me throw this pretty little scarlet shawl over your head, to be a complete defence against the night air! I declare that it makes you look like an opening rose-bud; I never saw a headdress more picturesque and becoming!"

Emmie smiled, and the brother and sister quitted the house together, sauntering down the steps which led from the door to the carriage-drive.

"We can see nothing here," observed Vibert; "we must go right round to the back of the house, and make our way over the lawn, till we get just beyond the group of yew-trees. There we shall have a clear view of the moon."

The first touch of shadow was dimming the round disc of the moon when the brother and sister stepped forth on the snow. But the orb was hidden from them, first by the house, and then by the trees around it, until they should reach the spot indicated by Vibert. The short quick walk was not a silent one; Vibert's thoughts were engrossed by a subject much more interesting to him than the moon.

"Emmie, I must be off to London to-morrow," said he.

"To London!" echoed Emmie in surprise. "What has put such a sudden flight into your mind?"

"I've many reasons for wishing to go up to town. Patti is to sing to-morrow night at a grand concert; I am dying to hear her again, and Standish—kind fellow!—has given me a ticket of admittance. Then I've shopping and business to transact which I cannot possibly put off. I shall only stay for one night in London, and I will not go to a hotel. Aunt Mary told me, you know, that she could always offer me a room in Grosvenor Square."

"Papa will not like the needless expense," began Emmie.

"Expense! how I hate the very word! But you have smoothed that matter for me, darling," said Vibert, pressing the arm that was locked in his own. "Papa shall not have a shilling to pay."

"But you would miss two days of study."

"No great loss, if one may judge of what they would have been by those that have gone before them," laughed Vibert. "I have not fatigued myself lately by any overwhelming amount of hard work."

"I fear not indeed," said his sister.

"But I'll work double when once I've had my full swing of pleasure," cried Vibert. "I can pass Bruce, at least in classics, if I make an effort to do so. I know that I've been an idle fellow ever since we came to Myst Court; but when Standish goes I'll have nothing to do but to study, and I'll be bound I'll astonish you all with my learning."

"We have only been here for a month," observed Emmie; "it is too early for you to think of returning to London. You had better far put off going for a while."

"I told you that I could not put off!" cried Vibert impatiently. "My concert ticket will not keep, nor my business neither. You might as well tell yon moon to put off her eclipse!"

By this time the Trevors had reached the spot beyond the yew-trees, where nothing obstructed their view of the radiant orb. The dark shadow of earth was slowly cutting its sharply-defined outline on her disc, and each minute her clear light was becoming more and more sensibly obscured. There is something very solemn in the sight of that natural phenomenon which science can foretell, but which all created powers combined can neither prevent nor for one single moment delay. Even the light gossip of Vibert was silenced as he gazed. Nothing appeared to be moving on the snow-covered earth, or through the still air, save when a bat, with its peculiar flickering motion, darted between the moon and those who stood with upraised eyes, silently watching the deepening eclipse. Behind the trees rose Myst Court, showing, not its broad stately front, but the back offices, which were irregular in construction, and some of them built at a later date than other parts of the mansion. This side of the house possessed no beauty whatever by day, save what climbing ivy might give; but by moonlight its very irregularity gave to it a picturesque charm which was wanting to the more handsome but flatter front of the dwelling. Emmie turned round to glance at a part of her <u>new home</u> with which she was very imperfectly acquainted, as she had never entered the mansion at that eastern side. She admired the effect of moonlight on the snow-covered ivy which mantled the walls— silver gleams which threw into strong contrast the deep black shadows which fell from projecting gable or overhanging roof. Even the chimneys seemed transformed into twisted columns of ebony and silver.

"I never thought that Myst Court could look so romantic," said Emmie; "it was worth while coming out at night to see it as we see it now. But the air is chilly," she added, and, to draw her scarlet shawl closer over her braided hair, the maiden for a moment drew her arm from that of her brother.

"Ha! I had forgotten the telescope!" exclaimed Vibert; and with that want of thought for others which with him was a branch from the root of selfishness, the youth darted off to bring the glass, leaving his sister alone beside the shadowy yew-trees.

Emmie had not thought of fear so long as she had leaned on her brother's arm, so long as the lively Vibert was close beside her; but his departure—so sudden, that she had no time to cry "Do not go!" before he was gone— awoke her dormant terrors. To find herself in utter solitude, standing on the snowy lawn beside the gloomy yews, within bow-shot of a dwelling said to be haunted, whilst the very moon was suffering eclipse, was a position which might have tried stronger nerves than those of Emmie. All the horrible tales that she had heard on the night of her first arrival, the colonel's ghastly legends, Jael's stories of apparitions seen in that very house which now dimly loomed before the eyes of the maiden, the dark hints of dangers thrown out by Harper—all rushed at once on the mind of the timid girl. She made a few quick steps in pursuit of Vibert; but he had vanished from her sight round the corner of the house. Emmie was afraid to skirt half of the spacious mansion alone, yet equally afraid to remain in such dreary solitude, to await her brother's return. A breeze stirred the branches of neighbouring trees; Emmie started at the sound of the rustle. The tall bushes in their shrouds of snow began to her excited imagination to assume the form of spectres; Emmie almost fancied that they began to move towards her! And now—it is not imagination—a dark figure is slowly moving along the gravel-path, whitened by snow, which divides the lawn on which Emmie is standing from that back part of Myst Court to which her gaze is directed! Emmie's first emotion is that of terror, her next is that of relief. She recognizes the sound of a short dry cough, which has nothing unearthly about it; and by the faint light of the half-eclipsed moon sees the outline of a familiar form most unlike the shape in which a spectre might be supposed to appear. Emmie feels no longer alone. There is Mrs. Jessel, coming at no unwonted hour, with basket on arm, doubtless to carry away what may remain of the evening's repast.

Never before had Emmie so welcomed the appearance of Mrs. Myer's late attendant, the obsequious, voluble Jael. Lightly the young-lady tripped over the soft white snow, whilst Mrs. Jessel was engaged in opening some back-door which lay in the deepest shadow behind a projecting part of the building. Emmie's step was noiseless as that of a fairy, and her form was unseen by Mrs. Jessel, whose back was turned towards her. Jael turned a key, pushed open a door, and entered the house, leaving the door ajar. Emmie followed the woman into the dwelling, guided by the sound of her creaking boots and her short dry cough. The passage which the two had entered was dark, but Emmie naturally expected that some inner door would quickly be opened, and that she should find herself in the light and warmth of her own kitchen, for whose cheerful interior Mrs. Jessel of course was bound. How welcome to the ears of Emmie would be even the coarse loud tones of Hannah! The young lady was somewhat surprised when the footsteps which she was following led up a narrow staircase, instead of turning towards what she supposed to be the direction of the kitchen. Still, as it was certain that Jael, after living for years in the mansion, must be acquainted with its every turn and winding, and as it was equally certain that she must be going to some lighted part, Miss Trevor went on, feeling her way by the iron railing up the narrow stone stair, listening to the creak of the boots and the occasional cough, which told that her guide was in front. Emmie felt a strange repugnance to address Mrs. Jessel in the darkness, therefore groped on her way in silence, expecting every moment to be ushered into the light. Here we leave her for the present, and go for a while to the study of Mr. Trevor, where he and his elder son are quietly engaged with the lawyer's papers.

CHAPTER XX.

AN ALARM.

 "It strikes me that there are unusual sounds in this generally quiet house," observed Mr. Trevor, raising his head to listen, after he and Bruce had been for nearly half-an-hour employed in reading and making extracts.

"I have been noticing them too," said Bruce. "I suppose that Vibert is in one of his wild merry moods, and that—"

Ere he could finish his sentence, the door of the study was suddenly flung wide open, and Vibert rushed in, with anxiety painted on his face.

"Emmie—is she with you?" he breathlessly cried.

"Emmie!" repeated Mr. Trevor, rising in sudden alarm. Bruce dropped the paper which he had held in his hand, and sprang to his feet.

"Did she not go with you to watch the eclipse?" asked the father; "when did you miss her?—where did you leave her?" The questions were asked in a manner and tone that expressed anxiety.

"I left Emmie on the sward by the yew-trees," said Vibert, answering the last question first.

"Surely not alone?" interrupted his brother.

"I was back in three minutes, but she was gone. I called—loudly enough—but there was no answer! I rushed back to the house, and have since been hunting all over the place—upper rooms, lower rooms, kitchen, and all! The servants know nothing about Emmie, but are looking for her in every corner!"

"The grounds must be searched with torches without a moment's delay," cried the father, loudly ringing the bell of the study. Bruce hurried to the door with such anxious haste that he almost came into collision with—Emmie!

"Here she comes herself, our wandering fairy, to give an account of her doings!" he cried, drawing back to let Emmie pass him and enter the lighted apartment. "She has only been playing at hide-and-seek."

Bruce spoke gaily, but almost before the last word had left his lips his manner changed, for he looked on his sister, and saw at a glance that no mirthful frolic had caused her late disappearance. Had the poor heroine of the story of the oaken-chest contrived by some superhuman effort to burst her living tomb, even in such ghastly guise might she have appeared before her wondering friends.

Emmie had entered the study with rapid steps; she now threw herself into the arms of her father, and buried her face on his breast, as if seeking for protection and safety. The poor girl uttered no sound, but her bosom heaved convulsively, and her clinging hands trembled as if with ague. Emmie's scarlet shawl had fallen back on her shoulders, and over it flowed her dishevelled hair. Emmie's attitude was so expressive of terror, that she might have been deemed some fugitive who had barely escaped with life from some scene of slaughter.

"My child—my sweet child—what ails you? what has happened to alarm you thus?" said Mr. Trevor soothingly, while Bruce dismissed the servants, who had, in a body, answered the summons of the bell, only bidding Susan bring a glass of cold water. "Emmie has merely had some little fright," he said to himself, as he returned to the table.

But that the fright had been no little one was but too evident when Emmie raised her head, and turned her face to the light. Her countenance was colourless, even to the lips, and ghastly as that of a corpse, whilst her eyes stared wildly, with the pupils dilated, as if seeking some object of terror. Mr. Trevor made his daughter sit down close by his side, and put his arm fondly around her, whilst with his left hand he gently stroked and chafed Emmie's icy-cold fingers.

"My poor little trembling dove, what has frightened you so?" he inquired.

Emmie's lip quivered, but she was unable to speak.

"I'm sure that I'm monstrously sorry that I left you for a moment!" cried Vibert. "I'm a thoughtless fellow, I own; but no harm could possibly have come to you, if you had

75

quietly remained where you stood. Where did you hide that I could not find you? Surely you must have heard me calling your name?"

Emmie shivered, but gave no reply.

"Do not trouble her with questions now," said her father; "she is in a weak and nervous state,—but this will set her right," he added, as he proffered to Emmie's lips the glass of sal-volatile and water which had been quickly brought by Susan.

The cordial revived the poor girl; her eyes lost their wild excited expression, and the lips regained a more natural hue, though the cheeks remained very pale. But when Emmie was again questioned as to what had caused her alarm, she but gasped forth, "Don't ask, don't ask!" and burst into a fit of hysterical weeping, which lasted for several minutes.

"She had better go to rest at once," said Mr. Trevor, when the fit had somewhat subsided; "quiet sleep is what she most wants. We will take her to her own room; and, Susan, do not quit the side of my daughter to-night."

Supporting the trembling Emmie, who did not even turn to bid her brothers good-night, Mr. Trevor then left the study, followed by Susan.

"Something strange must have happened," said Vibert, when the three had left the apartment.

"I see no reason to think so," said Bruce, who had resumed his seat by the table, and had taken up again the paper which he had dropped. "Emmie's timidity is like a disease, a kind of waking nightmare, and it would be as idle to look for external cause for her terrors as it would be for those experienced in a bad dream. What could have been more unreasonable than her dread of occupying a bright pleasant room, because a gentleman had died of hydrophobia in the one next to it, and that fifty years ago!"

"And with such a good thick wall between the two apartments," observed Vibert, who was standing with his back to the fire, "so that there is not so much as a key-hole through which ghost or goblin might creep."

"I cannot say so much," remarked Bruce; "there is a door of communication between the two rooms, though, by the way, the key-hole does *not* go right through it, for it can be opened but on one side."

"A door of communication!" exclaimed Vibert. "I never knew that before." ·

"Nor did I," observed Bruce, "until the workmen from S—— had to move in my presence the large heavy press which had stood in that room for I know not how many years. As they were dragging it off to place it in the apartment prepared for poor dear Emmie, I noticed a key-hole in one of the panels which had hitherto been covered by the oak press. When the workmen had departed, I tried whether the key of the door which opens on the corridor would fit into this newly-discovered key-hole."

"And did it fit it?" inquired Vibert eagerly.

"Exactly," was his brother's reply.

"Does any one but yourself know the secret of the door in the panel?" asked Vibert.

"No; nor do I care that the servants should know it, nor Emmie, who is sufficiently nervous already as to what regards the so-called haunted chamber. I have hung a large map over that part of the panel in which is the key-hole; and as the housemaid never ventures to move what I place on the walls, the fact of there being a door of communication between the two rooms is not likely to be discovered even by her."

"And with the power to enter at will into the haunted chamber, had you not the curiosity to tread the forbidden ground?" cried Vibert.

"When I first found that the key fitted the key-hole in the wall, I turned it, and pushed open the small panel-door," replied Bruce; "but I did not pass into the bricked-up room."

"You looked in?"

"But saw nothing, for the place was pitch-dark," answered Bruce. "I only observed that the air was close, as might be expected when coming from a chamber from which light and air had been carefully excluded for the last fifty years."

"And so you have been a whole month with only a door between you and the mysterious apartment to which such strange and thrilling stories belong!" cried Vibert. "I suppose that you intend thoroughly to explore its inmost recess."

"I see no use in so doing," was Bruce's reply. "As the relation to whose bequest my father owes the possession of the house so anxiously tried to ensure that no one should enter that room, it seems scarcely honourable to take advantage of her ignorance of the existence of that small door in the panel."

"Pshaw! that is a mere romantic scruple," said Vibert. "I could not withstand the temptation to explore the haunted chamber."

"I have a lack of curiosity," observed Bruce Trevor.

"Or a lack of something else," cried his thoughtless young brother, in a provokingly satirical tone.

Bruce was in an irritable mood on that evening, and at no time would have patiently borne what sounded like an imputation on his personal courage. Who should dare to taunt him with lack of daring, or the slightest taint of that superstitious fear which he scorned even in Emmie?

"If you cannot speak common sense, you idiot," Bruce fiercely exclaimed, "keep your idle twaddle for those who may mistake it for wit!"

"How now, boys? what's all this?" cried the loud, angry voice of Mr. Trevor, who, re-entering the room at that moment, had heard Bruce's passionate words, and seen his fiery glance at his brother. "Bruce, you forget yourself strangely."

Bruce bit his nether lip hard. He would not bandy words with his father, but still less would his proud spirit brook such sharp reproof even from a parent. The young man rose, quitted the study, and with a swelling heart went to his own apartment. Bruce bitterly, though silently, accused his father of partiality and injustice; the young man was blinded by pride to the fact that Mr. Trevor had had good and sufficient reason for finding fault with his son's intemperate language.

"What caused this quarrel?" inquired Mr. Trevor of Vibert, after Bruce had quitted the room.

"Oh, Bruce is in a huff,—it is no novelty," replied Vibert. "He thinks that every one is wanting in common sense but his own oracular self."

Mr. Trevor paced up and down the study for some minutes with a troubled mien and furrowed brow. He had many things to disturb his mind; he was seriously grieved at Emmie's hysterical state, and in the dissension between his sons found a new cause of perplexing annoyance. Vibert marked his father's vexation, and characteristically enough managed to take advantage of it for the furtherance of his own wishes.

"I should like to keep out of the bear's way till he has had his growl out," observed Vibert, watching his father's countenance as he spoke. "I have lots of things that I want to do in London to-morrow. I would sleep at Aunt Mary's in Grosvenor Square, and come back on the following day."

The youth had thrown out a feeler, and saw by his father's face that Mr. Trevor would not be likely to offer violent opposition to the trip upon which his son's heart was set.

"You will be wanting more money, you young spendthrift," was Mr. Trevor's remark, but made in an easy, good-humoured way.

77

"No, I have plenty left," answered Vibert.

The unexpected announcement was an agreeable surprise to the parent, who was not aware that Vibert's supply had been borrowed from Emmie.

"You might consult your aunt about Emmie," observed Mr. Trevor, pausing in his walk, and then resuming his seat. "I am not easy regarding the health of your sister; Myst Court is too dull for her, I fear, and its loneliness serves to fill her mind with idle fancies."

"Yes, yes, I'll tell my aunt all about Emmie," said Vibert, trying to look as thoughtful and sympathetic as his pleasure at getting his own way would permit. "It is so much easier to explain all these delicate matters by speaking than by writing," he added.

"And you will take up my watch to Golding to be repaired," observed Mr. Trevor. "I do not like to trust one so valuable as mine to conveyance by post."

"I will take it with all the pleasure in life!" cried Vibert, who would eagerly have undertaken the charge of all the clocks in the house had they needed just then a journey to London.

The matter was quickly settled; it was arranged that Vibert should start by an early train.

"What a lucky chance it was that Bruce should have barked at me just as papa came in!" thought the triumphant Vibert. "I'll be off before daylight to-morrow, or the hard-headed, hard-hearted chap would find a thousand reasons for not letting me go after all."

CHAPTER XXI.

INDECISION.

 "Vibert gone to London,—and so suddenly!" exclaimed Bruce, when, on the following morning, he heard from his father of his brother's early departure. "Wherefore did he go? He did not mention to me a word of his intention to make the journey."

"You scarcely invite his confidence," observed Mr. Trevor.

"There is more money thrown to the dogs," muttered Bruce.

"No; Vibert has shown more consideration for my purse than usual," said Mr. Trevor. "He has made no call upon it for this little expedition to London."

Bruce looked steadfastly into the face of his father for several seconds, but not in order to read anything there. The young man's mind was busy with its own thoughts; a slight smile came over his lips,—the smile of one who has detected a little plot, and knows how to foil it. With an inaudible "I smell a rat," Bruce turned and walked up to the window.

"Vibert need no money to carry him to London! As well might we believe that the train in which he travels requires no steam," thought Bruce to himself. "I happen to know that his purse was empty yesterday morning. My belief is that Vibert is in this house at this moment, or at any rate not further off than S——. He has some silly practical joke in his head connected with the haunted chamber, and means to throw me off my guard by a feigned absence in London. What folly possessed me to tell a wild hare-brain like Vibert of the little door in the panel? But it is no matter; whatever frantic freak he may have in his head, he at least shall find me prepared."

Emmie came down to morning prayers looking very pale, and with the violet tints under her languid eyes, which were tokens of her having passed a sleepless night. She presided as usual at the breakfast-table, but in a dreamy, listless manner, herself scarcely touching the viands. It was evidently an effort to the poor girl to join in the conversation, which her father purposely led to such topics as he thought might interest his daughter. Mr. Trevor talked of literature and arts, recounted amusing passages from his own history, and did his best to divert Emmie's mind, but with little apparent effect. Her eyes were constantly turned towards her brother with an anxious, questioning look, until, the morning meal being concluded, Mr. Trevor, perplexed and disappointed, left the room to speak to his steward.

Emmie then went up to Bruce, who was about to start on his daily walk to his tutor's.

"Bruce, dearest, you look ill," said Emmie, laying a tremulous hand on the arm of her brother.

"I might say the same to you, if it were not treason to utter anything so uncomplimentary to a fair lady," observed Bruce.

"Why do you look ill? Has—has anything painful occurred?" asked Emmie, in a hurried, nervous manner.

"I must act echo again," answered Bruce.

"Tell me, oh, tell me what has happened," urged his sister, who was not in the slightest degree disposed to enter into a jest.

"Nothing has happened, dear Emmie," replied Bruce more gravely. "I have had a little headache these one or two days; it is of no consequence. You have not the least occasion to look so miserably anxious as far as I am concerned."

To the young man's surprise, his sister's eyes filled and then brimmed over with tears. Emmie leaned her brow against his shoulder, and drops fell fast on the sleeve of his arm, which she was pressing with a nervous grasp.

"My dear Emmie, what can be the cause of all this sorrow? What ails you?" asked Bruce, grieved at the sight of distress for which he could not account.

"Oh, Bruce!" sobbed Emmie, pressing her brother's arm yet more closely, "promise me—promise me—" She stopped short, as if afraid to finish her sentence.

"What would you have me promise?" asked Bruce.

Emmie gave no direct reply, but inquired abruptly, "Have you a bell in your room?"

Her question was a real relief to the mind of Bruce, as it convinced him that Emmie's misery arose merely from some fanciful terrors in regard to the bricked-up apartment.

"Yes," he answered gaily, "and a gun besides, to say nothing of poker and tongs, pen-knife, and razors. If any unpleasant guests were to make their appearance, they should find me quite ready to meet them."

Emmie was crying no longer, but she looked pale and anxious as ever; something seemed to be on her tongue struggling for utterance,—something which she was afraid or unable to speak.

"It is time for me to be off," said Bruce, gently releasing his arm from the clasp of his sister.

79

"Bruce, stay. Tell me if you would again change rooms with me," cried Emmie, with a convulsive effort.

"I am very sorry that you do not like your new apartment," said Bruce, slightly knitting his brows.

"I do like it,—it is only too good for me," faltered poor Emmie.

"Then why quit it?" asked Bruce, with a little impatience.

"I thought that if you would not mind changing—" Again Emmie stopped abruptly, without concluding her sentence.

"Of course I will change rooms with you if you really wish it," said Bruce, willing to humour his sister, but making mental reflections on the fickleness and unreasonableness of the fair sex, of which Emmie was the only representative with whom he was well acquainted.

"But I do not wish it,—no, no,—not yet, not yet!" exclaimed Emmie, betraying terror at the idea of her brother complying with her request. The patience of Bruce was fairly exhausted.

"I wish that you would know your own mind," he said, with an air of vexation. "Really, Emmie, you should try to overcome these ridiculous fears and fancies. Where is your spirit,—where is your faith?"

Emmie turned away her head with a shivering sigh.

"We must send you to London for change of scene," observed Bruce; "a few weeks with Aunt Mary will drive all these unreasonable terrors out of your mind."

"Oh, let us all go—at once—to-day!" exclaimed Emmie, clasping her hands. "Let us all leave this horrible place."

"For my father or myself to leave Myst Court at present is simply impossible," said Bruce, in that tone of quiet decision which, as Emmie well knew, expressed a resolution which it was useless for her to attempt to shake.

"Then I will not leave you,—no, no!" she murmured. "Let us all at least be together."

"If we be in danger from any foe, corporeal or spiritual, your slender arm and more slender courage will scarcely avail much for our protection," observed Bruce, with a smile. He had regained his good-humour, and sought to rally Emmie out of her fears by assuming a playful manner.

But the attempt was vain; Emmie only burst again into a fit of weeping, and hastily quitted the apartment, brushing past her father, who was just returning to the breakfast-room after his interview with his steward.

"I am extremely annoyed about Emmie," said the affectionate parent, addressing himself to Bruce; "I cannot comprehend what has taken such a strange hold on her mind."

"Mere fear, I believe," answered Bruce. "She has never struggled to overcome it, and now in this gloomy old place it has gained complete mastery over her reason."

"The mere incident of her having been left alone on the lawn for a few minutes last night seems scarcely to account for my child's terror," observed Mr. Trevor. "Surely Vibert, thoughtless as he is, cannot have had the senseless cruelty to play on his sister's timidity any practical joke." The same idea had occurred, to Bruce.

"Vibert is capable of any folly," thought the elder brother; but after the experience of the preceding evening, he did not put the thought into words.

"I shall keep my girl as close by my side as possible," observed Mr. Trevor. "Perhaps this strange fit of melancholy may pass off; if not, I must arrange for her going to Grosvenor Square. Her departure would leave a sad blank in our little circle at Christmas-time, but my own gratification must not weigh in the balance against my child's comfort and health."

"Where is your faith,—where is your faith?" moaned poor Emmie, repeating to herself again and again her brother's question, as she paced up and down her own apartment, wringing her hands. "Oh, miserable doubt and mistrust! I might once have met my enemy on the ground of duty, and by prayer and resolute effort have gained some strength to meet more serious trials; but I let my fears subdue me without a struggle to cast them off, and now I lie prostrate,—a helpless victim bound in their chains. Usefulness marred, peace destroyed, a horrible dread on my mind, a reproving conscience within my breast, I seem now unable even to pray! I have let go the Hand that would so gently have led me; darkness is thick around me; I cannot find my Heavenly Guide! I dread to keep silent, yet dare not speak. Oh, that horrible, blasphemous oath!"

But it is time that the reader should be made acquainted with the circumstances which led to Emmie's present state of misery. We will therefore return to that point in the story where we left the maiden silently tracking in the darkness the steps of Jael up the dark and narrow stone stairs.

CHAPTER XXII.

THE HAUNTED CHAMBER.

Emmie's light footsteps were unheard by Mrs. Jessel, probably on account of the creaking noise made by her own. Had the form before her been that of Susan, Miss Trevor would at once have addressed her; but she had a dislike to entering in the darkness into a conversation with a woman who had told her so many ghost stories. Emmie therefore delayed speaking to Jael until they should both have entered a lighted apartment.

The top of the flight of stone steps was soon reached; Mrs. Jessel turned the handle of a door, and on her opening it a light streamed from within, casting its yellow reflection on the wall by the staircase. Jael entered the room before her, and Emmie heard her say, "What! at work still?" as she passed into the warmth and light.

Not in the least degree doubting that the woman had addressed one of the household, and eager to find herself once more amongst familiar faces, out of the darkness and chilly night air, Emmie quickly followed Mrs. Jessel into the room. No sooner had she crossed the threshold than she stopped short in surprise and alarm, gazing in motionless terror at the unexpected sight which met her eyes,—for Emmie stood in the haunted chamber!

The room was of good size, and, like that which it adjoined on the side opposite to that by which Jael had entered, was panelled with oak. The apartment was warmed by a stove, and lighted by a shaded lamp, which cast a dull radiance on antique furniture and various objects of whose nature and use Emmie, from her hurried glance, could form no definite idea. Her attention was concentrated on a point close to that shaded lamp. It stood on a table, and on every object that lay on that table threw an intense light. Seated almost close to it, bending over what seemed like a sheet of copper, with a graving instrument in his right hand, and a magnifying glass in his left, his long grizzled hair falling over his brow as he stooped, Emmie beheld the object of her special dread, the hollow-eyed, weird-looking Harper!

He raised his head; he saw the unexpected intruder; his glistening eyes were fixed upon Emmie, and, like those of the serpent surveying its victim, their gaze seemed to deprive the poor girl of all power of motion. Emmie, had she not been paralyzed with fear, would have had time to start back, spring down the stairs, and rouse the family by her loud call for assistance. But in the extremity of her terror the timid girl neither stirred foot nor uttered cry. She stood, as it were, spell-bound. In a few seconds her opportunity for flight was lost. Jael, seeing Harper's look, turned round, beheld Emmie behind her, and instantly closed and bolted the door. The poor maiden found herself a helpless prisoner in one of the rooms of her father's house.

"Utter a sound and you die!" growled Harper, dropping his graving instrument, and grasping the large knife which had been lying open on the table before him.

Emmie clasped her hands and sank on her knees.

"What made you bring her here?" said Harper fiercely to Jael, adding epithets of abuse with which I shall not soil my pages.

Jael looked alarmed, and declared that she had never guessed that the girl was following her up the secret staircase. "And now that she has discovered your hiding-place, what is to be done?" cried the woman.

"Dead men tell no tales," muttered Harper, in a tone which made the blood of Emmie appear to freeze in her veins.

"No, no; you must not harm her,—you cannot touch her," said Mrs. Jessel. "Such a deed could never be hidden; you would only ruin us all. Her father and brothers would search till they found her, if they had to pull down every brick in the house with their nails!"

Harper looked perplexed and undecided.

"Make her promise secrecy, and let her go free," said Jael.

"And trust my safety to a woman's power of holding her tongue! Not I; I will take a surer way,—if I swing for it!" cried Harper, starting from his seat.

"You have listened to your wife's advice before now, and found it good," said she whom we have called Mrs. Jessel, interposing herself between her husband and Emmie. A rapid conversation then passed between the Harpers, held in a tone so low that Emmie could not distinguish a word, though she had a fearful consciousness that on the result of that conversation her own life must depend. The terrified girl could not collect her thoughts, even for prayer, unless the voiceless cry of "Mercy, mercy!" which was bursting from her heart, was an appeal for help from above.

At length her fate was decided. Harper approached the crouching form of Emmie, and thus addressed her, still grasping the knife in his hand.

"Will you take the most solemn oath that tongue can frame never to give hint, by word or sign, of what you have seen this night? Will you swear silence deep as the grave?"

"Anything—everything—I will never betray you!" gasped Emmie, grasping with the eagerness of a drowning wretch at the hope of safety thus held out.

Harper made the shuddering girl repeat after him, word for word, an oath of his own framing, accompanied by fearful imprecations invoked on her own soul should she ever break that oath, even in the smallest point. If the wretched Emmie so much as hesitated before pronouncing words which seemed to her not only horrible but almost blasphemous, the cold steel was shaken before her eyes, as a menace of instant death.

When the oath had been taken by the poor maiden, Harper gruffly bade her rise. Emmie could not have done so without the help of Jael.

"Now, hark 'ee, girl," said the ruffian, and as he spoke he grasped Emmie's wrist with his left hand to enforce his words, "I have a hold over you besides that of your oath. If you break it—but by a whisper, but by a look—I have the means here of blowing up the house over your head! And I will do it, rather than myself fall into the clutches of the law. Or if you should think to find safety by flight, I would pursue you to the furthest end of the island, ay, or beyond it! In the grave alone should you hide yourself from my vengeance!" Then, turning to his wife, Harper added, "Now, take that girl back to the place from whence you brought her, and tell her that if she flinch from keeping her oath, I shall not flinch from keeping mine!"

With that terrible threat still sounding in her ears, Emmie found herself again on the narrow stone staircase, with the cold draught of air from the lower door, which she had left open, rushing up from below. Mrs. Harper was supporting the poor girl, or she must have fallen.

"Pluck up a brave heart, Miss Trevor; all is safe as long as you keep silence," said the woman.

"Is all safe,—my father, my brothers? Oh, is there no danger for them in this horrible house?" exclaimed Emmie, who had no clear idea as to the nature of the work in which Harper was engaged, save that it assuredly must be evil.

"Every one is safe so long as you are silent," answered Jael Harper.

"But Bruce—my brother—who sleeps next door to that room,—oh, if he were to discover what is passing in the haunted chamber!" exclaimed Emmie in anguish. "If he were to find out—"

"He has never found us out, and he never will!" interrupted Jael, who, having supported Emmie down the stairs, was now emerging with her on the gravel path, where the moon, passing from the shadow of earth, now shed her full radiance around them. "Think you that my husband does not take every precaution to prevent discovery? There is no chance of finding *him* napping. Master Bruce is regular in his hours as clock-work; we have no difficulty whatever in keeping out of his way."

Bruce's methodical habits had, indeed, rendered his occupation of the room next the haunted chamber no great restraint upon Harper, who was not even aware that there existed a door of communication between the two apartments. When Bruce started in the morning for S——, Harper's working-day also commenced. The man stopped his occupation on Bruce's return, till the sound of the dinner-gong assured him that the coast was clear, and that he could leave his temporary retreat on the secret staircase for the haunted chamber. There Harper was wont to remain till warned by the bell for evening prayer, when he usually quitted Myst Hall for the night, gliding silently through the shrubbery, sometimes shrouded in his wife's cloak and bonnet, and carrying her basket, lest he should chance to be noticed from the house. Jael's constant communication with Myst Court greatly facilitated the movements of her husband; and it need scarcely be added that they both fared well upon the provisions which Emmie had destined for the relief of the poor. The Harpers now scarcely regretted what had at first caused them serious alarm,—the determination of the present owner of Myst Court to reside on his own estate.

Emmie was somewhat relieved by the assurance of Jael that Harper's work, whatever it might be, would injure none of her family.

"My husband's business will no more harm any of your people than if he were blowing soap-bubbles," continued Mrs. Harper. "For years we have found that room quiet and convenient for—for whatever my husband has in hand. We hoped that, the house having the name of being haunted, no one would have come to trouble us here. We could not keep your family out, but we find that by caution and management the rat can live next door to the cat, ay, and nibble out of the cat's platter, without making her stretch out her claws, or so much as shake her whiskers. Hark! I hear a stir in the house; you are missed; they are searching for you no doubt. There's the front door open, you can see the light from it now; and I must not be found beside you. Go, and remember your oath, Miss Trevor; and remember what will come if you break it. Haman Harper is a man of his word!"

Dizzy and bewildered as she was, and ready to faint from the effect of the terror which she had undergone in the haunted chamber, Emmie yet managed to make her way to the entrance-door, which had been left open by Vibert. With trembling steps she passed through the hall, and thence to her father's study, where she appeared in the pitiable plight which has been described in a former chapter.

CHAPTER XXIII.

DEATH.

 The distress which Emmie endured from her fears and forebodings, was rendered more intolerable by the pangs of regret. After an emergency in which we have been suddenly called upon to act an important part, when that acting has proved a failure, how painfully the mind revolves and goes over the scene, reflecting on what might have been, what would have been, the result, had duty been more bravely performed.

"Had I had presence of mind,—the smallest presence of mind,—and that but for one half minute," thought Miss Trevor, "I should have made my escape, roused the household, and have been the means of destroying some dark conspiracy of which I now know not the end. I should have relieved myself for ever of these dreadful, haunting fears, and cleared from my home this mysterious shadow of evil. Had I thought of any one but myself, my miserable, worthless self,—had I but darted up a prayer to Him who was able to save me,—I should not have suffered myself to be bound by a horrible oath, which it is a sin either to keep or to break. How is it that I have so miserably failed in the hour of trial? Is it not that I have never earnestly struggled against the sin of Mistrust? I have perpetually yielded to it when it met me in the common duties of life; I have let my fears be sufficient excuse for neglecting the call of conscience; and how could I hope that God would give me the victory in a great and sudden trial? Weak women, ere now, have endured the rack and embraced the stake; but must they not have first exercised the self-denying martyr-spirit in the trials of daily life?"

Mr. Trevor, as he had proposed, kept his daughter much by his side during the day which followed her painful adventure. The father thought it better not to ask any questions which might distress the nervous Emmie, and for this considerate kindness the poor girl felt very grateful. Mr. Trevor tried to give Emmie employment and amusement in every way that he could devise. Emmie read to him, played to him, sang to him; but still it was too evident to the eye of paternal affection that the maiden's thoughts were wandering, and that her spirit was still oppressed.

"The day is fine, and mild for December; I will drive you over to the picturesque ruin which we have hitherto thought too distant for a winter excursion," said Mr. Trevor, when he and his daughter had finished their luncheon.

"If I might choose, papa," replied Emmie, "I would rather that you would take me to the cottage of Widow Brant."

"Ah! that's your poor *protégée*, Emmie; I have not seen her at her cottage door lately. Is she recovering her health?"

"I scarcely know, papa," replied Emmie faintly.

"I thought that you had taken her under your care, my love, that the poor creature has been supplied with food from our own table."

"Mrs. Jessel has often been with some—at least—that's to say—I hoped—I thought that she went to the widow," stammered forth Emmie. Since the discovery that Jael was the wife and accomplice of Harper, Miss Trevor had lost even the small amount of confidence which she might once have felt in this woman.

Mr. Trevor looked rather surprised and annoyed at Emmie's evident confusion. "I marvel, my child, that you should employ as your almoner and cottage visitor a person of whom we know so little," said he.

"She offered herself," observed Emmie, "and I was afraid to refuse Mrs. Jessel's services, lest I should give her offence. It was so foolish in me—so wrong! Poor Widow Brant is on my conscience, papa; but I do not like going alone to her cottage."

"Then why not take our good Susan with you?" inquired Mr. Trevor.

Emmie's dread of Harper had been so greatly increased by the events of the preceding night, that she now felt Susan's company to be no efficient protection. The young lady renewed her request that her father should, at least on this one occasion, be her companion on her walk to the hamlet. She felt safe when leaning on his arm.

"These visits to sick women are not in my line," observed Mr. Trevor, smiling, "as I am neither doctor nor divine. I do not neglect my tenants; I am willing to help them according to my means; and am proving at this moment my care for their interests by involving myself, for their sakes, in a very troublesome affair. But in a cottage I own that I feel like a fish out of water. Never mind, however; as you wish it, I am ready to-day to be your escort; my only bargain is that you shall take all the talking, my love."

The father and daughter soon set out together, sauntered along the shrubbery, and passed through the outer gateway. Emmie glanced timidly at the almost tumble-down hovel of Harper. It was shut up. No firelight gleamed through the cracked panes of the single window, from the chimney issued no smoke. The maiden saw that the tenant of that hovel was not within it, and guessed but too easily that he was at that moment ensconced at his mysterious work in the haunted chamber. She could scarcely pay any attention to her father's conversation, and answered almost at random the questions which he occasionally asked.

The door of Widow Brant's cottage was not closed. The sound of several voices was heard within as the Trevors approached the humble dwelling. Some women were in the cottage, and a gentleman in whom Mr. Trevor recognized the parish doctor of S——. The room was so small that the entrance of the two visitors made it seem crowded. Emmie's eye sought in vain for the widow, until she caught sight, in a corner of the room, of a form extended on a low bed, covered with clothes and rags instead of a blanket, and of a face on which were already visible the signs of approaching death.

"Why was I not sent for before?" said the doctor angrily to one of the neighbours; "this is just the way with you all: you give yourselves up to a quack till you have one foot in the grave, and then send for the doctor, and expect him to work miracles for your cure! Oh, I beg your pardon, sir," said the medical man, interrupting himself, and raising his hat on perceiving the presence of Mr. Trevor and his daughter.

"Is there no hope for the poor woman?" asked the master of Myst Court in a voice too low to reach the ear of the patient. The doctor, in his reply, observed less consideration.

"The disease has gone too far—too far—and the poor creature's strength is exhausted. She cannot struggle through now. She has been half starved with hunger and cold, and has had neither proper care and medicine, nor the food which was absolutely necessary to keep up her vital powers. I can do nothing in this case—nothing!"

Emmie had but paused to hear the doctor's opinion, and then, with a heavy heart, she glided to the bedside and bent over the dying woman. Emmie had but once before stood by a death-bed, and that was when she had been brought, while but a child, to receive a mother's last kiss and blessing. To Emmie the scene before her was inexpressibly solemn and sad.

The widow's life was ebbing away, but her mind was clear. "I thought that you'd have come again," were the faint words which struggled forth from her pale lips as she recognized the young lady.

Those words went to Emmie's heart like a knife. There had, then, been expectation and disappointment; the lady's visit had been watched for, hoped for, and it had not been made till too late! Hollow, wistful eyes were raised to Emmie's. Again the poor sufferer spoke, but so feebly that Miss Trevor had to bend very low indeed to catch the meaning of what she said.

"They say I'm dying—and death is so awful!" murmured the widow.

"Not to those who have given their hearts to Him who died for sinners!" whispered Emmie softly in the sufferer's ear.

"I've had no one to tell me of these things, and I be not learned. But—but I've not led a bad life; I've harmed no one," said the dying widow, grasping, as so many unenlightened sinners do, at that false hope of safety which can only break in their hands.

"She's al'ays been a good neighbour, and a decent, respectable body!" cried Mrs. Blunt, who was bustling about in the cottage, disturbing, by her noisy presence, the chamber of death.

"It's worse than useless for you all to come crowding here," said the doctor roughly. "Mrs. Wall, you may be wanted, but let the rest go out and leave the poor creature to the lady; can't you let a woman die in quiet?" And enforcing his words by emphatic gestures, the doctor soon succeeded in partially clearing the cottage. He then took his leave of Mr. Trevor, and quitted the place in which he knew that his medical skill could be of no avail.

"I will send Susan with blankets," said Mr. Trevor to his daughter. "Will you come with me, Emmie, or stay?"

"I will stay," replied Emmie with emotion; "would that I had come here before!"

For more than an hour the young lady remained by the dying woman, with her own hands beating up the pillow, spreading the warm coverlet brought by Susan over the wasted form, pouring wine, drop by drop, between the sufferer's lips. For more than an hour Emmie watched the flickering spark of life, and tried to whisper words of holy comfort, which the now dulled mind and deafened ear had no longer power to receive. Then came the last struggle, the gasp for breath, the death-rattle; the ashen hue of death stole over the widow's face, one sigh—and all was over.

"She is gone; you can do nothing more. Had you not better return home, miss?" said Susan softly, as Mrs. Wall closed the eyes of the corpse.

With tears and self-reproach Emmie Trevor quitted the lifeless remains of her to whom she might once perhaps have brought comfort, peace, and light, if not the blessing of restoration to health. The young lady was silent on her homeward way; her heart was too full to permit her to enter into conversation with her attendant. Emmie ran upstairs to her own apartment, shut the door behind her, sank on her knees beside her bed, and buried her face in her hands. Then her feelings gushed forth in broken confession and fervent prayer.

"I am verily guilty concerning my fellow-creatures," Emmie sobbed forth; "guilty before men, guilty before Thee, O my God! I have left undone what I ought to have done, and there is no health in my soul. Weak, selfish, and cruel, neglectful of the duties which lay so plainly before me, I am not worthy to lift up so much as my eyes towards Heaven; I can but say, *God be merciful to me a sinner!* But oh, Thou who dost pity, Thou who dost pardon, take not away from me for ever the talent which I have buried; say not, oh, say not to my miserable soul, *I was sick, and ye visited me not!* Help me to redeem the precious time which I have hitherto wasted, to overcome the sin which has beset and enslaved me! Increase my faith, deepen my love; hold up my footsteps, that I slip not on my perilous path; say to my weak, mistrustful heart, *Be not afraid; I am thy God!*"

Emmie wept freely while she thus confessed her sin and prayed, and then arose from her knees more calm. She was now able to collect her thoughts; and to strengthen her new-born resolutions she repeated to herself Trench's exquisite sonnet, which, at her uncle's request, she had, some time before, committed to memory.

"Lord, what a change within us one short hour Spent in Thy presence will suffice to make! What heavy burdens from our bosoms take, What parched lands revive, as with a shower! We kneel, and all around us seems to lower; We rise, and all the prospect, far and near, Stands forth in sunny outline brave and clear. We kneel—how weak! we rise—how full of power! Then wherefore should we do ourselves this wrong, Or others, that we are not always strong; That we should be o'erburdened with our care, That we should ever faint and feeble be, Downcast or drooping, when with us is prayer, And hope, and joy, and courage are with Thee?"

CHAPTER XXIV.

A MISTAKE.

It will be remembered that Emmie had, in the morning, tried the patience of Bruce by her strange indecision regarding a second change of apartments. It was now no superstitious fancy which made Emmie look upon the room next the haunted chamber as a post of peril. She entertained a dread lest Harper should on some night omit his usual precautions, and that Bruce should discover the presence of his dangerous neighbour. What then might ensue? The spirited young man would never suffer himself to be tied by such an oath as his sister had taken; and of the consequences which might follow his refusal Emmie trembled to think. It was this peril to Bruce which made Emmie regard a change of rooms as desirable on her brother's account, though certainly not on her own.

"It would be very dreadful to me to know that only a wall divided me from that wicked man who threatened my life!" thought poor Emmie. "How could I rest if I heard him stealthily moving about so near, even though aware that he could not possibly reach me?" Had the maiden known that there was actually a door in that dividing wall, her terror would have been yet greater. But Emmie believed that the corridor entrance being bricked up, there was no outlet from the haunted chamber but by the door which opened on the secret stairs. Ignorant as she was of the means of nearer communication between the two apartments, it was but the strain on her nerves that Emmie dreaded when suggesting her own return to the room which had been assigned to her at the first.

But this dread was so great, that, as we have seen, Emmie could not in the morning summon up courage to press the arrangement on Bruce. She had wavered, hesitated, drawn back. But Emmie had learned much during the last few painful hours; the effect which her uncle's warnings had failed to produce, followed the solemn teachings of conscience by the widow's death-bed. Humbly and prayerfully Emmie now resolved to bend all her efforts to conquer mistrust, to subdue the opposition of shrinking nature, and obey God's will at however painful a cost. Emmie determined to brave Bruce's displeasure at her apparent inconsistency and folly, and return to the hated room, in which her danger would at any rate be less than that of her brother.

But Emmie had on that evening no opportunity of carrying out her resolution. Bruce returned to Myst Court at his usual hour, but looking and feeling so ill, that he could not be troubled with anything in the way of household arrangements. He had one of the severe attacks of headache to which the young man was subject.

"I shall not be with you at dinner to-day," said Bruce to his sister; "like a bear, I shall keep in my den, and have my growl out by myself. I've my fire ready lit, my kettle on the hob, and my little tea-caddy on the table. I want nothing but quiet and rest, and shall be all right in the morning."

Bruce was proverbially a bad patient, and would never submit to what he called coddling. Emmie knew that he now meant what he said, and that she should only annoy her brother by offering to sit beside him, or bring him food which he would not touch. The brother and sister, therefore, bade each other good-night; and Bruce, taking a lighted candle, with slow step mounted the staircase, then drew back the heavy tapestry curtain, and passed on to his own apartment.

The fire blazed and crackled cheerily. Bruce, instead of going to rest at once, drew a chair in front of it, seated himself with his feet on the fender, and pressing his hot forehead with his hand, remained for some time in absolute stillness. He let his mind rest as well as his frame, not fatiguing it by following out any definite chain of ideas.

Thus young Trevor remained till he heard from below the sound of the gong which summoned the family to dinner. About five minutes afterwards, Bruce raised his head to listen to a different sound, much nearer to where he sat. It came from a place from whence he had never before heard the faintest noise. There was—he could not be mistaken—the voice of some one speaking in the haunted chamber!

Bruce's sensation on hearing it was not that of fear, scarcely even that of curiosity. When once young Trevor had taken an idea into his mind, he was wont to hold it with a pertinacity which savoured of obstinacy. Bruce was very slow to own, even to himself, that he had made a mistake. The notion now in the young man's brain was that his giddy brother had determined to try his courage by playing on him some practical joke. Vibert's sudden proposal to go up to London Bruce considered but as an attempt to throw dust into his eyes, and to put him off his guard; and the elder brother smiled to himself at the idea of Vibert's imagining that he really could take him in by so transparent an attempt at deception.

"Vibert is no more in London at this moment than I am," had been the reflection of Bruce. "He never thought of going thither till I casually let out that it is possible to enter the haunted chamber." And now, when a voice was heard in that chamber, Bruce but knitted his brow, and muttered impatiently to himself, "Could he not have kept his foolery for a better time; I am in no mood for nonsense to-night."

Another voice seemed to reply to the first, both speaking in low tones, and not distinctly enough for the import of their words to be understood by the listening Bruce. Still his suspicions were not aroused, for the power to mimic various tones was one of the accomplishments which added to Vibert's popularity in ladies' society. Then followed a creaking sound, as of the winding of a windlass, or the turning of the screw of a press. This puzzled Bruce, and made him alter his first intention of simply locking the door of communication between the two rooms, and so imprisoning the pseudo-ghost till the morning. Young Trevor, of course, knew nothing of the third door of the bricked-up chamber, or the secret staircase beyond it.

"I may as well put an end to this folly at once," said Bruce, rising and looking around for some convenient weapon with which to chastise, or rather to alarm, the disturber of his repose. He took up his gun, but did not attempt to load it. Why should he do so when he had no intention of startling the household and frightening his sister by the sudden report of fire-arms? Vibert would not be able to tell by a glance whether the gun were or were not loaded. The object of Bruce was to frighten, but not to injure his brother.

The next thing to be done was to get the door-key, which Bruce had left on his mantel-piece. He scarcely expected to find it there still, but there it was.

"Vibert must have taken the precaution of replacing after using it," thought Bruce, as he took up the key; "and he has been artful enough to leave my map still hanging up over the panel-door."

Very softly Bruce now lifted off the large varnished map from its nail, and laid it down on the floor. His object was, by his sudden appearance with his gun, to startle his brother. Noiselessly Bruce turned the key in the lock, noiselessly pushed open the door in the panel, then suddenly sprang into the lighted chamber, with a loud exclamation of "Ha! have I caught you at it?" To Bruce's amazement, as well as their own, he found himself confronted by Harper and Colonel Standish!

It is not to be denied that on his sudden recognition of these night-visitors, whom nought but an evil purpose could have brought to that place, to the heart of the youth "the life-blood thrilled with sudden start." But Harper had now no timid girl to deal with. Raising his unloaded gun so as to cover now the one man, then the other, Bruce in a loud voice demanded, "Villains! what do ye here?"

Seizing the instant when the gun was pointed at his companion, Standish made a dart forwards and struck up the arm of Bruce. In another moment the two were locked in a deadly grapple.

Even then Bruce Trevor retained his presence of mind. Wrestling and struggling as he was, with a hand stronger than his own griping at his throat, and stifling the cry of

"Robbers! help!" which would have burst from his lips, Bruce did his utmost to back through the doorway into his room. Could he but reach his bell-rope, he could bring his father and the servant to his assistance, and so overcome and perhaps capture his assailants. But in vain the young man struggled and strained every muscle in his frame, too closely grappled with by Standish to be able even to strike with the but-end of his gun. The strength of Bruce was failing, though not his courage; the odds were too heavy against him. While Standish, with throttling grasp, was pinning him against the wall, Harper, with some heavy instrument, came and struck the youth on the head. Bruce saw no more, felt no more than the one sharp pang of the blow. He fell heavily on the floor, at the mercy of the ruffians whose lurking-place he had on that night discovered!

In the meantime, the master of Myst Court was calmly sipping his claret, and telling to his daughter amusing stories of old adventures, all unconscious of the fearful scene going on within the walls of his own dwelling.

CHAPTER XXV.

STRANGE TIDINGS.

 When Emmie arose on the following morning, the landscape was covered with a soft mantle of snow. A few flakes were still falling, ever and anon, from a sky whence lowering clouds shut out the pale gleam of a winter daybreak.

Emmie arose with an earnest resolution on her mind—a resolution born of repentance, and gathering strength from prayer. She would no longer be the weak, selfish, useless being, whom every shadow could turn from the path of duty. She would listen for a Father's guiding voice; she would cling to the helping Hand; she would, through God's promised help, realize His protecting presence.

"I will beseech the Lord to enable me never, never again to mistrust His power or His love, or to doubt His promise that all things shall work together for good to His children," said Emmie to herself, as she opened her Bible; and in that Bible she read the touching history of those who once walked unharmed in the burning fiery furnace.

It was thus that the weak soldier of Christ put on armour to resist her besetting sin. She would, ere the close of that day, sorely need that armour of proof.

When Emmie had finished her reading, she rose and looked forth from her casement. She saw an open vehicle approaching along the snow-covered road towards Myst Court. Three men were seated within it, besides the driver. It was with no common interest that the maiden watched their approach.

"Policemen!—London policemen!—and with an inspector!" exclaimed Emmie in surprise, for she recognized the familiar uniform of the officers of the law. "What can be bringing them hither? Can Harper's secret have been discovered?"

Emmie's heart thrilled with mingled fear and hope. Had the officers of justice received information of some secret plot,—had they come to search the house,—would light be thrown on its dark recesses? Such was Emmie's hope, but still linked with a trembling fear. What might not Harper do, in his desperation, if he were driven to bay? Would he not conclude that her lips had betrayed his secret, that she had broken her solemn oath?

Emmie lost sight of the vehicle as it stopped before the large entrance-door of Myst Court, which was not overlooked by her window. She heard the policemen's ring at the bell, she heard her father's firm step as he descended the stairs to meet his early and most unexpected visitors. Emmie would have followed him at once, but the tresses of her long hair still floated down over her shoulders. The young lady was not independent of the help of a maid, and rang her bell for Susan.

Minutes passed, and no Susan appeared. There were sounds of steps and voices in the house, but not near Emmie's apartment. Her curiosity made her impatient; she rang again, and more loudly; and as there was still delay in answering the summons, Emmie resolved to wait no longer, and herself gathered up and twisted into a knot, as best she might, her long, luxuriant hair. She had just finished her toilette when Susan entered at last, looking flushed and excited.

"I beg pardon, miss," said the lady's-maid; "but I could not come sooner. The police are here, and they have been questioning me and the other servants."

"Have they come to search the house?" cried Emmie.

"Oh yes; they brought a warrant from London to do that," was Susan's reply.

Almost breathless with anxiety and hope, Emmie asked if they had searched the haunted chamber.

"That's the first place they went to," said Susan.

"And was any one there, any one arrested?" cried Emmie, trembling with eagerness to hear the reply, which might loose the knot of her perplexity, and free her for ever from haunting terrors.

"No one was found in this house, miss," answered Susan, with a look of distress. "There were strange presses and instruments found, as I heard, in the haunted room, such as must have been used in forging those dreadful bank-notes."

"Forging bank-notes! so that was the crime!" said Emmie under her breath. "And is any one suspected?" she inquired.

Susan at first looked perplexed, and avoided meeting her lady's questioning glance. She then answered, "There is a warrant out for the arrest of Colonel Standish."

"Colonel Standish!" echoed Emmie in surprise.

"The police had been at S——, at the White Hart, before they came here," said Susan; "but the colonel had gone off, no one knows where. He had not been seen or heard of since yesterday morning. He owes a large debt at the hotel, and his stealing off thus, without paying it, makes every one think him guilty about the forged notes."

"I never believed him to be a real gentleman," observed Emmie. "But," she added anxiously, "is he thought to have had no accomplice?" The maiden, bound by her oath, dared not so much as mention the name of Harper.

"I think that I hear master calling me," said Susan; and without answering her lady's question, she hurried from the apartment.

Emmie was standing near the window, and from it she now saw Joe leading her own pony-chaise from the stables towards the entrance of the house, and at a quick pace that told of haste. What was the vehicle brought for at so early an hour? Perhaps—so thought Emmie Trevor—to take one or more of the policemen back to S——. Yet scarcely so, for their own conveyance was waiting.

The maiden was not kept long in doubt. It was her own father that she saw in the chaise, a few seconds afterwards, urging on the pony to a frantic pace, plunging through the drifted snow as if life or death hung on its speed! Joe sat behind, while his master drove as Emmie had never seen her father drive before.

"What can be the matter?" exclaimed Emmie; "papa has forgotten even his greatcoat, and the weather is so cold, and it looks as if a storm would come on!" She watched the chaise till it disappeared behind intervening trees and brushwood.

Susan re-entered the room as her young lady, anxious and wondering, turned from the casement.

"Do you know where my father is going?" Emmie inquired of her maid.

"Master is going to London, miss," was the answer; "but I doubt whether the pony can gallop fast enough to take him in time for the train. Master was in great haste, or he would have come to bid you good-bye."

"What takes him to London?" cried Emmie.

"Oh, this bank-note forgery business," said Susan, the look of uneasiness passing again over her face. "Master called me to give you a message, miss. He says that while the police have charge of the house, he—he does not wish you to speak to them, miss, or question them about the matter which has brought them here. Master is anxious about you. He has ordered me to take care that no one should disturb or intrude upon you, Miss Trevor."

"The police are not likely to disturb the innocent, nor to intrude on ladies," said Emmie, smiling from the pleasant assurance of safety conveyed by their presence in the mansion. "If my father does not wish me to question them or see them, of course his will shall be obeyed. I must depend on you for my information, or—where is my brother, Master Bruce?"

"I cannot tell, miss; he is not in the house; he must have gone out," replied Susan in a flurried manner. The quiet, respectable, lady's-maid had never before been examined by a superintendent of police, and her usual self-possession had forsaken her on that eventful morning.

"Bruce must have heard something of this warrant against Standish," thought Emmie; "perhaps he has gone off early to S——, to help in the search after this daring impostor. I am glad that he felt well enough to do so; but how he could have received such early information of what has occurred, I know not."

Emmie now went down-stairs to the breakfast room; there was no family-prayer in the confusion of that strange day. Susan brought in a tray with her young lady's breakfast, in the absence of Joe. Emmie was not disposed to touch it. She lingered near the window, half hoping that Bruce might appear, or that her father, having missed the early train, might return to Myst Court. The policemen were very quiet; only the sound of a heavy tread, now and then, showed that they were in the house; but Emmie saw nothing of the officers of the law.

There were signs, however, that the unusual occurrences which had taken place at Myst Court had excited curiosity and interest in the surrounding neighbourhood. Knots of persons, not only from the hamlet, but apparently even from the town, came up the carriage-drive, as it seemed for no purpose but to stare up, open-mouthed, at the house. There was much shaking of heads and whispering amongst these spectators; but they had caught sight of the lady looking forth from the window, and nothing was uttered by them loud enough for its import to be distinguished by Emmie through the closed window.

Presently the wind rose in wild gusts, whirling the snow into blinding drifts; dark clouds were sweeping over the sky; all portended a violent storm; and the assembled crowd hastily retreated from the grounds of Myst Court, to seek refuge from the fury of the tempest.

"I would give anything to know whether Harper and his wife are under suspicion!" said Emmie to herself. "Susan is so strangely unwilling to give full information, she stammers as she answers my questions. I think that my father must have charged her to say nothing that could possibly agitate my nerves. He has desired that his weak daughter should be kept from excitement; and thus I, who have the deepest interest in all that is happening here, am more ignorant of what is going on than any servant in the household. I must question Susan again."

Emmie was about to ring the bell for her maid; but before she did so, there was a quick tap at the door, and, without waiting for the lady's "Come in," Hannah entered the room. The cook looked more excited than Susan had done; but while, in the case of the latter, there had been an appearance of perplexity, if not of pain, with a desire to speak as little as she could, Hannah's face, on the contrary, showed that she was not only brimming over with news, but that she had a vulgar pleasure in being the first to impart it. "Now I shall know all," thought Emmie.

"La, miss!" exclaimed Hannah, "to think of you taking your breakfast so quietly here, as if nothing had happened, when there be such goings on in the place!"

"Any one arrested?" asked Emmie eagerly. She dared not mention the names of Harper or Jessel, lest, by turning suspicion on them, she should indirectly violate her oath.

"No one took up yet, that I know of, but he in London," said Hannah. "Didn't master go off like a shot, as soon as he heard the news!"

"What news? who was taken up?" asked Emmie.

"La, miss! you don't mean to say that you've not heard of the scrape of poor Master Vibert, how he's been catched and put into jail!"

Emmie staggered backwards as though she had been struck. "Put into jail! my brother! and on what pretext?" she exclaimed, grasping the table for support.

"I'll tell you all about it—you ought to know, seeing you're his own sister," said Hannah, enjoying the excitement of the scene, and yet not without a touch of natural pity, on seeing the anguish which she inflicted. "Master Vibert went yesterday to London, you know; and when he got there, he went off straight to a jeweller (Golding, I think, is the name), and bought from him lots of jewels, diamonds, pearls, and all kinds of gim-cracks, worth more than a thousand pounds."

"Impossible!" exclaimed Emmie.

"But he did buy the jewels, and paid for them too with a lot of nice, fresh, clean ten-pound notes," said Hannah. "The shopman didn't suspect nothing at first, 'cause he knew the young gentleman's face so well, as he'd often dealt at the shop. But when the head of the firm, as they call him, came in the afternoon to look after the business (there's nothing like a master's eye, we know), he said the notes weren't real and honest bank-notes; and off he went at once to the biggest police-station in London."

"My brother has been the unconscious tool of a villain!" murmured Emmie, who felt certain that Vibert's vanity and careless security must have made him the victim of the impostor who had called himself Colonel Standish.

"The p'lice and Mr. Golding drove off to Grosvenor Square," continued Hannah, "for the jeweller knew the address; and a mighty bustle and fuss was caused by their coming, for there was an afternoon party, and the gentlefolk were amazed when they found that he who had been the merriest of them all was to be haled up afore a magistrate, on a charge of passing forged notes."

"Did not my brother at once clear himself from suspicion?" cried Emmie, the paleness of whose face was now exchanged for the crimson flush of indignation and shame.

"Master Vibert said that the notes had been given to him by a Colonel Standish; and that he had bought the jewels for Colonel Standish; and that he would have sent them off at once to some address in Liverpool, only he had waited to have out his dance."

"Then are the jewels safe in the hands of the police?" asked Emmie.

"Ay; I wish that this cheat of a colonel were so too," replied Hannah. "Hanging is too good for him, say I; for sure and certain it was his wheedling which made poor Master Vibert do so wicked a thing. Some of the police were sent off to Liverpool, and some hurried down to S——. And first they searched the colonel's lodgings, and then they came ferreting here."

"Did they easily find their way into the bricked-up room?" asked Emmie, who knew of no way of access into it but by the secret staircase.

"Bless you, miss, what could be easier, when the door was wide open 'twixt that room and Master Bruce's!"

Emmie started, and turned deadly pale.

"You may well start with surprise, miss; all of us were astonished to find there was any door in that wall. Lizzie declares that even she never knew that there was one, though she tidies the room every day. Master Bruce was so sly—he was—hanging the big map over the place!"

"How dare you speak thus of my brother?" cried Emmie.

"It ain't my speaking, but every one's speaking," said Hannah, firing up at the word of rebuke. "The police say as how young master could not have slept in the one room for a month, and have been innocent as a babe of what was going on in the other. Ay, they said that of him, Miss Trevor, before they'd found a lot of the odd kind of paper of which bank-notes are made in one of his drawers. I wonder young master did not throw it all into the fire before he absconded."

Emmie pressed her temples with both her icy cold hands. Her brain was reeling. Half unconsciously, she echoed the word "Absconded!"

"That's what the p'lice called it; and they're going to take out a warrant against Master Bruce," said Hannah. "It's plain he went off last night, for his bed had never been slept in."

This was to Emmie the crowning horror. There had been a door then—an open door—between her brother's room and that haunted by the presence of the unscrupulous Harper; and Bruce—the noble, the brave—had disappeared during the night!

"Leave me, leave me!" cried Emmie wildly; and, alarmed at the lady's ghastly looks, the bearer of evil tidings at once obeyed her command. Hannah had said more than enough, and now retreated in alarm, lest the effect of her words should have been to turn her young mistress's brain.

CHAPTER XXVI.

THE WEAK ONE.

Emmie remained for a few brief seconds as if transfixed into stone. More wretched was she even than her father, who had rushed off to London on hearing of the arrest of his younger son, without knowing that any danger or disgrace threatened the elder. It need not be said that Emmie never for one instant doubted the innocence of either; her present intense agony arose from her fear regarding the fate of Bruce.

"In that fatal room which he has occupied through my own selfish folly," so flowed the stream of thought like burning lava through the poor girl's brain, "Bruce has heard—has discovered the forgers. He would take no cowardly oath, and they have murdered him to ensure his silence. What a fearful fate may have overtaken mine own brave brother! But, oh! may merciful Heaven have shielded his precious life!"

Susan entered the room, alarmed by the account of the state of her mistress given by Hannah. She expected to find Miss Trevor either fainting or in hysterics, but to her surprise the lady was perfectly calm. This was no time to give way to weakness; the very extremity of Emmie's anguish subdued its outward expression.

"Go to the policemen, Susan; tell them that I am certain that my brother Bruce has been the victim of some foul deed," she said with distinct articulation though a quivering, bloodless lip. "Let every corner of this house, from attic to cellar, be searched; a thousand pounds' reward to whoever shall find Bruce Trevor!" Emmie waved her hand impatiently to urge speed, and Susan hastened from the apartment, scarcely more certain of young Trevor's innocence, or less anxious regarding his fate, than was his unhappy sister.

"There are two guilty ones who are likely enough to be able to throw light on this dark mystery," said Emmie to herself; "Harper, and that wretched woman his wife. But can I set the police on their track without breaking my oath, my horrible oath? Would Heaven, in this dreadful emergency, condemn me for that, or suffer that those awful imprecations which I was forced to utter should fall on my body and soul? Is there any other course open before me in this maddening misery of doubt?" Emmie made two hurried steps towards the door, and then paused.

"There is one other course; yes, I see it. I could go myself—alone—to the dwelling of Jael; there is something of the woman left in her still, she protected my life from her husband. Bruce may be living still, but kept in confinement,"—a gleam of hope came with that thought,—"not in Harper's hovel, which is too small and too close to others to be used as a hiding-place or a prison, but possibly in Jael's, which stands by itself. I will go thither. Threats, promises, entreaties, all will I use to win from her at least some tidings of my lost brother! If I go alone I break no oath, and Jael will be able henceforth implicitly to trust in my honour. She may confide to me things which she would effectually conceal from officers of justice. Yes, I will go alone. Oh, God of mercy, help and direct me!"

One measure of precaution suggested itself to the mind of Emmie, who could not dissociate the idea of personal danger from intercourse with any of those concerned in the forgery plot. She tore a leaf from her pocket-book, and wrote upon it the few following lines, to be left on the dining-room table. *"If there be tidings of my brother, or if I be long in returning, seek for me at the house of Mrs. Jessel."* "There is no breach of my oath in writing this," thought Emmie, as she added her initials to the lines which she had hastily penned.

Emmie's garden-hat and scarlet shawl were hung up in the hall; she sought no other equipment for her walk through the wood, though the clouds were hanging like a pall over the white earth, and the wind was now furiously high. Emmie did not pursue the path by the drive that would have led to the hamlet and the highway; there was a short cut through the woods to the dwelling of Jael, and the maiden took it, sheltering herself as best she might against the tempest which raged round her fragile form. The poor girl felt that she was on a dangerous enterprise. She knew not whom or what she might meet in the place to which she was going; she had not forgotten the gleam of Harper's sharp blade, or the fierce threat expressed in his eyes. It may be marvelled at that one so timid as was Emmie should venture without protection to a dwelling in which might be lurking those whom she knew to be criminals,—those who, as she fearfully suspected, might be murderers also. It was indeed sisterly affection that impelled Emmie onwards, but her support, her strength, was in prayer. Emmie was trusting now as she never had trusted before; she was leaning on, clinging to the invisible arm that could hold her up, to the love which would never forsake her.

It is not to be supposed that Vibert's miserable position was forgotten by Emmie in her terrors on account of his brother. But for Vibert the sister could do nothing but pray; his father was hastening to his aid: her whole energies, Emmie felt, must be concentrated on her own special work,—that of discovering the fate of Bruce Trevor.

Emmie had gone more than half-way to the dwelling of Jael, when the thunder-cloud above her burst in a storm compared to which that one which she had encountered on the evening of her arrival was but as the play of summer lightning. Never before had the trembling girl heard such deafening peals as those which now shook the welkin, while the rattling hail descended with fury. Branches above and on either side creaked and snapped in the gale, and some were whirled with violence across the path of the maiden. Emmie started, shuddered, and drew her shawl over her head for protection against the blast and the hail, but still she struggled onwards. She uttered no shriek, but she gasped forth a prayer; it was the moan of one in anguish, not the cry of one in despair.

That storm was one of the most terrible which had ever been known in England. The newspapers on the following day recorded many a wreck on the coast, many an accident in inland localities. They told of stacks of chimneys blown down, and a church spire struck by lightning; they recorded how cattle had been killed by the fall of a tree, and a sportsman in the field struck dead with his gun in his hand. Emmie always remembered that storm as a horrible dream, and wondered how she had been strengthened to endure what terrified nature so shrank from. But personal fear was partly neutralized by a yet more absorbing fear; to gain tidings of Bruce, Emmie felt that she would bear the shock of the fiercest storm that ever swept over the earth.

The maiden emerged unharmed from the wood, safe at least from danger of injury by lightning-struck tree, or branches torn off by the gale. She had been preserved through one terrible peril; and would not the Power that had helped her hitherto sustain and protect to the end?

Emmie had now reached a road which skirted an open heath, and the lone dwelling of Jael Harper stood not a hundred yards before her. It was a narrow, two-storied house, standing in a small garden; both house and garden were whitened with snow, as was the little path which connected the door with the road. The hail had spent itself in that sharp and furious downfall, but the blinding lightning flashed faster than ever its forked, jagged darts through the sky.

As Emmie with desperate resolution approached the garden-gate of that dwelling which was as fearful to her as a lion's den might have been, she noticed on the snow-covered road the tracks of cartwheels, and on the garden pathway those of feet. The latter were all in a direction which showed that though several persons might have quitted the house since the fall of snow on the preceding night, no one could have entered it. Emmie leaned for a few moments against the low garden-paling to gather her thoughts; the noise of the storm and the terror of her mind made it difficult even to think.

"Footprints from the door to the road, some larger, some smaller as if made by a woman, and some left by wide nailed boots, all pointing this way," murmured Emmie; "three persons must have left the house this morning, and I stand on the track of wheels. All then have absconded,—they have fled from justice; that den of wickedness must be empty." Emmie looked across the garden at the door with its iron studs and large old-fashioned knocker, and felt assured that the loudest summons on that knocker would not cause that door to open. The shutters of the windows were all closed, the house was evidently shut up and deserted. The young lady could not get in; wherefore, then, should she stay? Would it not be better to return home at once, and hear if the strict search after Bruce which must have followed her offer of large reward had been of any avail?

"Oh! why did I madly come hither?" exclaimed Emmie, personal fear again rising into terror, as she contemplated returning through the wood whilst the dreadful storm still raged. "That lightning! oh, how awful the flash! The heavens seem to be splitting asunder! But do not the lightnings obey God's bidding? Is it not the voice of my Father which I hear in the thunder? Even if it bring His summons to His child, should I fear to go unto Him?"

While her faith was wrestling thus with her fear, the attention of Emmie was attracted by a small object near her, almost covered with snow, which, strangely enough on that winter day, looked something like a rosebud. Its soft crimson hue contrasted with the whiteness of the snow under which it was lying half buried. There was something curiously familiar to Emmie in the appearance of that flower, which did not seem like a work of nature. The small thing, whatever it might be, was but two steps from the spot where Emmie stood leaning against the paling. Emmie turned towards the place where lay the object, and, though she could scarcely have given a reason for so doing, she stooped and raised it. With emotions which no pen can describe, the trembling girl drew out from the snow *a man's slipper*—a slipper which her own fingers had worked for her brother! Emmie sank on her knees with a faint cry of anguish. How had that slipper come there, and when? and, oh! where, where was he who had worn it? Did that deserted house conceal some fearful—

The chain of thought was broken by an explosive crash of heaven's artillery in the cloud above, and, almost simultaneously with the peal, a fire-ball struck the house, by the garden-gate of which Emmie was crouching, still on her knees. The noise was so tremendous that the maiden for a brief space lost sense of hearing and power of thinking; she was deafened and bewildered, and remained motionless and breathless, with the slipper clenched in her grasp. But the thunder-clap was soon over, and miserable consciousness of her position returned to poor Emmie. The sight of that slipper roused her to a more sickening fear than could be caused by lightning or thunder.

Emmie started to her feet, and again turned her wild gaze on the lonely house. It had been fast closed against her entrance, but (attracted, perhaps, by the metal on the door) Heaven's bolt had torn its way through; it had smashed through woodwork and brickwork, and made a ghastly breach, charred and blackened, as if a bomb had exploded there to make an opening for destroyers! There was nothing now but her own terror to hinder the maiden from exploring the lightning-stricken dwelling.

"O Father—mercy—help!" burst in almost unconscious prayer from Emmie's quivering lips, as she lifted the latch of the gate. With rapid steps she crossed the little garden by the snow-covered path, and over the charred and splintered wreck of a door made her way into the house which she had so much dreaded to enter. To Emmie it seemed as if she were borne onwards by some invisible power, and were scarcely a voluntary agent; but this sensation was the effect of excited fancy.

Emmie was now in the narrow passage of Jael's house; to her right was an open door, beyond which lay a room, dark indeed, for the shutters of its window were closed, yet not utterly so, for daylight forced its way in through chinks, and there was a faint reflected light from the wall of the passage. Into that room Emmie now turned, groping her way forwards with hands extended. Her object was to reach the window and throw open the shutters, and so gain fuller light by which to pursue her dreadful search for—perhaps a brother's corpse! But ere Emmie could feel her way to the window, her bare and icy-cold hand came in contact with something soft and damp—something resembling a human face! Emmie could not stifle a cry of horror. Her first emotion was that of terror, the next that of almost ecstatic hope, as the maiden's straining eyes traced through the deep gloom the outline of a form, not standing upright, but apparently leaning against or fastened to some heavy piece of furniture. This form, of which she had accidentally touched the face, was assuredly not dead, for the flesh had some slight warmth, and the head had slightly moved when her hand came in contact with it. Emmie sprang to the window, raised the bar, and flung the shutters wide open. What a sight did daylight reveal! On his knees, with his back to a table to which he was bound, while his mouth was gagged with his own neckcloth, Emmie, as she turned from the window, beheld her brother—her own lost Bruce!

Almost in the twinkling of an eye the prisoner's mouth was freed from its bonds. The exclamations "My sister! my preserver!" which burst from the young man's lips, showed that neither the sense of recognition nor power of utterance was lost. Emmie then attempted to free the arms of Bruce, which were bound with a rope behind him; but to accomplish this work required more time and far greater effort. The knot was not easily unloosed, and the slender delicate fingers of Emmie, though she exerted their utmost strength, could not for several minutes accomplish their difficult task. Whilst Emmie was straining at the tight knot, quickened in her efforts by a faint moan from her suffering brother, she noticed not whether lightning flashed or thunder rolled; she seemed for the time to have lost all personal fear; self-consciousness was swallowed up in anxious care for another.

At length the rope end was dragged through the last cruel loop, and Bruce Trevor was free. Emmie, with thankful delight, threw her arms round the neck of her brother, and, for the first time on that terrible day, burst into a flood of tears. Her brother feebly returned her embrace, and wept like a child. Emmie was surprised, and even alarmed, at the emotion to which Bruce Trevor gave way. Had it been Vibert who had wept—Vibert, ever impulsive, and without any self-control—Emmie would neither have wondered nor feared; but that Bruce, the firm Bruce, who since childhood had never been known to shed a tear—that Bruce should actually sob, showed that even his powers of endurance must have been overstrained at last, and that his strong nerves had been shaken by torture, either physical or mental.

And suffering was written on the young man's face; not only in the ghastly wound which Harper's blow had left on his brow, but in the hollow eyes, the haggard cheek, the lips which had lost for a while their expression of calm decision. Bruce had secretly prided himself on his firmness; he had to be taught that no merely human courage can be proof against every trial, as his sister had been taught that human weakness can be raised into heroism by the power of faith and prayer.

But soon the strong will struggled against human infirmity. Mastering his emotion by a convulsive effort, Bruce was the first to speak.

"How came you here? who is with you?" he asked.

"No one is with me; I think that God led me here," was Emmie's reply.

"He led you indeed," murmured Bruce. "The cords were cutting into my flesh, my position was torture; another half-hour and reason or life must have given way. But for you to come alone, in the storm, and to such a place as this, is scarcely less than a miracle—you, Emmie, who dreaded the lightning!"

"Blessed was the lightning! it did His bidding; it made a way for me to enter and save you," cried Emmie.

"But for that crashing bolt you would never have seen me alive," said Bruce. As he spoke, the young man turned his head with a quick, uneasy movement, like a sentinel at night who detects the sound of a stealthy tread. Emmie saw the movement, and her heart throbbed fast with sympathetic alarm. Could the forgers be returning to make sure of their victim? But the apprehension expressed in the face of Bruce arose from a different cause.

"Mark you not that smell of burning?" he said. "See the smoke rolling in through the doorway; the bolt has set the house on fire; we must make our escape before the building be wrapped in flames!"

Bruce was in so exhausted a state, and his limbs had been so cramped by the painful position in which he had for hours remained, that without the support of his sister's slight arm he could scarcely have moved even a few steps forward. Very strange was it to Emmie to find that her brother leaned upon her—that it was given to the weak to support the strong, to the timid to encourage the brave. The relative positions of brother and sister were reversed at that crisis of danger; the pride of man was brought low, whilst strength was given to the humble and meek.

Smoke, blinding and half-suffocating smoke, filled the passage through which Emmie now guided her brother's faltering steps. Sparks flew around, the heat was intense, the roaring sound of flames mingled with the noise of the storm. But there was no actual obstacle to the departure of the fugitives from the burning house, and over the wreck of the shattered door they passed forth into outer air. Here they felt comparatively safe; the snowy waste which spread around them promised protection at least from any danger from fire. The storm was gradually abating, and soon the roaring and crackling noise of the conflagration and the crash of falling timbers were more audible than the muttering of thunder rolling away to the west.

With awe that hushed them into silence, the Trevors watched for a while the progress of the fire. Flames burst forth from windows, and blazed up from roof, till the whole building seemed swathed in a fiery mantle, from which the wind scattered myriads of sparks. Fast as rose a column of black smoke from the conflagration, it was spread by the gale in a western direction, like a dark pall overshadowing the snow which lay on the heath. The Trevors had sought the shelter of a hedge, on the side opposite to that to which flames and smoke were driven; and thus not a spark fell beside them, though they were near enough to the burning dwelling to feel its glowing heat.

"But for you I should now have been *there!*" exclaimed Bruce, after an interval of silence, as he pointed towards the house, which every minute was becoming more like a burning fiery furnace. "I could not have stirred hand or foot; I should have remained bound, like victim at the stake, waiting till the flames should reach me. You have saved me from the most horrible of deaths; I owe my life to your courage."

99

"Not mine! oh, not mine! it was His gift!" exclaimed Emmie, with a gush of unutterable thankfulness and joy. "Oh! shall I ever again mistrust the power and the goodness of God!"

CHAPTER XXVII.

A NIGHT-JOURNEY.

The Trevors were not long to remain alone. The flames from the house, seen far and wide, soon drew to the spot the inmates of farms and cottages dotted over the neighbouring land. Amongst the first arrivals at the scene of the conflagration was that of Mr. Trevor's own servant, who was driving the pony-chaise in which he had returned from S——. Susan, who had found the paper left by Emmie, and who was alarmed at her young lady being out in the storm, had despatched Joe with all speed by the road, after heaping the chaise with warm wraps to protect Miss Trevor from the cold. Susan herself had accompanied Joe, in whose intelligence and promptitude no great trust was reposed by the old family servant.

Very thankful was Emmie for the arrival of the chaise, which afforded a means of carrying her brother quickly home; for Bruce was in so exhausted a state that she feared that he would faint by the way. The young man let Emmie spread her own cloak around him, and cushion him up with shawls; his submission to such offices of kindness was so unlike Bruce's former self, that Emmie saw in it a token of prostration of mind as well as of body. Not a word was uttered by either during the short drive back to Myst Court. Bruce leaned back with his eyes closed; his sister scarcely knew whether or not he were conscious of what was passing around him.

"I dare not tell him in his present weak state of what has happened to Vibert," thought Emmie, whose mind now recurred to the troubles of her younger brother, which had been for a while forgotten in the excitement of the late scenes.

Myst Court was soon reached. Bruce was gently assisted out of the chaise, which was then at once sent off to S—— to bring a surgeon. Bruce's wound had never bled much, as it had been inflicted by a blunt instrument. Susan had offered to bind it, but the sufferer had refused to let his injured head be touched save by professional hands. A ghastly sight the young man presented, as he slowly entered the hall of Myst Court, leaning on the arm of his sister; but it was then that he startled Emmie with the abrupt question, "Has Vibert returned from London?"

"Not yet," was her faltered reply.

"Then I must go thither at once. When does the next train start?—I have lost count of time—days, weeks seem to have passed since I was last here," said Bruce, with an evident effort to collect his scattered thoughts. He seated himself wearily on one of the large oak chairs in the hall, and in his own decided manner repeated the words, "When does the next train start?"

"Bruce, dearest, you are utterly unable to attempt to take such a journey," said Emmie soothingly. She feared that her brother's mind was beginning to wander. Bruce perhaps guessed her suspicion, for calmly meeting her anxious gaze he reiterated his question, "Only tell me, when does the next train start for London?"

"Not till after dark," replied Emmie.

"Then after dark I go up to London, unless Vibert return," said Bruce. "I must warn him—I must give notice to the police—I must telegraph at once," and with an effort the young man rose to his feet. At that moment the superintendent of police entered the hall, not a little surprised to see before him, living, the man for whose corpse he and his companions had been making most diligent search. The appearance of Bruce showed but too plainly how narrowly he had escaped the fate to which he had been supposed to have fallen a victim.

"What brought *him* here?" cried Bruce, glancing at the official, and then turning his inquiring eyes on his sister.

Concealment was no longer possible; Emmie began to break gently the evil tidings which had come that morning from London, but had scarcely uttered a sentence before Bruce anticipated all that she was about to tell him.

"Vibert has been arrested," he cried, "the dupe of the villany of a forger. Emmie, I must go to the study with this officer; I can give him information of the greatest importance. He will send telegraphs to London and to Liverpool, and he and I will go up to town by the next train. There is a nefarious plot to be unravelled, and the events of last night have placed the end of the clue in my hand."

His sister saw at once that opposition would be useless. The more ill Bruce felt himself to be, the more resolved he was to speak and act while the power to do so remained. Till he had had his conference with the superintendent, the sufferer would take neither rest nor refreshment, save copious draughts of water, eagerly swallowed to quench his feverish thirst. Bruce's hand trembled violently as he replenished the tumbler again and again; but this was but the weakness of the nerves,—the will of the soul was as strong as ever.

"Will you not suffer us first to bathe and bind your poor head?" suggested Emmie, who could not look on the injured brow without a thrill of pain.

"There will be time for all that," exclaimed Bruce with impatient gesture; "more important matters press,—is not our brother's honour at stake?"

The condition in which Bruce Trevor appeared, and the circumstances under which he had been found, had removed from the mind of the police official all suspicion that he could ever have been leagued with the forgers. He had evidently barely escaped with life from the hands of the ruffians, and their shallow device for implicating him in their guilt was transparent to all. The superintendent eagerly received from Bruce such information regarding the forgers as was likely to lead to their apprehension before they should have time to make their escape from the shores of Britain.

To Emmie, in her anxiety for her brother, the interview held in the study seemed to be painfully long; but Bruce had not been half an hour in the house when a policeman, despatched in haste by the superintendent, was on his way to S——, commisssioned to telegraph from thence to Liverpool and to London.

Then, the immediate strain on his energies being over, Bruce collapsed for a brief time into a state of utter prostration. When the surgeon arrived from S——, he found his patient stretched on the drawing-room sofa in something between a sleep and a swoon, with his pale, anxious sister watching beside him.

Emmie remained present while the surgeon performed his part, giving such trifling aid as she could. When Dr. Weir had done his work and left the room, Miss Trevor followed him into the hall, most anxious to know his opinion as to the extent of the injury which her brother had sustained from the blow.

"The wound is not in itself of so *very* serious a character," said the surgeon gravely, "if the brain itself have not suffered. But there is a strong tendency to fever, and the patient should be kept as quiet and as free from excitement as is possible."

"But he actually insists on travelling to London to-night," cried Emmie; "and it is so difficult, so impossible to resist the will of my brother when he thinks that a duty must be performed."

The surgeon shrugged his shoulders. He, like every one else at S——, had heard of Vibert's arrest, and could understand that no light cause drew his brother towards the metropolis. He had seen already also something of his patient's decided character, and recalled to mind the well-known words of one who, when told that to travel might be to die, replied, "It is not necessary that I should live, but it is necessary that I should go." Bruce had a few minutes before in Dr. Weir's presence, expressed a similar sentiment.

"To oppose him would, I fear, bring on the very evil which we would guard against," said the surgeon, after a minute's reflection. "I dare not, under existing circumstances, absolutely forbid the journey to London." Perhaps Dr. Weir, in giving his reluctant consent to what he saw that he could not prevent, was but making a virtue of necessity.

"Then I will accompany my brother," said Emmie.

As soon as the surgeon had departed, Emmie began to make preparations for the journey, which should at least be made to Bruce as comfortable and as little fatiguing as it was possible for a night-journey in the depth of winter to be.

"My young lady is a changed being," thought Susan, as she found Miss Trevor actively engaged in packing her brother's carpet-bag. "After all the dreadful news which she heard this morning, after her exposure to the most fearful of storms, after the horror of finding her brother half-murdered, and the narrow escape of both from being burned to death, I should have expected to have seen my mistress either in violent hysterics, or in a burning fever! But here is Miss Trevor able to think of all, arrange all, care for all, speaking no word of fear, showing no sign of weakness! I never thought that my lady could have learned so soon how to 'glorify God in the fires!'"

Before the arrival of the close vehicle ordered by Emmie to convey her brother and herself to the station, the sister made one more earnest attempt to dissuade Bruce from making an effort which, in his present state, would probably bring on serious illness. Was it indeed, she urged, so needful for him to appear in person in London?

"Emmie, I have wronged a brother, and shall I not do what I can to right him?" was Bruce's reply. "Yes," he added, "though I knew that to go to him now were to go indeed to my grave." Emmie attempted no further remonstrance.

The vehicle came, and the travellers started. Susan accompanied the Trevors as far as the station, to take their railway tickets, and look after their comforts. Emmie would have been thankful to have taken her faithful attendant with her all the way to London, but difficulties stood in the way. Not only had money run short (for Emmie's purse had been empty, and her brother's had been so poorly supplied that they had had to borrow from their servant), but Miss Trevor was afraid further to encroach on the hospitality of her aunt, whose house might already be full.

Few persons travelled in winter by the night train, which was chiefly used for luggage. Bruce and Emmie had the railway carriage to themselves, and the invalid was thus able to recline as on a couch. Very few words passed between the brother and sister during that long wearisome journey; Bruce was reserving the small residue of his strength for the morrow's effort, and as the light of the dull lamp fell on his almost corpse-like features, Emmie felt that it would be cruel to disturb him even by a question. She scarcely knew whether her brother were thinking or sleeping; but what a full current of thought was passing through her own mind, as the train rolled on through the darkness! Emmie reviewed the events of that—to her—most eventful day with emotions of horror so mixed with fervent thankfulness, that she could not herself have told which was the uppermost feeling. Emmie had, as it were, had lions close to her path, but had found that the lions were chained; she had looked on death very near, but her spirit had been so braced by prayer that she had not fainted at his awful approach. She had, for once, conquered mistrust, and by doing so had been the blessed means of saving the life of her brother. But was she to rest content with one victory over besetting sin, or could she suppose that the enemy, though once foiled, would not perpetually be returning to his too familiar abode? Had vivid light been thrown into her heart's haunted chamber, only that she should again resign it to darkness? Must not the young Christian be now constantly on the watch, and resolutely and prayerfully resolve that the thought "I fear" should never again turn her feet back from the path of duty?

Emmie was so absorbed in such reflections that she almost started when her brother broke silence at last.

"Emmie, what induced you to go to that house, and alone?" asked Bruce suddenly, opening his languid eyes, and fixing their gaze on his sister, who occupied the opposite seat. "Had anything occurred to make you suspect treachery in that most false of women?"

The question took Emmie by surprise, and she was about to return a frank reply, when there came the remembrance of her oath, like the galling of a hidden chain worn by penitents of old. Even all that had passed had not set the conscience of the maiden free from the burden of that dread oath.

"I cannot tell even you, Bruce, why I suspected Jael,—why I went through the wood in the storm,—but the thing which decided me to make my way into the house and search there for my brother was finding one of his slippers close to the garden-gate."

A faint smile, the first seen on his lips during that fearful day, passed over the face of Bruce. "Then it was not for nothing," he said, "that I contrived to detach that slipper from my foot as the villains bore me past the hedge to the gate. It was so dark that they did not notice the trace I was leaving behind me. But wherefore can you not tell me, Emmie, the cause of that suspicion of Jael which led one so timid as yourself to her dwelling in the midst of a storm so terrible, that when the bolt struck the house I thought to have been buried under its ruins?"

"Oh! Bruce, do not ask me!" murmured Emmie, shrinking from the searching gaze of her brother's eyes.

"I understand," said Bruce to himself, after a pause in which he had recalled Emmie's mysterious disappearance on the night of the eclipse, and her subsequent agony of terror. "You are bound by some promise," he continued, again addressing his sister; "there had been one moment of weakness, but how nobly redeemed! Emmie, my preserver, fear no questions from me; it is enough to know that you dared danger and death for my sake!" The look of deep grateful affection which accompanied the words repaid Emmie for all that she had suffered.

This brief conversation alone broke the silence of the Trevors ere their arrival in London. The tedious journey at length was over, the train had reached the last station. Emmie had never before travelled without being relieved of all the petty trouble which a long journey involves; now, on a night in winter, she had charge of an invalid, and had the care of all arrangements needed for his comfort. When, trembling with cold, the travellers stepped out at last on the platform, it was Emmie's part to see about luggage and cab, and then to procure at the refreshment-room wine for her almost fainting companion. Such matters, indeed, seem to be trifles; but they formed part of the discipline which was raising a self-indulgent girl, accustomed to be the object of constant attention and care, into the thoughtful and self-forgetting Christian woman.

While the church clocks of the metropolis were striking the hour of midnight, Emmie and her silent companion were passing the comparatively deserted streets on their way to Grosvenor Square. Few persons were abroad at that hour, especially in the wider streets of the West-end, save the policeman on his beat, or the waifs and strays who have no better home than the casual ward of a workhouse. The minds of both Bruce and his sister were now full of the subject of Vibert's arrest, and painful anxiety to know whether their younger brother were not at that moment the occupant of some prison-cell. The Trevors had left Myst Court just before the arrival of a telegram from their father which would have relieved their minds from this fear. Vibert had been taken before a magistrate, but his case had been remanded till the following day, when, as it was hoped, news might be received of the arrest of Colonel Standish. Heavy bail had been offered for the unhappy youth's reappearance before the court, and the securities had been accepted. Vibert had therefore been permitted to accompany his father back to the house of his aunt.

CHAPTER XXVIII.

THE BROTHERS' MEETING.

 With drowsy driver and weary horse, the cab rolled slowly on, till at length the rumble of its wheels broke the stillness of aristocratic Grosvenor Square. Bruce roused himself as the conveyance stopped at the door of Mrs. Montalban.

As the coming of the Trevors was unexpected, none of the servants were likely to be up to answer at once the summons of the bell. No light shone in the hall, all was shut up; and the driver stood clapping his arms to keep out the cold, until some sleepy lackey should rouse himself to obey the unwelcome summons.

But there was one person in that mansion too nervous and too much excited to have made any preparations, even at past midnight, for retiring to rest. Vibert was pacing up and down his room when the cab was drawn up at the door; to him the bell, heard at so late an hour, announced tidings which must relate to his own unhappy affair. It was Vibert who, pale with anxiety and distress, rushed down the six flights of stairs, hurried into the hall, drew back the massive bolts, unloosed the chain, and threw open the door, while Mrs. Montalban's footman was yet rubbing his sleepy eyes and yawning, before he attempted to ensconce himself in his livery coat.

"Emmie! Bruce!" exclaimed the astonished Vibert, as by the flickering light of the bed-room candle, which he had brought from his own apartment, he recognized the travellers who now entered the hall. "For what have you come, and at such a time?"

"To stand by you," answered Bruce, grasping the hand of his younger brother.

Those brief words—that grasp of the hand—were to the wretched Vibert like the first gleam of light bursting through clouds of darkness and storm. Of the bitter drops which had filled the cup of misery which, since his arrest, Vibert had drained, perhaps none had been more bitter than the thought of the contempt which his elder brother would feel for one who had stood in a police-court, accused as a felon. Not that Vibert supposed that Bruce would believe him capable of knowingly passing forged notes; but what a selfish prodigal—what a contemptible dupe—what a disgrace to the family, would he not appear in the eyes of his high-minded elder brother! Bruce, with his lofty sense of duty,—his own character so pure from reproach,—how he would despise the companion and tool of a profligate forger! Vibert, notwithstanding his affected disregard of the opinions of Bruce, really looked up to him with respect, though that feeling was largely mixed with that of dislike. The youth was vain of his own personal advantages; love of approbation was strong in his soul, and he had resented the stern Mentor-like superiority assumed by his elder brother. Now that all Bruce's warnings against Vibert's folly had been more than justified by the event, the younger brother winced at the idea of the stern judgment on his conduct which would be passed by him who had warned in vain. The brother's withering sneer—so thought Vibert, who was selfish even in his misery—would be harder to bear than even his father's deep mortification, or Emmie's burst of distress. Now to find sympathy and support, where he had looked for upbraiding and scorn, touched the heart of the poor lad, and filled his eyes with tears.

Bruce's dislike to "cause any fuss in the house" made him decide at once on accompanying Vibert back to his room, where, as the younger Trevor said, there were a sofa and a fire. Emmie was to steal up softly to the apartment of her cousin Cecilia, whose habit it was, as she knew, to sit up reading novels till midnight. There was to be no noise—no whispering on the stairs—to rouse the family from their slumbers. Vibert wondered at the earnestness with which Emmie recommended Bruce to his care; it was strange to the poor lad, absorbed as he was in his own trouble, that his sister should appear to be more anxious about Bruce than unhappy about himself. A feeling of shame had made Vibert scarcely glance at his brother when he met him in the hall, and he scarcely noticed with how feeble and slow a step Bruce now mounted the long flights of stairs. If Vibert thought at all on the subject, as, candle in hand, he led the way to his room, he deemed that his brother was giving to Emmie, who accompanied Bruce to the upper landing-place, the support which he was in reality receiving from the slender arm of his sister.

Bruce entered his brother's room, into which he had been preceded by Vibert, with difficulty reached the sofa, and then sank upon it, his brain reeling, and every object seeming to swim around him. He threw off the travelling cap which, light as it was, had sat like a weight of lead on his brow; and then, indeed, Vibert noticed that his brother's head was bandaged.

"What has happened to you, Bruce?" he exclaimed. "You look as if you had just walked out of your grave!"

Bruce simply replied, "I had a blow;" and Vibert's mind went back at once to his own affairs. The youth, as he stirred the fire to a brighter blaze, kept up what could scarcely be termed a conversation, as he himself was the only speaker. Bruce did not take in the meaning of half the rapidly-uttered words which fell on his ear,—to his feverish brain they were as sounds heard in a dream; but he was a silent if not an attentive listener, and that was enough for Vibert.

"Can you imagine a more horrid affair than this has been?" exclaimed the younger Trevor. "I had no more doubt that those notes had been issued from the Bank of England than I had of my own existence. But I need not tell you that. No one who knows me could for a moment suspect me of a dishonourable action, though, as I am ready enough to own, I have acted with consummate folly. How could I have let myself be so deceived by a worthless adventurer? I cannot even now understand how Standish gained such an influence over my mind!"

Bruce might have replied—"By working on your vanity and self-love;" but the young man had neither the strength nor the inclination to make such a remark. Vibert went rambling on with his painful story; he had been longing for some one to whom he could pour out his heart, and was agreeably surprised at not being interrupted by any caustic remark from his brother.

"The blow fell upon me in so horridly public a way!" cried Vibert. "Just imagine the scene. There was the large drawing-room full of people,—my aunt was giving an afternoon party. We had the Montagues, Carpenters, stately Sir Richard,—the countess and all! The music had struck up; the couples were placed; I had asked Alice for the first dance; she and I stood at the top. We were laughing, chatting, and just beginning to dance. Suddenly the music stopped,—musicians, dancers, every one looking in one direction. A policeman—astounding apparition!—was making his way up the room! Even then I was not in the least alarmed. I remember that I turned to Alice, and jestingly asked her whether she was to be taken up for stealing hearts! It was no jesting matter for me! When the fellow in blue laid his grasp on *my* arm,—when he said that his business was with *me*,—I should have liked to have struck him to the earth; and then—I should have liked the floor to have opened beneath me!" Vibert, as he spoke, plunged the poker fiercely into the heart of the fire. "Only conceive," he continued, "what it was to have to walk down that long room, with a policeman's hand on my collar, and to feel (I dared not look about me to see) that every eye was watching my movements! I did indeed catch a glimpse of my aunt in her purple velvet, with her face as full of horror as if she had seen the Gorgon's head! I did hear Alice's exclamation of pity,—that was almost the worst of all; for such pity is akin to contempt! Then my poor uncle, stammering and confused at the dishonour done to his family and house, would fain have got me out of the clutch of the grim policeman; but he could not effect anything then, though his bail and my father's were accepted on the following day when I had been before the magistrate. I was led off from that grand house—from that gay throng—to—to—O Bruce! can you imagine your brother in the lock-up for a night! I wonder that I did not go crazy! And then to have to appear on the next day in a police-court, on a charge of felony! Horrible! horrible!—most horrible! I should wish, when this affair is over, to shut myself up in a hermitage, where no one should ever see or hear of me again. I shall never be able to endure meeting one of those who beheld me carried off to jail in charge of the police!"

Vibert turned suddenly from the fire as he concluded the sentence, and saw his brother stretched on the sofa, quite unconscious of his presence, sleeping the sleep of exhaustion.

CHAPTER XXIX.

CHARGED WITH FELONY.

he remarkable circumstances attending the arrest of Vibert Trevor, his high connections, and the official position which his father had for many years held, made the affair in which he was implicated cause a very great sensation in the upper ranks of London society. Never before had the police-court in which Vibert was for the second time to appear been so crowded by the wearers of fashionable bonnets, sable muffs, and ermine tippets. Never before had so many carriages (some of them bearing coronets) blocked up the narrow avenues to the magistrate's court. The police had some difficulty in clearing a way for aristocratic ladies through crowds of roughs assembled to see "a gent in the hands of the bobbies!" Expectation was on the tiptoe. To many of Vibert's gay companions—the young men with whom he had played at billiards, the pretty girls with whom he had danced—the sight of him standing at the bar to answer a charge of passing forged notes, gave a thrill of excitement more delightful than could have been afforded by the most sensational novel, or the most charmingly tragical play.

Information was circulated amidst the mixed throng, where news was eagerly passed from mouth to mouth, that the police at Liverpool had been unsuccessful in their attempts to discover and arrest the person who had called himself Colonel Standish. No person of that name, no one answering to the description given of his person, had inquired after the box of jewels at the place to which Vibert was to have sent it. No individual called Standish had taken his passage in any vessel about to sail for America. The police were eagerly on the alert, but had, it was said, discovered no clue that could lead to the arrest of the principal criminal.

"The monkey who used the cat's paw to pull the chestnuts out of the fire, has got clear off to the jungle," observed a fashionable-looking young man, who had been one of Vibert's most particular friends. "Poor Grimalkin is caught with the nuts in his claws, and will have something to bear in addition to the pain of the burning!" The speaker, as he ended the remark, raised his gold eye-glass to his eyes, to enable him to see more distinctly every nervous twitch on the face of poor Vibert, who, attended by his father, uncle, and brother, at that moment approached the bar.

"Ah! how changed the poor boy looks—how shamefaced!" whispered Alice to a companion; for Alice was there in her fashionable hat with its scarlet feather. "To think that I should have danced and talked nonsense with one who is standing where all the low thieves and pickpockets stand!" The little lady rose on tiptoe to have a better view over the shoulders of those in front of her; but had the grace to hope that the poor prisoner would not turn his eyes in her direction. There was no danger of his so doing, the wretched youth could not raise his eyes from their fixed stare on the floor.

"Vibert's brother looks more ill than the prisoner does," observed the companion of Alice; "he has a bandage on his head. One would think that Bruce had been brought to the bar for prize-fighting, or for leading the roughs in a row!"

"Hush! hush! he is going to be sworn as a witness,—some one is giving him a glass of cold water; I wish that I could hand him my scent-bottle," whispered Alice, who was touched by Bruce's evident struggle to overcome physical suffering and mental exhaustion by the force of strong will.

Bruce was sworn as a witness. Very simply and concisely he gave evidence as to what the reader knows already. He told of his hearing a noise, entering the chamber next to his own, seeing the forgers, and receiving, while struggling with Standish, a stunning blow from some heavy instrument wielded by Harper.

Harper's name had not even been mentioned in the evidence given on the preceding day, Vibert not being in the slightest degree aware of the strange old man's complicity in the crime of forging bank-notes. Bruce's narrative, given in a low but clear and steady voice, commanded breathless attention. The silence observed in the crowded court was scarcely broken even by the rustle of a lady's silk dress.

"You say that you were stunned by the blow given by this man Harper," observed the magistrate. "Did you long continue in an unconscious state?"

"I know not how long I remained senseless," was the answer of Bruce; "probably the cold night air revived me, for I found, when I came to life, that the two forgers were bearing me into the wood. I lay perfectly still, and they doubtless considered me dead, for the men uttered words to each other which I was certainly not intended to hear."

"Can you recall to memory any of those words?" the magistrate inquired.

Bruce had a tenacious memory, and what had passed on that eventful night had been as it were branded on it, never to be erased. He at once replied to the magistrate's question.

"The first words which I remember hearing were some spoken by Harper—'How could you trust Vibert Trevor to pass my notes?' said he.

"'I trusted him no more than in angling I trust the fly on my hook,' answered Standish. 'I use him to make the gudgeons bite; but the fool knows no more of the nature of the work to which I have put him than does the senseless fly that covers the barb.'"

A thrill of satisfaction went through the court. Mr. Trevor could not restrain a faint exclamation of thankfulness at this clear testimony to the innocence of his unfortunate son drawn from Standish himself.

"Proceed, sir, with your evidence," said the magistrate to Bruce Trevor. The witness went on with his story.

"'How then is the lad to forward the jewels?' asked Harper.

"'He is to direct them to me under my assumed name,' replied Standish; 'but I shall be too wary to claim the box myself. Aunt Jael, whom no one suspects, will call at the office for the jewels, and bring them to us at the White Raven, where we shall keep close till the *Penguin* sails.'"

"Did you hear anything more regarding the plans of these men?" the magistrate asked.

"No; but I had heard enough to put the police on the right scent on my return to Myst Court," answered Bruce.

This was all the evidence which young Trevor could give which bore directly on the charge against his brother; but so much of interest remained to be learned, that the examination went on.

"What do you suppose that this man Harper and his accomplice intended to do with you, when they carried you through the wood?" asked the magistrate.

"They intended to throw my corpse into the pond on the heath," answered Bruce in the same calm tone. "I knew as much from what they muttered, though I cannot recall the words; and I reserved myself for one last desperate struggle for life. As we left the wood,

108

Harper found out, perhaps by some involuntary movement that I made, that I was alive. I was set down under a hedge, and there followed some conversation between the two men regarding my fate, of the nature of which I could guess more than I heard. There was something said about 'gallows' and 'hanging for it,' so I concluded that the ruffians thought it a more serious matter to be tried for murder than for the forgery of bank-notes. The men lifted me up again, and carried me into the house of the woman hitherto called Jael Jessel, whom I now found to be the wife of the one and the aunt of the other. In that house I was blindfolded, gagged, and bound to a table. Half swooning as I was, I knew little of what was passing around me, save that I judged from the sounds that I heard that the forgers were moving their goods and leaving the place. How many hours I passed alone after their departure I cannot tell. A great storm came on, and at last a fire-bolt struck the dwelling, shattering the door, and setting the place on fire. Then followed the entrance of my sister, who, alarmed at my absence, was searching for me, and who found me in the helpless condition in which the forgers had doubtless hoped that I would have remained for days undiscovered. I was scarcely likely to have survived till the evening, had not timely succour arrived."

Before Bruce had quite finished giving his evidence, tidings were brought to the magistrate from Liverpool, which excited such interest amongst the crowd thronging the court that an irrepressible murmur of satisfaction arose. The police, following the clue given by Bruce Trevor, had arrested at a low public-house, called the White Raven, three persons answering to the description given of Harper and his associates. The woman, it appeared, had inquired at the coach-office for a box directed to Colonel Standish, which, it could not be doubted, was that which was to contain the jewels. Other suspicious circumstances seemed to place it beyond question that the individuals now in custody were Harper, Standish, and Jael. The first named had been recognized by a policeman as an engraver, who had been taken up before on a charge of forgery, but who had been dismissed for want of sufficient evidence to convict him. Jael, it appeared, was his wife; and Harper had found in her nephew, Horace Standish, *alias* John Stobb, an unscrupulous accomplice in carrying out his guilty designs. It afterwards appeared that the Harpers and their confederate had taken their passages in the *Penguin* under three different assumed names.

Vibert still stood as a prisoner at the bar, but he was not long to remain in so humiliating a position. The magistrate, who had from the first doubted the young man's guilt, was now convinced, by Bruce's testimony, that the prisoner had never been an accomplice in the crime of the forgers, but in pure ignorance had passed false notes so skilfully engraved as almost to defy detection. The magistrate therefore dismissed the charge against the prisoner, and Vibert once more was free.

A louder hum of approbation, accompanied by some clapping of hands, followed the order for Vibert's release. But to Vibert that release brought no joyful sense of freedom, and the favourable verdict no feeling of exultation. The youth was humiliated—even to the dust. He had only escaped condemnation as a felon, by being convicted of acting as a fool. He had been the easy dupe, the senseless tool of a designing villain. His emblem was the gaudy fly hiding the hook of the angler! Under such circumstances the congratulations of the so-called friends who now pressed around him were to Vibert but as a stinging insult. His one wish was to escape all notice, to fly from his fellow-creatures, and to hide his head where no one should know of his folly and the disgrace to which it had brought him. Many hands were held out to the late prisoner, words were spoken which were meant to be kind; but Vibert would not notice the hands, nor listen to the words. He bent down his head till his long hair almost hid his cheeks, which were glowing with shame. Vibert pushed his way through the crowd, scarcely able to draw a full breath till he had reached the street, rushed into his uncle's carriage, in which Emmie was anxiously waiting, and pulled down the blinds to shut himself out from the sight of mankind.

CHAPTER XXX.

TREMBLING IN THE BALANCE.

 nother and a yet sharper trial was further to humble and sober the once gay and thoughtless Vibert. If ever a gush of warm gratitude had arisen in his heart, it was drawn forth by the generous effort made in his behalf by his elder brother. Bruce, when in a state of exhaustion and suffering which rendered him fit only for the silence and repose of a sick-chamber, had taken a long journey in winter, and had then encountered the fatigue and excitement of giving evidence in a police-court, acting as one who felt that he had no leisure to be ill, that it was a time for action and not for repose. Bruce had been as a rider forcing his horse to a leap almost beyond its strength; the brave steed just clearing the stone wall, and falling on the opposite side, crushing its rider beneath its weight. An effort had been made, successfully made; but reaction was certain to follow, and in the case of Bruce Trevor terrible was that reaction. Ere nightfall straw was laid down before one of the houses in Grosvenor Square to deaden the sound of passing wheels, and the most skilful physician in London was counting the quick throbs in the pulse of a patient in a high delirious fever.

Emmie had never before watched by a sick-bed; she had been far too young at the time of her mother's last illness to have had anything to do with nursing. All those who best knew Emmie, with her delicate nerves and timid character, declared that she was utterly unfit to nurse in a case that required both strength and courage; for Bruce's ravings were often those of a maniac. He had sometimes to be held down in his bed by main force. But the painful lessons of the last few days had not been taught to Emmie in vain. The timid nervous girl had learned to go to the Fount of Strength, and the firmness and faith which she thence received astonished her father and Vibert. When her younger brother would quit the sick-room, unable to endure the harrowing sight of Bruce struggling like a demoniac, Emmie remained at her painful post. The sound of his sister's voice, the gentle touch of her hand, would sometimes soothe the poor sufferer when nothing else had the slightest effect.

"How can you bear to see him thus?" exclaimed Vibert once to his pale but tearless sister, after one of Bruce's most distressing paroxysms of brain-fever.

"I try to trust and not be afraid," the poor girl faintly replied. "I try to trust him to God, to my—his Heavenly Father. I repeat to myself, *God is love*. He can—oh! He *will* make all things, even this most fearful anguish, work together for good to those who trust Him!"

110

But for the ravings of fever, when the mind of Bruce had lost all power of self-control, never would mortal but himself have known the extent of the sufferings which he had endured whilst in the power of the forgers, and during the hours of torture when he had remained pinioned and gagged. In the police-court Bruce had described with calm brevity the events of that trying night and morning. But when reason had fled from the sufferer, what images of horror those events had branded on his mind was apparent to all who approached him. The dreadful scenes through which Bruce had passed were, in the delirium of fever, acted over and over again: now he was struggling with fearful violence to unloose a murderer's grasp on his throat, calling for help in tones so piercing that they thrilled to the hearts of those watching beside him, and even reached the ears of passengers in the street. Then the sufferer seemed to be listening, gasping and trembling as he listened, to sounds which none but himself could hear. Bruce would mutter words about the pool—the deep, black, icy-cold pool—and clutch the bed-clothes, as if to save himself from being dragged down to a watery grave. At another time the fever-stricken youth would imagine himself as being again bound in the house of Jael, would writhe and struggle to free himself from imaginary cords that cut into his flesh as he struggled; and anon would convulsively start, as if again he heard the thunderbolt strike the dwelling close to his head.

Day after day passed, night after night, in dreadful transitions from frenzy to stupor, deathlike stupor, only exchanged for more fearful frenzy, till even Emmie could scarcely wish for a prolongation of the terrible struggle. Humbly and submissively she prayed that if her loved brother were indeed now passing through the river of death, one ray of reason might gleam through the awful darkness around him, and that the waves and billows might indeed not go over his head.

But Bruce had youth in his favour, and all that man's skill or woman's tenderness could throw into the opposite scale to that in which his life appeared to be gradually sinking. With alternations of hope and fear, the watchers by the sick-bed marked the trembling of the balance, scarcely able to believe that from so fearful an attack of fever the sufferer ever again could rise. But the crisis came at last, and the worst was over; the maddening fever quitted the suffering Bruce, but left him helpless as an infant, and more nervous than the most weak and timid of women.

For weeks Bruce could hardly endure the noise of a step crossing his room; a shadow alarmed him, a voice would make every nerve in his frame quiver. The doctor said that for long his patient would be incapable of any mental exertion; he who had been so steady and regular in his work, was condemned to the idleness and inaction which, to a character like that of Bruce, was in itself a most humiliating trial and disappointment.

As soon as the invalid could be with safety removed from London, he was sent to a watering-place in the south of England. Emmie, whose health had suffered from her devoted nursing, accompanied her sick brother. After a while she exchanged places with Vibert, and rejoined at Myst Court her father, who was actively fulfilling his duties as a landlord and benefactor to the poor. In the latter character Mr. Trevor needed the help of his daughter, whose health was now sufficiently restored to enable her to become his able assistant.

Vibert had not seen his brother for more than a month when he joined him at Torquay, and with the sanguine expectations natural to youth he hoped that the change of air and scene, and the effect of so many weeks passed in perfect repose, might have brought back health and strength to the shattered frame of Bruce Trevor. The youth was disappointed to find how slow had been the progress made by the invalid towards recovery. It was not merely the hollow eye, the transparent skin, the faint voice and feeble step that told how far removed convalescence was from vigorous health, for it seemed to Vibert as if his brother's firmness of mind, and even his moral courage, were gone. Bruce so shrank from any allusions to the sufferings of the past, that Vibert, who had come full of news which he was eager to impart, found that he must avoid even mentioning the names of the Harpers. For some time Bruce did not hear the result of the trial of the forgers, who had all been convicted and condemned to various terms of imprisonment.

But if Bruce's shattered state was distressing both to himself and to others, it was evident that the character of the young man was ripening under the trial. Bruce had been proud in his self-dependence, impatient of the weakness of others; he had trusted in the power of his own strong will to overcome all difficulties before him. He was now, in conscious infirmity, learning to cast himself simply, humbly, unreservedly upon the strength of his God. The proud soul had had to learn that the kingdom of heaven can only be entered by those who come in the spirit of a little child, and that the haughtiness of man must be brought down, that the Lord alone may be exalted.

"There are many things in life that one can't understand," observed Vibert one day, when he had just placed a footstool before the brother who had formerly taunted him with an effeminate love of luxurious ease. "It seems natural enough that I should have had some rough discipline, seeing what a thoughtless, selfish life I had been leading, till I was pulled up sharp by that horrid affair. But you—the steadiest fellow in Christendom—you, who never broke bounds, or turned to the right or the left—I can't see why the heaviest strokes should be laid upon you, or what good such a long trying illness can possibly do you."

"Vibert, do you remember what our uncle wrote on those fragments of paper when we were together at Summer Villa?"

Vibert nodded an affirmative reply.

"I have often thought over his words," continued the invalid; "they conveyed a salutary warning, all the more needed because it raised my anger against him who had laid his finger upon the tender spot. Vibert, I, as well as yourself, had my haunted chamber within the heart, and it has needed the thunderbolt which has smitten me so low to burst open a way for the light to enter."

A few months before nothing could have extorted from the lips of Bruce Trevor such a confession.

CHAPTER XXXI.

CHANGES.

The last month of Bruce's stay at Torquay was passed at the house of a relative; Vibert had returned to his studies, Emmie's presence and help were required at home by her father, and the convalescent no longer needed constant attendance. It was arranged that Bruce should remain at the sea-side till his uncle's return from his voyage, when he and Captain Arrows should travel to Myst Court together.

It is bright sunny noontide in April; earth has long since cast off her fetters of ice and mantle of snow, and the voice of the west wind has called forth innumerable flowers to welcome the spring. The apple-trees and cherry-trees are full of blossom, and the meadows are sheeted with gold. If some clouds flit over the sky, their light shadows but add the beauty of contrast to sunshine. If soft drops occasionally fall, they but make the fair earth the fairer.

Two travellers have just stepped on the platform of the station of S——. The pale thoughtful face of the one is familiar to us as that of Bruce Trevor; in the healthy, bronzed, intelligent countenance of the other we recognize that of Captain Arrows.

"Ah! a hearty welcome to you both!" exclaimed Vibert, who had been awaiting the arrival of the train with impatience. "As the day is so mild and bright, I have driven over in the pony-chaise to meet you. I want the captain to have a good view of the country as we drive to Myst Court."

The gentlemen were soon in the chaise, which could only conveniently accommodate three; Joe was to follow with the luggage. The captain and Vibert sat in front; Bruce preferred occupying the small seat behind.

Vibert was in the highest spirits, talking and laughing as he drove. It was well that the pony knew the way, and required no guiding. The youth often turned half-round in his seat, to address himself to his brother.

"Doesn't this remind you, Bruce, of my first coming to meet you at this station, when I ran off with Emmie, and nearly broke both her neck and my own? What a storm we had then to welcome us into our home!"

"We've had worse storms since," thought the silent Bruce Trevor.

Vibert continued his animated conversation with his uncle, pointing out all the landmarks around, telling of the improvements made by his father, and giving lively anecdotes of the people whose dwellings they passed.

"There now—yon unsightly square fortress of brick is the castle of old Bullen, the giant whom my father, armed with a roll of law-papers, boldly attacked and subdued. The stream which runs through our land has ceased to run purple and crimson; it is now a case of 'Never say *dye*.' You see yonder builders busy at work? They have made good progress with the new cottages, designed on the most approved plan. Bruce, don't you recollect the wretched pig-sties of hovels that stood in that place?"

Bruce's pale face was lighted up with interest and pleasure; the plans for the cottages had been made by himself, soon after his arrival in Wiltshire. That these plans were actually being carried out, had been purposely kept a secret from him, in order to give him a pleasant surprise.

"Yon field seems to be divided into allotments," observed Captain Arrows.

"Yes; that's one of the schemes of my father for improving the state of his peasants; he says that he had the notion from Bruce."

"And how does Emmie like her new life?" asked the captain.

"Emmie! why, she's a changed being—changed from the pale, clinging jessamine, into a bright apple-blossom!" cried Vibert. "Emmie is busy from morning till night; she drills her awkward squad of pinafored children in the barn, till a proper school can be built, and has actually coaxed them into washing their faces! She has a book like a parish register, with all the tenants' names put down, age, number of children, and all that sort of dry information; which seems, however, to interest her. Emmie ventures to enter the dirtiest cottage; but, somehow or other, soap and water are more freely used now than when she first came to the place. Emmie is a kind of guardian, or rather guardian-angel, to the poor. Why, she has even tackled an old ploughman, who was notoriously fond of his glass; and

113

if he gives up gin and whisky, it will be all owing to the influence of the young lady. You will be as much surprised at the change in Emmie, as my father was yesterday, when old Blair told him that I was a steady, promising young man!" Vibert leaned back in his seat, and laughed so merrily, that had not the pony at least been steady, the accident of the first evening might have been repeated, by the chaise being upset into a ditch.

Bruce neither shared the merriment nor joined in the conversation. Though young Trevor's health had by this time been greatly restored, his shattered nerves had not completely regained their tone. Bruce regarded Myst Court with extreme aversion, from the painful associations connected in his mind with the place, and would have been most glad had his father sold the estate at once. No one knew the shrinking dislike, almost amounting to loathing, with which Bruce thought of reoccupying the room next to that hateful bricked-up chamber in which he had suffered so much. The young man knew that other rooms in Myst Court had by this time been repaired and furnished, and twice had he taken up his pen to write a request that his apartment might be exchanged for another, and twice he had thrown down the pen, ashamed to betray such childish weakness.

"I scorned, even in poor Emmie, what I deemed silly superstition," thought Bruce. "There is nothing that teaches one to feel for the infirmities of others like suffering, as I now do, from one's own."

Bruce's aversion to the room adjoining the haunted chamber arose, it need scarcely be said, from a different cause from that which had made his sister dread to occupy the apartment. There was neither superstition nor mistrust in the mind of Bruce; he had no fear of apparitions; but he did shrink from reviving the images of horror impressed on memory, which, during his illness, had excited his brain to the point of frenzy. No one knew of the mental struggle in the mind of the convalescent; not to his nearest and dearest friend would he confide a weakness for which he despised himself. Bruce's post of duty was at Myst Court, and he deemed it a matter of comparatively small importance whether he disliked that post or not. Young Trevor's habitual self-control was now exercised in overcoming the infirmity left by long illness; and while Bruce was accusing himself of being a despicable coward, he had at no period of his life exercised more that courage which

"Triumphs over fear, And nobly dares the danger nature shrinks from."

Mr. Trevor and his daughter met the travellers at the iron gate which has been repeatedly mentioned as opening into the grounds of Myst Court. Emmie's face, radiant with smiles of welcome, and blooming with happiness and health, did indeed rival the soft beauty of the apple-blossom. Captain Arrows and his nephews quitted the chaise; and while Vibert on foot led the pony, the whole party sauntered at an easy pace along the carriage-drive, Emmie keeping close to the side of her newly-restored brother. With what tender, thankful joy she looked upon him whose step, but for her self-conquest, would never have trod that path again!

The trees on either side of the road were opening their budding leaves to the sunshine; the woods were full of the song of birds; and amidst the copse clusters of violets, primroses, and wood anemones, enamelled with their varied tints the carpet of moss.

"You see Myst Court in its beauty," said Vibert to his uncle, as a turn in the road brought the party in view of the stately mansion. "My first sight of the haunted house was on a stormy night in November, when poor Emmie and I arrived dripping and half-drowned, and Bruce welcomed us home with a scowl and a growl.—Now, Bruce, does not the garden do credit to Emmie? Look at the flowers in those classically-shaped vases, and the beds all ablaze with crocuses, purple, golden, and white!"

"The garden is greatly improved," said Bruce, forcing himself to speak in a cheerful tone.

114

"But what will you say to the interior of the house? it is there that most has been done," cried Vibert. "Emmie has now her own boudoir, and I think that you will own that it is a gem! I've done much of the ornamenting part myself, and am not a little proud of my taste."

Vibert was so impatient to show the boudoir that, after the party had entered the hall, he insisted with boyish vehemence upon their at once proceeding up the broad oaken staircase, which on their first coming had led only to the sleeping apartments and the corridor upon which they had opened. Vibert, leading the way, drew back the heavy tapestry curtain, beyond which lay the two rooms which have so often been mentioned. The first apartment was that which Bruce had occupied, and which he was to occupy still; but it was not here that Vibert stopped. A little beyond it was an open door, and through the doorway the eager youth led the party into a fairy-like apartment, where sunshine streamed through the diamond-shaped panes of a mullioned window, while shining mirrors reflected graceful ornaments within, and pictures wreathed with garlands of spring wild-flowers, or imaged on their clear surfaces the beauty of the woodland without.

"I call this Emmie's boudoir; but she insists that it shall be your study, Bruce," cried Vibert. "It's a pretty fairy-like retreat for you to read or for her to sing in."

"Surely this must be—*the haunted chamber!*" exclaimed the astonished Bruce.

"The disenchanted chamber, without its gloom or its spectres," observed the smiling Emmie.

"But there was a codicil to the old lady's will which obliged us to keep this room bricked up," observed Bruce.

"That codicil was a forgery," interrupted Mr. Trevor. "Harper, as unprincipled in devising schemes of fraud as he was skilful in carrying them out, had in this forged codicil attempted to achieve a double purpose. He made over to his wife a house and property to which she had no real claim, and he for a while contrived to secure to himself what was called the haunted chamber. Here were left his graving tools, his printing-press, and whatever else was required for his nefarious work; and here he pursued his occupation, shielded from interruption by the superstitious fears which his wife took pains to instil. The guilty man, with his associates, now reaps the reward of his crimes."

Bruce looked around him with admiring wonder. It was impossible to recognize the place, which he had only once seen before, when fire and lamp-light threw a red glare on instruments of guilt, and the threatening countenances of ruffians disturbed at their unhallowed work. Turning towards his sister with a brightening countenance, young Trevor exclaimed, "What a change is made by admitting the pure light of heaven!"

And it is with these words, taken in a loftier sense, that I would now close my story. Its object has been to lead the reader to search the haunted chamber of his own heart, to discover there the lurking ministers of evil who may, unknown even to himself, have made it their secret abode. Let us resolutely and prayerfully resolve, at whatever cost of humiliation or shame, to know ourselves, to recognize and face the sin that so easily besets us. Let the brickwork of ignorance be thrown down, and let not spiritual sunshine be shut out from the self-deceived heart. *Pride, Self-love*, cowardly *Mistrust* of God's wisdom and goodness, are natural to our fallen nature; but the entrance of His Word into the heart is as that of the glorious beams of the day,—joy, brightness, and holiness follow the admission into its deepest recesses of the pure, life-giving light of Heaven!

Made in the USA
Lexington, KY
23 November 2018